Subjects: CSH: Detective and mystery stories, Canadian (English)—Ontario—Ottawa. |
CSH: Short stories, Canadian (English)—Ontario—Ottawa. | CSH: Canadian fiction
(English)—21st century. | LCGFT: Detective and mystery fiction. | LCGFT: Short
stories.

Classification: LCC PS8323.D4 C37 2025 | DDC C813/.08720897138409052—dc23

I0635782

CRIME WRITERS OF CANADA PRESENTS

A CAPITAL MYSTERY

EDITED BY: BERNADETTE COX AND MIKE MARTIN

FEATURING

LIS ANGUS

BRENDA CHAPMAN

GARY COFFIN

ANNA DI MEGLIO

STEWART DUDLEY

BARBARA FRADKIN

BERNADETTE HENDRICKX

ELIZABETH HOSANG

P. R. ISFELD

JOE ITALIANO

JENNIFER JORGENSEN

KATHY MACLELLAN

NANCY PAWELEK

A.E. PITTMAN

MADONA SKAFF

ADRIENNE STEVENSON

KATIE TALLO

RUBY URLOCKER

MAYA VALENZUELA

JOANNE WHITE

MELISSA YI

INTRODUCTION BY RON CORBETT

OTTAWA PRESS AND PUBLISHING

MYSTERY

A CAPITAL MYSTERY ANTHOLOGY
Ottawa Press and Publishing
Copyright © Mike Martin 2025

ISBN PRINT BOOK: 978-1-990896-35-4
ISBN EBOOK: 978-1-990896-36-1

Cover design: Joanna D'Angelo
Book formatting and interior: Joanna D'Angelo

Printed and bound in Canada

Library and Archives Canada Cataloguing in Publication

Title: A capital mystery / edited by Bernadette Cox and Mike Martin.

Other titles: Crime writers of Canada presents

Names: Cox, Bernadette, editor. | Martin, Mike, 1954- editor

Description: Includes index.

Identifiers: Canadiana (print) 20250263130 | Canadiana (ebook) 20250263149 | ISBN 9781990896354 (softcover) | ISBN 9781990896361 (EPUB)

A CAPITAL MYSTERY

EDITED BY

BERNADETTE COX & MIKE MARTIN

OTTAWA PRESS
AND PUBLISHING
MYSTERY

CONTENTS

ACKNOWLEDGMENTS

We wish to acknowledge the encouragement and support of **Crime Writers of Canada** and **Capital Crime Writers**. This project would not have been possible without their assistance.

Crime Writers of Canada is a national non-profit organization for Canadian mystery and crime writers, associated professionals and others with a serious interest in Canadian crime writing. Their mission is to promote Canadian crime writing and to raise the profile of Canadian crime writers with readers, reviewers, librarians, booksellers and media. For more information please visit:

crimewritersofcanada.com

Capital Crime Writers is made up of writers at various stages of their career. Some are pre-published. Some are thrilled to see their name on published short stories. Others enjoy seeing their first novel or one of many in print. It is also made up of people simply interested in mystery and crime fiction. For more information please visit:

capitalcrimewriters.com

Finally, we give special thanks to our proofreader extraordinaire, Alex Zych.

INTRODUCTION

One of my most vivid childhood memories is reading a story in a grade five classroom at D. Roy Kennedy Public School, an elementary school on Woodroffe Avenue.

The story began — *"I like the lower towns, the place across the tracks, the poorer streets not far from the river. They represent failure, and for me failure here has a strong appeal. On my first day out, I walked along St. Patrick Street."*

I stopped reading. St. Patrick Street? There was a St. Patrick Street not far from where I used to live, before moving to what was then considered far-west Ottawa (Baseline Road was the edge of the known world.)

I continued reading, while at the same time wondering about the story's locale. *Nah, it couldn't be.* Then I read the sentence fragments that started the third paragraph of Norman Levine's *In Lower Town*:

"Towards the river. Down King Edward Avenue. Black trees in the middle, their branches dripping. Dirty snowbanks around the trees."

Dirty snowbanks on King Edward Avenue? My gosh — this story takes place in Ottawa!

You can do that?

That has stayed with me all these years — my childhood memory

— the utter astonishment I felt when I realized someone had written a story about Ottawa.

Not only written such a story but had it published in an anthology of Canadian short stories.

You can do that?

Well, as it turns out — yes, you can. The anthology you are holding is the latest proof.

A Capital Mystery has 21 short stories — some written by well-known authors, some by just-breaking-in authors — but what they have in common is the mystery takes place in Ottawa.

Or the Ottawa Valley, the Gatineau Hills — you will recognize the geography of these stories, the places and people.

Edited by Bernadette Cox and award-winning author Mike Martin (Sgt. Windflower Mystery Series) these stories run the gamut, from cozies to noir, police procedurals to locked-room puzzles.

A Capital Mystery, I feel confident in saying, has a mystery for everyone.

I hope you enjoy these stories as much as I did when I first read them. And perhaps share the wonder I once felt while reading a short story in a classroom on Woodroffe Avenue.

Yes, you can write stories about Ottawa.

What's more — they can be quite good.

Ron Corbett
Publisher
Ottawa Press and Publishing

OTTAWA PRESS AND PUBLISHING
ottawapressandpublishing.com

COLD SHOCK

1

BARBARA FRADKIN

take a deep breath of the sharp, cold air and try to calm down. Even the anticipation of him sends a spike of fear through me. But I should be okay. It's a quiet, peaceful evening, and I've decided to wait on a bench near the lighted parking lot leading to the pedestrian bridge. The snowy expanse of the park glows silver in the crescent moonlight, broken only by the outlines of trees near the edges. In front of the bench lies the Rideau River, snow-covered and silent. It looks peaceful, too, but I know beneath the layers of snow and ice, its rapids flow fast and cold.

I've always loved Strathcona Park, and we often brought the twins here when we lived in a student apartment nearby. Coming back here feels like returning to a happier time, where I first met Russ and where it all began. That's one of the reasons I suggested meeting here, hoping its magic would bring out the best in him. Or at least tone down the worst. He was dismissive of the meeting at first. Talking never got us anywhere, he said in reply to my text. At least your bargain-basement lawyer doesn't scream and cry and play the victim card.

Just the memory of that contempt causes another spike of fear. But I'm stronger now, I texted back. We need a reasonable discussion for the good of the boys. Even as I typed those words, I knew that was impossible. He doesn't care about the good of the boys. He ignored them, first busy with medical school and then with establishing his surgery practice. They are useful to him only as a weapon against me, and with the help of his lawyer buddy, he's winning the war. If I have any hope of remaining part of the children's lives, I have to persuade him that I'm not the fragile, overwhelmed and incompetent mother I was when he kicked me out.

He loved me once, or rather loved the delicate, naive girl he first met. Yet now that very frailty he once loved is what he hates most and uses against me in our battle. I'm not going to give you a penny, he said, because you have to learn to stand on your own two feet, and that won't happen as long as I prop you up. Instead, you'll bleed me dry and teach the twins to do the same.

I take another deep breath. It's no use dwelling on the past and on the mess I made of things. I have to think of my future, my boys' futures. That's what this meeting is about. I shiver as the wintery moon slips behind a cloud, casting the park into deeper shadow. Nine o'clock was his idea, not mine. He's a busy man, after all, and I'm not a priority. Even now he's late, as if to drive home that point. The park is deserted, all the students driven away by the cold. I'm freezing and rapidly losing my nerve. Cursing loudly, I'm about to give up when I hear the soft purr of a car and the crunch of tires over ice. Headlights sweep over me briefly.

I wait for the car door to slam before I turn to watch him approach, his expensive sheepskin jacket unzipped, his red cashmere scarf trailing and his black curls glossy in the pale light. Not a grey hair on his head to mar the youthful charm that used to captivate me. We're both 35, but my beautiful, wavy red hair has faded to a dingy greyish brown. For God's sake, Mel, dye it, he'd say. You make it look like I married my mother!

I didn't have the energy or the inclination to please him, so I didn't dye it. But now, as part of the New Me, I splurged on an expensive cut and auburn dye job, "to bring out your lovely sea-green eyes," the stylist said.

My expensive cut is crammed under a tuque against the cold, but in a reckless moment, I yank it off and shake the curls loose. I've put on some makeup and covered my ratty parka with a colourful pashmina.

He stops at the sight of me, his usual haughty frown replaced by surprise. He doesn't say hello or 'you look nice', but he reaches into his parka pocket and pulls out a small bottle of Scotch. Waving it at me, he says, "I thought this might help you relax."

I feel my mood crumbling. It's Glenfiddich, a rare treat I could only afford by stealing from the food budget and feeding the boys mac and cheese. My dream Scotch, and I know he brought it tonight to remind me not just of what I am but of the power he holds. I want to say no, but the words stick in my throat. I have to keep control because tonight is too important. Tonight is the beginning of the New Me. If he wins tonight, I'll lose the rest. So I pick up the tatters of my self-confidence, turn away and gesture up the path that runs alongside the river. It's snow-covered but well trampled.

"It's a nice night, but I'm cold. Let's walk."

With a shrug, he takes a swig of Scotch and falls in beside me. "You've fixed yourself up. New man?"

"No, just new self-confidence."

"Was this little get-together your therapist's idea?"

I ignore the condescension in his tone. In his eyes, therapy is for the weak and needy. "No," I lie. "I've had a chance to take stock of myself."

"Good for you. It doesn't change anything, Mel. I'm still going for full custody."

My eyes smart. Staring straight ahead, I keep walking as the path reaches the edge of the park and heads into wooded darkness. On my right, tall apartment buildings loom above the trees, and on my left, the steep riverbank plunges to the river below. I suddenly notice how alone and invisible we are, and I pick up the pace.

"I just want to talk, Russ. Without the lawyers, without all the bitterness that has built up. To see if we can find some common ground for the boys' sake."

"The boys are a handful because they've been raising themselves. They need stability and firm discipline, and they need a good male role model. They'll be teenagers soon."

And you're the perfect role model. Arrogant, manipulative, cruel. I want to point out that boys need a female model, too, to learn compassion and tenderness, but I don't want to antagonize him. That never works out well for me, and tonight of all nights, I need to keep him happy.

He takes another sip and glances at me with a gleam in his eye. He holds out the bottle. "If you're cold, this will help."

I can smell the alcohol on his breath, the delicious aroma making me dizzy with need. In the dark I slip on an icy patch and, without thinking, reach out to grab his arm. "Sorry," I stammer, snatching my hand away.

"Lighten up, Mellie. It's just you and me."

The smell of the Scotch lingers in the air. Can I have a sip—just one sip—and still keep control? Would it help his mood if I join him in an amicable drink? More importantly, can I stay ahead of the game he's playing? "Okay," I say, "just a small sip, just this once."

He hands me the bottle, his hand touching mine. I raise the bottle, and the sharp, fruity liquid burns my lips. Aware of the shrewd glint in his eye, I close my eyes, tilt my head and pretend to take a deep drink. The taste on my lips is exquisite.

"Better?" he says softly, using that rich, mellow voice that used to melt my reserve.

"Yes," I murmur, and mean it. We walk on. Footing is tricky, and the path is in darkness, but I know that a few feet to my left, the ground drops steeply to the river below. Nervously I scan the tall apartment buildings through the screen of skeletal trees, but there are few lights in the windows overlooking the river.

I take a deep breath to brace myself. "I'm going back to school."

He stops in his tracks. I rush on before he can belittle my choice. He always told me I couldn't handle the pressures of graduate school while the twins were young. When they were first born, it made sense to put his own medical school training first, but over the years I lost myself. Lost my edge, my quick mind, my own dreams. I hardly remember the woman I dreamed of being. Is her brain too rusty and her spirit too broken to pick up the pieces now?

The thought terrifies me, but once I found myself in a decrepit one-bedroom basement apartment, surrounded by cheap novels and cheaper wine, with only an anti-social cat and the inane chatter of daytime television for company, I finally began to wonder. At first it was a relief to be alone, without his oppressive, brooding presence, but the absence of the boys was an ache that no amount of wine and pills could assuage.

Bit by bit, I started to imagine a life beyond my filthy apartment and booze-addled days. I was alone in the world. I'd left my home and family in New Brunswick when I went away to university. They were thrilled with my marriage, but they knew only the charming, successful Russ, not the contemptuous bully behind closed doors. If they noticed, on their occasional visits, my descent into despair and helplessness, they would probably blame me. And if they knew how it ended, they'd have shaken their heads and muttered dark warnings about old Aunt Margaret who was not right in the head.

"Forensic sciences," I say defiantly. "I'm going to start slowly. I need to upgrade my biochemistry, biology and maybe organic chem, but..."

"And how are you going to pay for this?"

"Well, it will be part-time at first. I'll keep my job."

"I thought you lost your job."

"I got another. I'm... I'm working on it, Russ. I'm going to get a bigger apartment with two bedrooms, so maybe eventually I can have the boys—"

"No."

I quiver. I'm losing. "I know what I did was—"

"Unforgivable."

"But I'm working on it. Turning my life around. I'm off the booze—"

He snorts and pulls out the bottle to take a long sip. Savouring it.

Watching me. I grit my teeth. "But I want to prove to you, and the courts, that eventually I can be a part of their lives."

"They were traumatized. They don't even want to see you."

My worst fear is that he'll turn them against me. Through a blur of tears, I slip on the ice and teeter near the edge of the bank. The river below is frozen, but in March the ice will be thin. I force myself to steady my step and control my tone. I mustn't fight with him! How can I get things back on track?

"I know they're upset. I totally understand that. I'm not going to rush them into anything."

He takes another swig of Scotch and walks on. Only a slight wobble in his step gives him away.

The path slopes down toward another park, and it's slippery as I hurry to catch up. "I don't want to fight, Russ. I want to get past all that. I understand how you feel, respect how you feel." I nearly choke on the words. "I didn't used to be like this. Remember...?"

I stumble on the rutted path and reach out to grab him. This time I don't pull away. My skin crawls as I link my arm through his to steady myself. "I've been thinking about how we used to be, before the kids, before life got so busy. The fun we had, the laughs, the simple things." I press against him affectionately. Breathe in the familiar earthy smell of his jacket. We cross the flat section of the park where the river widens into a small bay. He takes another sip— how many is that now?—and to my surprise, he offers me the bottle again. I try to hide my craving as I take another tiny sip, but all my senses hum.

I'm not lying about the laughter and the joy in simple things. To all our friends, we were the perfect couple, meeting over lab work in second year biology and getting engaged right after undergraduate school. We were smart and beautiful: him with his thick black hair, sultry eyes and bad boy smile; me with my red hair, porcelain skin and fragility. I don't know exactly when I became a burden instead of a playmate, an irritation instead of a joy. Probably when I was pregnant, flattened by exhaustion and morning sickness, my beautiful hair fading and my perfect skin erupting in zits. He buried himself in his studies and became impatient that I couldn't even drag out the vacuum cleaner or cook a decent meal. It didn't help that the smallest criticism made me burst into tears.

I hoped the arrival of the twins would bring out his nurturing side, but his contempt and coldness only got worse as I tried to cope with two screaming babies. Women have been doing this for millennia, Mel! Pull yourself together.

A glass of wine after dinner became my reward for surviving the day. Soon there was a second after I got the twins to bed. No fancy sleep training for them. Let them cry it out, Russ insisted. They've got to learn. Then he'd retreat to his study with his headphones. As I listened to the wails, I topped up my wine.

That's how it started. Not that I ever wished for a different life; I love my little boys with a fierceness that surprises me. I promised myself things would get better once Russ finished his residency and the boys were older. Then we'd finally be a proper family. Sometimes, just sometimes, it almost felt like that. I learned to be careful not to arouse his anger so the boys would never see the brandished fist or the twisted arm. Despite threats, he never hit them; cruel put-downs and ripped-up schoolwork were enough.

Now I try to put those awful memories aside and find happier ones. Pointing to the shoreline, I force a light laugh. "Do you remember how Timmy and Jaco used to play with their boats in the little bay there? They had such fun."

He stops to gaze out over the icy bay, his expression thoughtful. Is he softening? I venture further, into the heart of the matter.

"Do they have to go to Upper Canada College, Russ? Ashbury has a good reputation, and it's right near your house." I hold my breath, afraid I've pushed too far.

"We've been over this, Mel. This hasn't been easy for me either. I work long hours, and leaving them with a housekeeper is no way to keep teenage boys out of trouble."

They're not teenagers yet. They're only 10! "Well...maybe I could—"

"No, you can't."

He strides off, pulling me along the path into the darkness, with the steep riverbank on one side and a row of elegant townhouses on the other. From their balconies, the owners have a spectacular, private view of the river. I always dreamed of living here within easy reach of the university and downtown. The houses are quiet now, their owners cocooned inside reading or watching television.

I'm running out of options. He's so intransigent, so convinced he's right that he'll never see my side, never understand the black despair that drove me to that ultimate choice.

With an effort, I keep my arm linked through his and rest my cheek against his chest. "Any more of that Scotch?"

He pulls out the bottle and takes another swig before holding it out. "Not much left, but here."

"Thanks, but you finish it." It's a small bottle, but he's managed to consume almost all of it. He's drinking more than he used to. Is it my imagination or is there a slight stagger in his step?

He drains the bottle, tucks it away and pulls a small silver flask from another pocket. "I brought emergency backup. Here."

Since when does he need emergency backup? Or a secret flask? I hide my shock with an elaborate show of delight. As I savour a few small drops, I stop to look down at the shore and spot the limbs of an old tree leaning over the ice. The snow around it is trampled with footprints.

"It's beautiful here, but I'm getting a bit tired. Should we go back, or...?"

He studies the river. "Let's sit for a while first. There's a good spot down there."

He holds my hand as we slither down the icy bank to the river's edge. "It looks as if other people had the same idea," he says, pointing to the footprints.

We sit side by side on the tree bough, and for the first time, I notice the wind sweeping up the river. I pull my parka tight. "It's cold, though."

He wraps his arm around me, and involuntarily I tense. Old habits die hard. I sneak a quick peek at the townhouses above.

Through the lacey screen of bushes, I can make out blue light flickering in a window, but no one will be able to see us in the darkness.

"Boarding school will be good for them, Mel," he says as if he's discussing broccoli for dinner. "The discipline, the team spirit and lifelong friendships."

What should I say? If I contradict him, I might ruin his good mood. Or worse, trigger his cold rage. I try to match his amiable tone. "They're still so young."

"You've babied them."

I was trying to make up for you, I wanted to shout. But he's right. My parenting was wildly erratic, ranging from complete neglect that forced them to scrounge through half-empty cupboards for a can of something edible for supper to taking them on extravagant shopping sprees on the days Russ gave me money. Showering them with kisses one day and shutting myself in my bedroom the next.

Until that fateful day.

As I wallow in my guilt, he's watching the river. On the far shore, a sprinkling of lights and the red and white flashes of moving cars are all that penetrate the dark. The traffic is a distant murmur.

"Do you know," he muses, "it can take only a minute, maybe less, for a person to be incapacitated in freezing water? When you first fall in, the shock can cause cardiac arrest or trigger a gasp reflex that fills your lungs with water. Even if that doesn't kill you, within 10 minutes you lose muscle strength and coordination in your limbs, so you can't swim. When that happens, unless you're rescued, it's game over."

A chill creeps through me. Is this just Russ showing off his superior knowledge, or is there a subtle warning in his words? I sneak another look at the townhouses. Is anyone watching? Does anyone even know we're here?

I decide to play it light. Faking a laugh, I point to the footprints in the snow heading out from shore. "It looks as if someone decided to test that theory."

He turns on his phone flashlight, illuminating the pockmarked surface of the snow. There's not just one set of prints but several disappearing into the darkness ahead.

"I don't see any prints coming back," I say, "so I assume they made it across."

"We would have heard something if they hadn't. The news is full of dire warnings to stay off the ice at this time of the year." He shares the flask with me. I watch him carefully for the familiar danger signs that he's tipping over the edge. I press closer to him, trying to hide my trembling. "I suppose you are right. Scary, though."

"The ice is still solid. I bet it would be fun. We could walk across to Vanier and take the river path back up the other side to the bridge where we started."

"Now there's a brilliant idea," I mutter.

He reaches for my hand. "Come on, Mel. It would be an adventure. It's so peaceful out there, like we're miles from civilization."

Behind me, I hear the quiet opening of a door and a brief escape of music before it shuts again. Is someone out on the balcony? Have they heard our voices? An instant later, I glimpse the orange glow of a cigarette.

"They'll see us," I whisper.

"Who cares? Is it a crime to walk on the ice?"

"No, but..."

He leaps to his feet, swaying slightly, and flings his arms wide. In the darkness, I can see the whites of his eyes. "It would be a rush. That's your problem, Mel. You worry too much, never take risks, never think big. You spend your life curled up in a little ball, frozen with fear. You won't apply to the forensic sciences program. You won't even finish the courses you need. You'll quit at the first sign of hardship, just like you quit school the moment you got pregnant. Take the easy way out, just like you did last summer."

I let him talk, not caring if the smoker overhears him. I can't stop him anyway, not once he's begun to spiral. Emotions rush through me. Shame at the reminder of that night when I took every pill in the house and left it to two panicked nine-year-olds to call 9-1-1. Hurt at his dismissal of that night—that night when I decided my boys would be better off without me—as just 'the easy way out'. Rage that he was so wilfully blind to my despair. Fear of what the future holds for my little boys in his hands. But beneath the emotions, a whisper of doubt sounds. What's the endgame of this rant? Is this whole evening—meeting me, talking about our future, plying me with Scotch—just a prelude to this moment?

Is he goading me into one last reckless, suicidal act?

He takes my hand. "I'll rescue you, you know, if you fall in. I would never let you drown."

No you won't, no matter what powers you think you have. I've walked this river path dozens of times in summer and winter. The powerful current would sweep me beneath the ice in seconds.

Feeling the pressure of his grip, I glance up once more at the balcony. The orange glow is gone. Taking a deep breath, I stand up. "Okay, let's do it. But turn the flashlight back on so we can see how safe it is."

"The moonlight on the snow is all we need." He steps out onto the ice, pulling me with him. "It's beautiful. You walk ahead, and I'll take some photos."

I balk and break his grip. "I need both hands for balance. You go ahead and make sure it's safe."

"No, I want—"

"I'll be right behind you."

With a shrug, he sets off. He moves at a cocky jaunt over the snow-covered ice, occasionally kicking it to test its strength. The darkness is lightened by the crescent moon and the canopy of stars reflecting off white snow, creating a spooky pallor. I follow at a cautious distance, studying his footprints for signs of seeping water.

About halfway across, he turns to me. "Hurry up, Mel! Stay close to me. I can't help you if you're way back there."

My heart beats faster. "I'm coming, but it's scary."

"It's beautiful! And we're getting there." He spreads his arms to turn in a circle, and his boot sinks deep into the slushy snow. He leaps backward, swearing, as the ice cracks. Water pools around his boots. "Mel," he shouts. "Help me!"

I scramble backwards as the crack widens and the ice opens up, plunging him into the frigid current. He doesn't even cry out. His eyes bulge in panic, and his arms flail briefly against the breaking shards of ice before the current sucks him relentlessly under. I stand for a few more seconds, watching the water churn against the edge of the hole until all trace of disturbance is gone.

Then I begin to scream, long and loud, as I pull out my phone to call 9-1-1.

Barbara Fradkin, a retired child psychologist with a fascination for why we turn bad, has published over 30 short stories and 21 novels, several of which have been shortlisted or won Awards of Excellence from Crime Writers of Canada. She is probably best known for her long-running series featuring quixotic Ottawa Police Inspector Michael Green. This gritty series has earned two Best Novel Awards of Excellence, as well as two additional nominations. The twelfth, SHIPWRECKED SOULS, was released in 2025. Her Amanda Doucette series features an adventurous foreign aid worker who battles her own trauma to help people in trouble.

THE SPARKS STREET SAPPER

2

A.E. PITTMAN

Isabelle parked next to the cluster of cops and broken glass at the Sparks Street pedestrian mall. She sighed as she looked at the bookstore's busted front door. This wasn't how she had imagined her first case, and it certainly didn't seem like the kind of thing you would get called out of bed for. But she was determined to make a good first impression. So she tried to look professional as she stepped out of her unmarked car, adjusting her black leather jacket to ensure everyone could see the shield on her belt.

Constable Isaac Davis, a balding and slightly overweight patrol officer, was leaning against a sandstone column beside Bytown Books. He acknowledged her with a nod. "Detective Paradis."

"Hey Isaac, how's it going?"

"No complaints. Congrats on the promotion."

"Thanks," she smiled. "I'm supposed to be working with," she checked her notebook, "Detective Sergeant Brown. Is he around?"

"Not yet."

"OK, I might as well get started without him. Were you first on scene?"

"Yup. Alarm came in at 03:03. I was just around the corner on Elgin, so I got here at 03:07. Cleared the shop. Nobody inside."

"Really? After getting here that fast, you didn't even see our bad guy running away?"

Isaac shrugged. "Sometimes takes 10 minutes before an alarm is even relayed to us. You know that."

"True," Isabelle replied without conviction. "OK. What else can you tell me?"

"Looks like a smash-n-grab. Perp broke in through the glass door, busted the cash register and a book display cabinet. Owner is coming down to confirm what's actually missing. Luckily we've actually got a witness to this one."

Isaac walked behind the sandstone column into a record store and returned with a tall lanky man who had dark beady eyes and a crooked nose. "This here is Charlie Packard, night cleaner at Vinyl Groove. Says he saw our perp."

Isabelle took out her notebook. "OK, great. Mr. Packard, I'm Detective Constable Isabelle Paradis. What can you tell me about the break-in?"

"I was mopping the floor out back when I heard glass smashing and an alarm going off. When I came out front, I saw a homeless guy going into Bytown Books."

"What time was that?"

"A little before 3 a.m., I guess."

"OK, and what did he look like?"

"Small scrawny guy. Wore camo gear with Canadian flag patches. And he had a green beret with something red pinned on it."

"What happened next?"

"Figured you guys were on the way, so I stayed in the record store with the door locked. Heard him busting stuff next door. Then he ran away. Oh, and his beret must have fallen off because he wasn't wearing it when he left."

"OK. What direction did he go?"

"Towards Elgin Street."

"You sure about that?"

"Yeah. Why wouldn't I be?"

Isabelle let Packard return to work; they could get a formal statement later. She wondered, again, about the timing. There were no alleys or structures on Sparks Street where a suspect could hide. Even if dispatching the alarm had been delayed, how could Isaac have missed a suspect running towards Elgin?

An ident tech came up to Isabelle. "Checked for prints, nothing useful. But the smudges suggest that whoever knocked the cash register over was wearing gloves. I'll send you the report later."

Isabelle watched the ident tech leave. Why would their suspect be wearing gloves? Most homeless people wouldn't have bothered with that precaution.

She decided to take a closer look at the crime scene. The shop had a counter with a variety of coffee machines, the walls were lined with stacks of used books, and it was furnished with comfy couches and a dozen wooden chairs scattered around small tables. On the floor, next to pieces of the cash register, Isabelle saw a green beret with a red maple leaf pinned to it.

Isaac cleared his throat. "I'm pretty sure that hat belongs to Captain Canada."

"Who?"

"A street person matching the description of our perp, usually hangs out around the ByWard Market."

"OK. Does he have a real name?"

"Not that I know of."

This wasn't exactly the crime of the century. But Isabelle liked the prospect of presenting her new boss with a case that was essentially solved. Going through a mental checklist, she asked Isaac to follow up with a formal statement from Packard.

"No problem," he replied. "By the way, your partner just got here."

Having recently spent an entire paycheque on her wardrobe, Isabelle couldn't help but notice her partner's attire. His greyish London Fog overcoat was fraying around the edges, his brown pants were faded, and his wire rim glasses made him look like a nerd. Still, it wasn't her place to judge his fashion choices. She squared her shoulders and introduced herself. "I'm your new partner, Detective Constable Isabelle Paradis."

Her boss smiled, lighting up his face, and replied with a friendly Jamaican lilt. "Yes, Yes. It is certainly a pleasure to meet you. Please call me Devan. May I call you Isabelle?"

"Sure."

Devan's phone rang. He took it out of his breast pocket, pressed mute and put it away. That seemed odd to Isabelle because the call display said O'Connor—as in Deputy Chief Mickey O'Connor, head of major crimes.

Isabelle bit her lower lip. "No disrespect, but why are we here for this? And why is senior management calling you about it?"

Devan gave her a half-smile. "Politics. The Chamber of Commerce is complaining about a spike in property offences, and this particular crime scene is only a block away from Parliament Hill. So I suspect senior management will be monitoring this case fairly closely. What have you learned so far?"

Isabelle outlined what she knew about the break-in and told her partner about Captain Canada.

"Good work," Devan said. "Let's take another look at our crime scene."

As they walked towards Bytown Books, Devan stopped in front of Vinyl Groove. He adjusted his glasses and stared at bits of soil on the cobblestone sidewalk.

Isabelle hadn't noticed the dirt before. "OK. So that's interesting," she began, "but I can't make out any helpful details like tread or shoe size."

The owner of Bytown Books, Kimi Wolfe, came up to them. Kimi was an attractive woman, wearing a moose-hide jacket with a medicine-wheel button pinned to its lapel. She grimaced as she glanced at her shop's broken door, then turned towards the detectives.

Devan told his partner to check out the shop with Ms. Wolfe. Then he ran across the boulevard, waving his arms to flag down a street-cleaning truck that was driving by.

Kimi Wolfe raised her eyebrows but didn't ask. She proceeded to look around Bytown Books with Isabelle and confirmed that nothing had been disturbed except the cash register and the display case. Less than a $100, mostly in $5 and $10 bills, had been stolen, and the only thing taken from the display case was a second-hand book titled *Construction of the Rideau Canal by the Royal Engineers*.

Devan came in, gazing at the wall of books like a kid in a candy store. Isabelle briefed him on what Kimi had said, figuring that gave them enough to arrest their suspect. Instead of leaving, Devan asked the shop owner about the stolen book.

Kimi sighed. "What can I tell you? It was just a book. I bought it for $20 at an estate sale for some retired civil servant. Apparently he bought the book because it mentions his great-great grandfather, who actually helped Colonel John By build the canal."

"What does the book look like?"

"Large, black binding, gold letters on the cover. Thing is, it wasn't even for sale. I was only using it to draw customers into my shop to buy coffee."

Devan's eyes lit up. "How?"

"Trivia. I left the book open in the display case. Every week I turned the page so customers could read a different section while waiting in line. And every week I posted a new question based on facts from the pages on display. Customers who correctly answered a question got their names put in a draw for a gift card."

Isabelle looked at the trivia question posted on the board: What is the name of the Bytown cemetery where many canal workers were buried?

"Is there perhaps another book in your shop that is roughly the same size as the one that was stolen, so I can understand how large it is?"

Wolfe looked around and then pointed to a thick volume titled *Political History of Eastern Europe*. "It's about the same size as that text-book. In fact, I bought both of them at the same estate sale."

Devan handed the book to Isabelle, who looked at it with feigned interest. The book was too large to comfortably hold in one hand, so she put it on the counter.

"Are you, perhaps, able to think of anyone who showed a particular interest in the stolen book?" Devan asked.

"Well, Presley Stirling kept trying to buy it," Kimi replied.

"Do you know why?"

"He studies local history. Actually runs Bytown's Haunted History Tours, just down the street."

Devan nodded. "Does anyone else come to mind?"

"No. Except, well, there's a diplomat. Pavel, Pavel Igorevich." She blushed. "Everyone talks about the trivia questions. But he always took it a step further. Like last week, he told me that the answer for the trivia question was the Barrack Hill Cemetery. The book refers to that. But Pavel also knew that Sparks Street was built on part of that cemetery. Anyway, Pavel's getting transferred back to Russia and he was joking that he wanted the book as a souvenir."

Isabelle wanted to get the investigation back on track, so she asked if anyone matching the description of Captain Canada had been hanging around Bytown Books. Kimi shook her head and said she didn't recall seeing anyone like that around her shop.

The detectives left Bytown Books, and Isabelle grinned up at her boss. "Not much of a file, but at least it's pretty much done. All we've got to do is find and arrest this Captain Canada character."

"I am not so sure. The theft of cash makes sense, I guess. But why would our suspect run off with a big bulky book that is not worth much money? And are we supposed to believe that he wore gloves to avoid being identified but still left his hat at the crime scene?"

"OK. There may be a few loose ends. But all the evidence points to Captain Canada."

Devan smiled. "Alligator lay egg, but him no fowl."

The detectives took Devan's car and, after asking around, found their prime suspect lying under a hot air vent near a service entrance for the Élisabeth-Bruyère hospital.

Captain Canada rubbed his eyes and squinted up at the detectives. There was no book in sight, and his only possession appeared to be a Styrofoam cup filled with loonies and toonies.

Devan crouched down and presented his badge. "We are from the Ottawa Police Service; we need to ask you a few questions."

"Didn't do nothin'. Man's gotta sleep somewhere."

"We are not here to discuss your choice of accommodation. Could you please tell me your name?"

"Captain Canada!"

Devan responded quietly, "What name did you go by when you served as a combat engineer in the army?"

"How ya know about that?"

Devan pointed to a tattoo on Captain Canada's left wrist: Ubique. "The motto for Canadian combat engineers, I believe."

Captain Canada stroked his tattoo. "Glenn McKenzie. Master Corporal Glenn McKenzie."

"May we call you Glenn?"

He looked down and nodded.

"Glenn, what do you know about a break-in at a shop on Sparks Street a few hours ago?"

"Sparks Street? Nothin'. Been here since midnight."

"Can anyone confirm that?"

Glenn gestured towards some empty boxes a few feet away from him. "Yeah, all my invisible friends."

Devan convinced Glenn to agree to a consent search, and the detective confirmed that their suspect did not have any cash apart from the coins in his cup. Devan then pointed to the green beret that Isabelle was holding in a clear evidence bag. "Does this hat have any significance to you?"

"Hey, that's mine!"

Isabelle discretely took out her handcuffs. That admission put their suspect at the scene of the crime. Case closed.

Devan adjusted his glasses. "Glenn, do you have any idea how your hat ended up in a book shop that was broken into a few hours ago?"

"Someone must've stolen it while I was sleeping. But it's mine. I want it back!"

Devan frowned. "I am sorry Glenn, we need your hat for our inquiries right now. I will touch base with you soon."

Isabelle followed Devan back to his car. She put her handcuffs away, feeling uneasy about their lack of progress on what seemed like a fairly simple case. She heard Devan's phone buzz and noticed him put it away when he saw the call was from O'Connor. Pissing off the head of major crimes didn't seem very wise to Isabelle, and she was beginning to worry that her new partner's behaviour could impact her career prospects as well.

Isabelle tried to not sound sarcastic. "OK, so we're not even taking him in for questioning."

"I would like to follow up on a few other points first."

She bit her lower lip. "With all due respect, Devan, what points, exactly, do we need to follow up? I mean, we have an eyewitness who says he saw our suspect break into Bytown Books. Our suspect admits that the hat left in the shop belongs to him. He clearly needs the money. And he has no alibi. It seems to me that the facts speak for themselves."

"You are not wrong. But I believe those facts raise some interesting questions."

Isabelle exhaled slowly. "What questions?"

Devan smiled. "Well, as our most newly minted detective, what questions come to your mind?"

She had to, literally, count to ten. "All right. Well, Captain Canada doesn't have the cash from the shop. And he doesn't have the book. So I guess we could ask where that stuff is."

"Good. Anything else?"

"Why steal the book in the first place? I mean, it's not worth much and would've been hard to carry. Hey, our guy used to be a combat engineer, and the book is about army engineers. Maybe there's a connection!"

"That is a very astute observation."

Isabelle smiled. "OK. But does any of this really matter when we have an eyewitness statement which is corroborated by physical evidence?"

"I suspect the outcome of our investigation will matter a great deal to Glenn McKenzie if he gets charged for the offence. And, frankly, I do not find the evidence you have cited to be as conclusive as it might seem."

The detectives went to Tim Hortons for coffee and a couple of bran muffins. After reviewing the facts of their case, Devan said he wanted to interview the people who had expressed an interest in the stolen book. Isabelle thought that was a red herring, but Devan was the senior investigator. So they headed back to Bytown Books.

Kimi pointed out Pavel Igorevich when he entered the shop. Short and stubby, the diplomat shook his head sadly as he glanced at the busted book cabinet. He told Kimi that he was sorry this had happened to her and then left after buying a cup of tea.

The detectives followed the Russian out of the shop. Devan presented his badge. "Mr. Igorevich, we are making inquiries about the book that was stolen from the display cabinet. I understand you had an interest in it."

Igorevich lifted his chin slightly. "Officer, I have, how you say, diplomatic immunity."

"I recognize that; however, I would appreciate your assistance, that is if you are interested in helping Ms. Wolfe."

Igorevich looked towards the owner of Bytown Books. "Da. Well, do not see how I can help."

"Ms. Wolfe told us that you asked if you could have the book."

"Da. Wanted it as, how you say, keepsake."

"But Ms. Wolfe seemed to feel that you had a particular interest in the subject matter covered by the book."

"Of course. Am student of military history. Construction of canal for strategic purpose, yes. That was interest. Colonel By built canal. Glorious accomplishment. Then recalled to England. Wrongly accused of, how you say, fraud and stealing. Could have been great Russian novel I think."

"Am I correct that you are being transferred out of Canada soon?"

Igorevich looked towards Kimi Wolfe again. "Regrettable, but true."

"I read about the expulsion of five Russian diplomats for espionage. Are you one of them?"

"Bahh. Politics. Must go now."

Isabelle jotted down notes as Igorevich briskly walked away. Clearly her partner had visions of some kind of super-spy conspiracy over this used book. She had to admit that the Russian seemed evasive. But her money was still on the homeless guy.

Presley Sterling, a portly man wearing a beige jacket, wobbled towards them as they entered his office for Bytown's Haunted History Tours. "May I be of assistance?"

Devan presented his badge. "We are making inquiries concerning the break-in at Bytown Books."

"Really? I must say, it is reassuring that the authorities are taking this so seriously. Please, make yourselves comfortable." Sterling sat behind an old metal desk and motioned for the detectives to sit in two upholstered green chairs.

Isabelle sat down and took out her notebook. Devan surveyed a bookshelf of historical textbooks. Then he adjusted his glasses and studied a large framed map of Ottawa dated 1831, when the settlement was still called Bytown.

"Thought you already had your man. Some homeless chap," Sterling began.

Devan replied, "Where did you hear that?"

"Charles Packard. He's been a member of my historical society ever since he was a guard at the Bytown Museum."

Devan nodded. "I see. Actually, we have made no arrest to date. Ms. Wolfe told us that you wanted to purchase the stolen book. What was the nature of your interest in it?"

"Well, I certainly didn't steal the thing if that's what you're suggesting!"

"I am not suggesting anything. I am asking a question."

"Sorry, quite right, just doing your job and all that. First time dealing with inquiries of a criminal nature, you understand. Anything I can do to help, of course. Well, to answer your question, I had hoped to add the book to my collection. You see, I've been looking for a copy of that particular publication ever since they found the unmarked graves."

"Unmarked graves?" Devan asked.

Sterling smirked. "Over the last decade or so, construction projects near Sparks Street have stumbled onto dozens of unmarked graves from the 1800s. Most of them were for canal workers and their families, but they have also found the remains of some sappers. Do you know what a sapper is, Detective?"

Devan was still looking at the map. "Soldiers who serve in a combat engineering regiment."

Sterling pursed his lips. "Yes, quite. Well, in any event, there are several ghost stories about the sappers who died building the Rideau Canal, so I thought the book might provide useful insights."

"I see. Do you, by chance, have any theories on who might have wanted the book enough to steal it?"

"If it wasn't the homeless chap, I'd be looking pretty closely at that Soviet spy, Igor something or other."

"Mr. Pavel Igorevich?"

"Yeah, that's him. He's getting kicked out for trying to compromise government officials. And, unless I'm mistaken, the stolen book used to belong to an employee who worked for Canada's foreign service."

Isabelle sighed. How much more time were they going to waste on this espionage nonsense? She noticed her partner was smiling as he took out his iPhone and tapped something into a search engine.

When they left Sterling's office, Isabelle decided to speak her mind. "OK. So you're the boss. I get that. But you're getting calls from our deputy chief, which you're not answering. We have a solid suspect, who we have not arrested. And we seem to be spending our time going off on tangents. What's the game plan here?"

"I can understand your concerns Isabelle. I am, in fact, working on a theory. I will not share it with you at present because I want you to continue your inquiries with an open mind, but I am reasonably certain that we will be in a position to arrest someone within 24 hours if we split up our tasks."

Devan gave Isabelle two assignments and told her to get some sleep once they were done. He would pursue his own inquiries, and at midnight they would meet at the Elgin Street Diner to compare notes.

As they parted ways Isabelle saw her partner look at his buzzing phone, only to let the call go to voice mail.

Isabelle grimaced as she looked at her notebook. Tasks assigned to junior investigators were usually just loose ends that needed to be resolved. But her inquiries had failed to do that and had only left her with more questions.

And then, just as she was about to head home, she was cornered by Deputy Chief O'Connor, who was upset. Very upset. Why had his calls not been returned? And why had no arrest been made yet? She didn't want to throw her new partner under the bus. So she simply replied that she didn't know why his calls hadn't been returned. Which was true. And she tried to calmly explain that no arrest had been made because her partner wanted to be thorough. Which, despite her own misgivings, was also true. The deputy chief had scowled and stormed off, muttering comments about his ability to make or break careers.

Isabelle went home and took out her frustrations on a punching bag. After a shower and nuking some leftover lasagna, she got around five hours of sleep. Then she got up and went to the Elgin Street Diner.

The restaurant was brightly lit and smelled like freshly baked meat loaf. Isabelle walked up to the booth where Devan was sitting. "Thanks for nothing!"

"What do you mean?"

"Our beloved deputy chief tore a strip off me because you haven't bothered to return his calls."

"I am really sorry about…"

"I've worked hard to get where I am," she interrupted, "and I don't appreciate getting caught in the middle of whatever dispute you seem to be having with him."

Devan bit his lower lip. "I am sorry. O'Connor has a track record of demanding quick results, regardless of the facts. In this case, given the political nature of his interest, I avoided talking to him because I was worried he would order me to arrest Glenn McKenzie."

Isabelle sighed. "So do you actually believe this guy's innocent?"

"I do and I will tell you why. But first, I would like to hear about your inquiries."

"OK. Well. I had a good conversation with the museum librarian, but I'm not sure what to make of what she told me. And I'm not too happy with Packard's statement, now that I've taken a closer look at it."

Devan asked Isabelle to elaborate on her findings and smiled as she told him about the additional questions her inquiries had raised. He explained his theory, told her what he had learned and showed her a scanned document on his iPhone. Then he looked at his watch. "I believe it is time for us to effect an arrest."

From the shadow of an unlit entranceway, they watched a white panel van that was parked in front of Vinyl Groove.

Packard carried two large sacks out of the record store, put them in the van and returned to the store. The detectives walked behind the sandstone column beside Bytown Books and waited until Packard came back with two more sacks.

"Those look heavy," Devan commented.

Packard froze and looked behind him. "Oh, it's just you guys." He put the sacks into the van and closed the door. "What's up?"

"Just confirming a theory."

"What theory?"

"That you lied when you claimed you saw someone breaking into Bytown Books."

Packard crossed his arms and leaned against the panel van.

"I had my suspicions," Devan continued, "and Detective Paradis confirmed my assessment when she reviewed your statement. You claimed that you heard breaking glass and then saw a man wearing a green hat go into Bytown Books."

"So."

"Well, the glass would have been broken by someone standing right where we are now. And as we have just demonstrated, this pillar would have blocked your view."

Packard shrugged. "It all happened pretty fast, but I think you're right. I only saw him run away afterwards."

"Then you could not have seen him wearing his hat because that was left inside the shop."

"Why would I lie?"

"To distract us from the reason you broke into the shop: the book. The Bytown Museum had a copy of the same book, but their librarian told Detective Constable Paradis that it went missing while you worked there. Then you quit your position as a museum guard for a lower-paying job as a night cleaner at Vinyl Groove."

Packard pretended to yawn.

"I wondered what could be so important about this book, so I contacted the archives at the Royal Engineers Museum in Gillingham, England. They sent me a scanned copy of the book from their collection. Do you know what I discovered?"

Packard smirked. "No idea."

"An entire chapter was dedicated to allegations of theft. Colonel

By suspected the regimental quartermaster was pilfering gold coins from the safe but was never able to prove it. The book speculates that the quartermaster hid the stolen gold in a sapper's unmarked grave and that the quartermaster died of malaria without ever retrieving the coins. The book describes the location of the unmarked grave, but the landmarks it refers to no longer exist. So there was no way to locate the unmarked grave and the missing gold—until the other graves were found under Sparks Street. Using that discovery as a landmark, you were able to locate the sapper's unmarked grave under Vinyl Groove."

Packard wasn't smirking anymore.

"I talked to Vinyl Groove's owner earlier today. We found your excavation work, covered by floor boards and boxes. You have been digging in the basement every night and getting rid of the dirt. Some nights, like last night, a little soil spilled in front of Vinyl Groove, a pattern the street cleaner has noticed over the last few months."

Packard started to look around, like a trapped animal.

"Everything was going according to plan until history buffs started reading a copy of the book next door. You were afraid that one of them would figure it out."

Devan looked at Packard for a moment. "You know, breaking into Bytown Books and damaging Vinyl Groove property are criminal offences. Disturbing an unmarked grave is probably worse. But I think you'll spend more time in jail for trying to frame an innocent veteran for the crime."

Packard shrugged. "Maybe I've been digging underneath Vinyl Groove, a minor mischief charge. But you got no proof that I broke into Bytown Books or that I tried to frame that homeless guy."

"Well, there is the surveillance footage."

Packard laughed. "Nice try. Look around, no cameras anywhere around here."

"That is true. But there is a surveillance camera near the hospital's service entrance, where Glenn McKenzie was sleeping last night, and the video footage shows you stealing his hat."

Packard tried to push Isabelle out of the way, but she twisted his arm and drove him face down onto the sidewalk.

Devan was grinning as his partner handcuffed Packard. "Good work Isabelle. Now that we have made an arrest, do you think I should call Deputy Chief O'Connor?"

"I figure it can wait a couple hours," she replied. "I mean, I don't think he'd appreciate getting called in the middle of the night for something like this."

"I suppose not." Devan chuckled and took out his phone.

Everyone was at the press conference except Devan. He apparently had a prior commitment. Isabelle grit her teeth as Deputy Chief O'Connor droned on and on in an auditorium full of reporters and dignitaries, happily taking credit for Packard's arrest and the discovery of a major archeological find. It was, by all accounts, a good news story. The unknown sapper's remains had been reinterred in Beechwood's military cemetery. The recovered gold coins were being catalogued and would soon be on display in the Bytown Museum. And the Crown attorney figured Packard would be doing federal time at Joyceville.

Isabelle's dressy suit was getting increasingly uncomfortable as she drove back to headquarters. It had been a long day, and she was already late for a wine and cheese event that Deputy Chief O'Connor had ordered everyone to attend. But she pulled over beside Major's Hill Park when she saw Devan sitting on a bench and giving a green beret back to its owner. Isabelle loosened her jacket and smiled as she strolled in the sunshine towards the park bench.

A. E. Pittman is an emerging author whose stories (while entirely fictional) are influenced by his life experiences as a lawyer and a police

officer. He has previously published a story in the January 2023 edition of Mystery Magazine.

DEAD END

3

STEWART DUDLEY

The tree is one of the main reasons Penny bought the property—that and the garden and the delicious rumours about a haunted house. She wanted a house with character. With history. She wasn't going to find that on a suburban street in Barrhaven. Sean ignored the not-so-subtle barb when it was first delivered. His townhome backs onto a golf course in, yes, Barrhaven.

Five years into their relationship, Penny and Sean are content to live apart. He is only 10 minutes from her place in Manotick. The arrangement is ideal for two people in their mid-sixties, happy with companionship and its menu of benefits. They're both retired, she from teaching biology and anthropology at the University of Ottawa, he from a career with the Ottawa Police Service. She is free to garden by the river; he is free to golf in suburbia.

The tree—Penny's tree—is an oak near the bottom of her property. A Shumard oak, to be exact. *Quercus shumardii*, according to the arborist she had hired during the inspection. He'd guessed it to be 70 to 80 years old. Scarred only by the fleeting evidence of treehouses past, the tree has flourished in the flat section of the lawn just before it slopes down to the Rideau River.

Penny is busy now at the base of the oak. Sean watches from the kitchen window. She'd pushed a thick manila folder his way over lunch, the file she compiled on the history of the house, one of the last of the original homes with river frontage on Long Island.

He'd offered to help her in the garden, but it's been only a week since Doctor Omarro implanted two stents in his left coronary artery. Stents four and five to be precise. Sean feels that the surgeon may have missed a blockage this time. Angina is a crotchety old friend, and Sean has sensed it nagging more than once since the procedure. The stents were intended to fix that. He'll give them a couple of days, then check in with the cardio nurse. In the meantime, he will try to let Penny work alone. She'd insisted on it, and she isn't afraid to get her hands dirty.

Instead, Sean has made himself useful by baking lemon blueberry scones. The air is alive with the welcoming aroma of baking.

He returns to the file. Much of it he already knows. She's told him the stories often enough. Before she bought the property in 1996, she'd done more than her due diligence.

Renos to the old Victorian had doubled the estimates, creeping to eventually include major roof and foundation repairs, as well as complete electrical and plumbing upgrades.

Cha-ching, cha-ching.

"It's like digging up a grave," one contractor admitted. "You're never sure what you're going to find until you put a shovel in the ground."

Penny was told more than once that it would have been cheaper and easier to tear down and build fresh. But she's seen enough of that. To her, Ottawa is a city with no respect for the past—at least as far as architecture goes. She's been vindicated by the final product. The house stands out on the south end of the island for its authenticity and unassuming charm. That passing cars will stop in front of her home and skip others irks more than a few neighbours who believe their mega-million-dollar investments deserve more adoration.

The house is picturesque, but the gardens are the main draw. They always have been.

Doctor Earl Warner had the house built for his wife, Ella, in the 1920s. He ran his clinic out of the front rooms until the 1960s when he retired and sold his general practice to a young family physician. Both the Warners were gardeners, but credit for the design and upkeep of the property's landscaping went to Ella. For years she ran regular garden tours and hosted teas to raise money for charity. Early spring to late fall, the newspapers tripped over themselves to feature Warner blooms: lily of the valley, tulips, peonies, roses, delphiniums, asters, verbenas, gaillardias.

Penny could feel the garden's bones in the overgrowth when she'd first walked the lot with the realtor. She saw through the decades of neglect. It took 20 years, but she revived the garden, restoring some of Ella Warner's original design while adding her own touches.

Her file includes notes from interviews with a Mrs. Swindale who, by the late 1990s, had lived in the house next door for more than 60 years—first as a child and later as the homeowner, her parents having willed her their house in the 1970s.

Mrs. Swindale said she thought Doc Warner had planted the oak in Ella's memory. Five months pregnant, Mrs. Warner had been swept away by the river's rushing waters during the 100-year spring flood of 1938. The date put the age of the tree about right. But the pregnant wife—washed away and never found? According to Penny's batch of newspaper clippings, that tragic anomaly hadn't sat right at the time. The Rideau could rage during spring runoff, but it wasn't deep between Manotick and the Rideau Falls where it joins the Ottawa. The papers kicked up a fuss, maintaining that the body should have turned up. A little over a year later Canada was at war, and Mrs. Warner's disappearance was eclipsed along with so many other domestic mysteries.

Like others who have spent a lot of time on the Rideau River, Sean knows its knotted banks hide many places where a body could become permanently entangled.

He returns to the window. *Here we are again*, he thinks, *cleaning up after another 100-year spring flood.*

This year's ice and water had clawed the bank on the south side of the oak's root bed, as if stealing a slice of pie. The moment the water receded, Penny sprang into action to build a retaining wall and then backfill in support of the oak. The old tree has yet to tip, as far as Sean can tell, although Penny won't let him anywhere near it to inspect.

The flood seems to have taken a chunk out of her as well. She's been acting strange since the water levels hit record highs. The house was never in danger. Penny is usually more resilient in the face of adversity. Perhaps it was the existential threat to more of the garden.

It is just like her to get emotionally caught up with a tree.

A dozen pages into the file, Sean comes across a glossy brochure urging him to choose the greenest funeral option—soil transformation. In just eight weeks, his body could be transformed into a cubic yard of human compost.

Here's a flyer about planting your ashes in a sapling's root ball, and another on biodegradable burial pods in which your dead body is placed in the fetal position "beneath the young tree of your choice."

Okay, now I get it, he thinks. *Tree-hugging on steroids. That's my girl.*

Sean looks up to the view through the garden and down to the water. Penny is finishing her wall, which curls around the far side of the oak. She's anchored the barrier with cables sunk deep into the riverbank. She's laid every block herself—a fortress against the next 100-year flood.

The millionaire contractor two doors down had been a gentleman and ferried the blocks, crushed stone and topsoil from the driveway to the waterfront with his shiny new Kubota tractor. Of course, he had also taken the opportunity to remind Penny that his offer on her property still stands. Apparently, he's ready to sweeten the deal.

"Tea's on," Sean calls from the patio door.

She waves.

All that's left is to backfill the tree.

Now and then they spend the night together, sometimes in separate rooms, sometimes the same room. Penny had signalled Sean not to forget his overnight bag on this Saturday. She orders dinner in from the Black Dog. They each go a single glass deep into a good bottle of red and watch an episode of *The Diplomat* before heading upstairs.

Sean checks his watch—2:47 a.m. He realizes he'd fallen asleep almost immediately after they'd made love. Their frolics don't usually end so abruptly.

He rolls back onto his pillow and finds Penny awake beside him, sitting up, pillows against the headboard.

He squeezes her hand. "Sorry about that."

She squeezes back.

"You're the one who should have passed out after spending all day in the yard."

"I'm not the one who was just released from the heart institute. I was worried we might have gone at it a bit too hard."

"I love it when you talk sexy."

"Ha. I'm just relieved to see you awake and alive."

"So you haven't slept yet."

"The house is making too much noise."

Sean holds his tongue. Penny never says she believes the stories about the house being haunted, but it seems every week she drops a hint about some strange goings on, especially here on the second floor. She hears unexplained creaks on the stair landing, phantom knocks and wind noise when the air is still.

Sean has never experienced anything remotely otherworldly in the house, except for a few memorable lovemaking episodes.

She switches on her bedside lamp and brings the file onto her lap.

He sits up beside her.

"All this talk recently about making sure we have our affairs in order," he says. "I have to ask you again, love, are you okay? You're not hiding something from me?"

To his surprise, she takes a moment to consider his question.

"You can tell me anything," Sean says.

"You worked for the police."

"Honey, I managed the vehicle fleet. As a civilian. I was never a cop. What, you've robbed a bank or something?"

Her head tips forward.

He grins, reaching for a brochure. "It's these burial pods, isn't it? You went and bought one." He laughs. "I poked around on the web enough today to learn there's nowhere around here you can use them." He nudges her. "It's okay, I understand—I guess. It's not so strange for some, wanting to be buried with a tree."

"I think it would be magic." She caresses his arm. "Imagine, feeding the roots of a tree like Shumard."

Yes, the oak has a name.

"Well, if we're good for anything," Sean says, "I guess it would be fertilizer."

She slips on her reading glasses. "This is more serious than that."

"Oh?"

Her expression says she is weighing a heavy decision. "Promise not to get all bent out of shape," she says. "No trips to ER tonight."

He signals scout's honour.

She pulls her tablet from the bedside table and swipes to photos. The damage to the waterfront embankment is worse than Sean had thought. Too many tree roots exposed. One good windstorm could send the oak into the Rideau River.

"What do you see?"

He takes the tablet, zooms in on one image. "Roots."

"Look again."

What am I supposed to see? He alters the angle of view. "Okay, here and here kind of look like bones."

"They are bones."

"You're the one with the doctorate in biology. Fox. Badger. Porcupine. Even coyote. Lots of animals burrow into tree roots. Sometimes they go there to die."

"That photo gives you no sense of scale. I'm no forensic pathologist, but I do know human bones when I see them."

Sean feels the buzz of this news trickle into his system, the first adrenaline since the surgery, like a rush of ice in his veins.

"Here." She taps the screen with the tip of a ballpoint. "Part of a hip. Thigh bone. A couple of vertebrae."

"We have to call the police." He reaches for his phone. "You're sure about this?"

She places a hand on his arm. "Now? Not now, Sean. It's three in the morning."

He is out of bed in a flash of disbelief. "How long have you known about this?"

She shrugs. "A week?"

"Jesus Christ, Penny."

"I know, I know. It's unsettling."

"Honey, there's a dead body in your garden."

"Skeletal remains, Sean. Now get back here. You look silly hanging out there naked, and you promised you wouldn't get worked up."

"You shouldn't have told me something that would *get* me worked up." He bends over for his pants. "Show me."

"Now?"

Penny leads the way down the flagstone path, the flashlight's bright beam bouncing ahead of her, flaring in the mist. "Couldn't ask for a spookier scene."

The spring night's air is heavy with damp and the peaty fragrance of thawing earth. They are close to the river when she peels back a tarp, leans in, aims the flashlight and nods to the base of the tree. "Do you see?"

"Jesus Christ."

She moves the light to add dimension to the view.

"How can you be so calm?"

"I've worked on digs my whole life."

"This one's not in Kenya. It's here."

She shifts the flashlight's beam. "Look at that, how that root has threaded its way through the *obturator foramen*."

"The what?"

"The holes at the base of the hip bone. There. Nerves and blood vessels run through them to your legs. Now tree roots have taken their place." It's clear Penny finds this satisfying. "You can read a lot into that."

Sean turns to her. "What if it's her?"

"Ella Warner. Mm."

He digs deep for composure. "The doctor's pregnant wife. He said she'd been swept away in the flood."

"I'm thinking she may have miscarried. Or delivered prematurely right here. In the house. One night they were alone. It's early spring, maybe a storm. He can't get off the property. Something goes wrong. Maybe there's nothing he can do."

"Maybe he murdered her, you mean. Planted her in the ground with an oak sapling."

"Or prenatal depression," Penny continues. "She kills herself. A lot of stigma attached to suicide at the time. Doctor Warner is distraught. Can't think straight. All he can remember is that she wanted to be buried in the garden."

Sean takes a deep breath. "Have you touched anything?"

"The remains? No."

"Have you found any clothing, belongings?"

Penny studies him for a moment then nods. "A few bits of cloth." She digs in a pocket. "And this." It's a ring. She turns it in the light; Sean takes it from her fingers.

"It's a signet ring," she says. "A man's. I cleaned it. It's gold. But I haven't searched the crest yet."

He starts back to the house, the porch light his beacon. "We're calling the police."

"Can we have a cup of tea first?"

"I don't believe you."

"Sean... Slow *down*. You're not supposed to strain yourself."

"Stay with me now." Penny paces the living room in front of him. "Do we really have to call this in?"

"Penny."

"Give me a second. Listen. Drink your tea."

He complies.

"I made a decision to tell you about this, to trust you. I didn't have to."

"You're telling me this is some kind of test? Honey, the guy who built your house may have murdered his wife."

"They're all dead! It was 90 years ago. Warner was an only child; his wife came from Ireland via New York. No relatives. They had no other children. What's to be gained by calling 9-1-1?"

"Avoiding criminal charges."

"No one needs to know, Sean. I backfill Shumard. Poof. Nothing happened."

"*We'll* know."

Penny squats at his knee. "Honey, they will swarm my house and dig up my entire garden and cut down my tree." Saying aloud what she's been fearing for days brings her to tears.

She pounds the arm of the chair.

Sean jumps.

"I'm not going to let that happen," she says through gritted teeth. "*And* it'll be a media circus..."

"All this for a tree, Pen?"

"It's her!" She stands, wincing through the pain of sore legs. "She *is* that tree!"

"Ella. And—"

"And the baby, sure, yes, maybe. Don't you see? Their beauty is its beauty, too. They're alive in that tree."

In the fridge, the icemaker dumps a fresh load into its tray.

"You need to listen to yourself."

She drops onto the couch facing Sean.

"I choose not to see any crime here," she says.

"See, that's not so easy for me." Sean is struck that he and Penny may have found their wall.

"Forty-two million trees," she mumbles, eyes closed as if in prayer. "Cut down every day. Sacrificed."

He flips the burial pod flyer front to back. "So Ella Warner and her baby should be sacrificed for one oak?"

"They already were!" She's back on her feet. "We can't change that."

"Oh, damn it, Penny. What if it's not Ella Warner? What if it's someone who has surviving relatives? What if it's an Indigenous grave? Shouldn't we let them know—in, what is it, the spirit of reconciliation?"

She has no comeback.

"Your backyard is a crime scene."

"A 90-year-old crime scene."

"There is no statute of limitations for murder in Canada."

"There's no one to charge! It's a dead end."

"You've got that right. But the crime I'm talking about is you covering it up. For all we know, the good doctor buried bodies all over the yard. Maybe there are more recent graves." Sean hesitates. "Wait." He catches her eye, then shakes his head. "You—" He pulls himself up from the deep confines of his favourite chair.

Dizziness strikes him first. He tips and gropes to find his phone and the arms of the chair.

"Sean?"

A burning spike shoots from his chest up through his neck—a pain he's not familiar with.

She catches him and eases him back to the chair. "Where're your pills?"

In Barrhaven. He has new stents. Why would he need pills?

She snatches the phone from his hand.

He struggles for breath. *Don't leave.*

He sees her back away and run from the room; then his field of vision shifts. He's looking at himself from above, mere inches over his own head, which is flopped back against the chair. He rises higher, sees his arms and legs askew. He's lost all physical sense of himself. He has no feeling, only awareness that tells him someone else is with him—a form, a shade on the edge of his vision that vanishes the instant he looks for it.

Penny is back, fussing over him, checking his pulse. The shade withdraws, but Sean knows it's close. He tries to call out, but it's as though his lips have been sewn shut. Penny's hands go to her head. She paces the room, then shoves the coffee table aside, snaps open a blanket and spreads it on the floor. Sean watches helpless as she drags him onto the blanket, pushes his arms against his side. Penny, oblivious to the other presence, tucks in the edges as if she were wrapping a Christmas gift. Sean strains against his locked lips, all while rising higher and farther away. Penny rolls him once, twice. Rope appears. She loops it around his neck, his waist, his ankles. Then she grips the ankle rope and drags the shrouded form through the dining room and out onto the patio.

Sean wishes he hadn't lost so much weight. He floats overhead like a drone. No detail is lost to his view, but he is powerless to intervene.

An immense sense of futility settles over him.

The shade returns, edging farther into his vision, becoming increasingly opaque the closer they get to the oak. A woman. She leads the way down the path, a gossamer siren, checking back over her shoulder to make sure they're still with her. Sean watches his head bounce on the path to the big oak. At the tree, its roots snake from the earth to carry and cushion his body to lie in the wraith's welcoming arms. The first punches of topsoil slap his shroud. The woman strokes his head. He meets her beckoning, magnetic eyes as they tug his spirit and form back together. In that instant, he starts to fall to his place in the shroud.

Before the black hits, Sean's feeling returns, and he is cocooned in an angelic warmth. He also wonders why he ever thought he was a good judge of women's character.

Cold hands shock his face. She burrows into his mouth.

Sean chokes, coughs.

"Stop squirming. We have to get this under your tongue."

The burning sensation forces his eyes open. Penny's eyes are wet, scanning the pill bottle through reading glasses perched on the end of her nose.

"Judging by this evening, you're not taking that Viagra, which is a good thing." She tucks the bottle into her cardigan. "Ambulance is on the way." She fusses, sniffs. "I told you it was a good idea to leave some of the nitro here."

Penny adjusts the cushions, draws a blanket over him and brushes hair from his forehead. "My darling man. You hold on for me."

Sean reels at the chill of another cold hand against his face.

"Whoa there; it's just oxygen." The paramedic adjusts the mask. "Sean, I'm Marcie. This is Jason. We'll be your chauffeurs this morning."

Marcie catches Penny's eye. "When did you give him the nitro?"

"Maybe, I don't know, 10 minutes before you arrived," Penny says. "But the pain didn't stop, so I gave him another one."

A radio squawks.

"Readying for transport," Marcie reports.

Sean's eyes open as slits.

"There he is. Breathe deep for me, okay?"

The paramedics ease him onto the gurney, and Penny wraps her hands around his clenched fist. Jason tucks in the sheet, then laces the straps across Sean's legs. "Marcie," he says, chin-pointing to the patient. "He wants to say something."

Marcie lifts the oxygen mask.

Sean's eyes go to Penny. He opens his fist to reveal the ring.

Penny takes it. "Put it back?" She sees a nod.

Sean's eyes swing to Marcie as they wheel him to the door. "Did you know this house is haunted?"

Marcie resets the oxygen mask. "Now, Sean, not by you it isn't."

The paramedics ease the gurney down the front steps.

"I saw those brochures," Marcie says. "Jason's aunt recently did a biodegradable burial in California."

"Whatever makes your garden grow," Jason adds.

Marcie pats Sean's shoulder. "But you, my good man, are not heading for the compost just yet."

"You'll take him to the Civic?" Penny asks.

"Yes, ma'am. Want to ride with us?"

Stewart Dudley's first novel, The Cutting Room, was named among Kirkus Reviews' Best Indie Novels of 2014. It was also a finalist in the English fiction category at the 2015 Ottawa Book Awards. His crime novel, Six Days to Say Goodbye, is to be published independently in 2025.

THE INCIDENT IN BYTOWN

4

NANCY PAWELEK

A lice sat on the settee, looking around impatiently. It was always the same at every party. Men stood in one large group talking in low, urgent voices, and women chatted in animated voices in clutches of two or three on the other side of the room.

Alice sipped her drink. She was weary of the gossip that preoccupied the women, and from what she could overhear, the men's conversation was neither as interesting nor as important as their postures suggested.

If only Penelope were here.

For almost seven weeks, Alice had stayed with her Uncle Percival, Aunt Mary and cousin Penelope in Bytown. Every day Alice had found cause to chide Penelope for her impulsive behaviour. Now, however, Alice would give anything to have Penelope beside her.

Alice's mind wandered back, to five weeks before, to the incident in Bytown...

"Set the stools down there," Alice instructed, "and I shall set up the paint box."

Determined, Penelope struggled with the two stools for a full minute before Alice stopped what she was doing, sighed at her cousin's efforts and walked over. "Honestly, Penelope. You don't have to force things. Just try another way—or ask for help." She showed her how to open the stool but noticed Penelope wasn't listening. She had stretched out her arms and was taking in the view.

Alice left her to her reverie and continued setting things up. "We shall only *sketch* tonight," she said as she laid out a piece of muslin and began arranging the stools and a table on it. "You should also take notes, remembering the colours. Tomorrow, at home, we shall do a rough sketch with paints, and if the weather holds, we shall bring the sketches back in a day or two and fill in details."

"So why did we bring all the paints with us, then, if we aren't painting tonight?" Penelope asked.

"To help us remember the hues of the colours we observe this evening." Alice stood back, admiring the way she had set everything up. "You dab bits of colour on the sketch, like a visual cue."

"Oh. I see."

"We are doing the background tonight, and tomorrow we will come a bit earlier and try to sketch the men as they work."

"Is it hard to draw the men—to catch the movement, I mean?"

"Well, that's why we sketch and practice until we get it right. Come now, sit down."

Penelope obeyed her cousin, taking her place beside the little table where Alice had laid out in orderly rows the graphite for sketching, the paint tubes, some small flat sticks and a well-used, grey rubber eraser.

Alice had also set down a flat piece of wood, which had symmetrical smudges of colour in a circular pattern on it. Penelope touched the colours gingerly to feel if they were wet and then, realizing they were not, pulled back her fingers.

"That's my colour wheel," Alice explained. Primary colours—red, blue and yellow—with different variations and the shades of green, purple and orange in between."

"Do I get a sheet of paper?" Penelope asked.

Alice placed a flat but uneven piece of wood onto Penelope's lap. A piece of paper had been fastened to it with wooden pegs.

"Now what?"

"Well, you use that to draw what you see. Start by sketching out the shoreline, the buildings and trees. You can erase your lines if they're not quite right. That's the way I was taught, and it worked for me. We shall see what you come up with on your own, and then I will critique it."

"So, I just—?" Penelope hesitated, making swishing motions with the paintbrush she had selected.

"Plunge right in, cousin, yes," Alice said, finishing Penelope's sentence, taking the brush from her and handing her a stub of charcoal.

"With this?"

"Yes. Use it to sketch what you see, *then* you use the paints afterwards to note the colours."

Alice took her own piece of wood and placed it in her lap. She sat up straight, breathed in deeply and then blew the air out through pursed lips. She took in the scene before her with satisfaction. "Very good. The sun is just about to set. That is the light I like best of all." Alice turned to her cousin to see if she was paying attention, but Penelope's head was already bent down over her paper.

"Excuse me, may I sit down?" a man's voice said next to her.

Alice looked up, her reverie interrupted. "Yes, of course." She looked at him sideways as he settled himself in beside her on the settee. She noticed he sat himself at an angle to face her, so she shifted her position in a similar way to speak to him directly. She had been introduced to this young man by her father after the Sunday service a few weeks before. "It's Henry, isn't it?"

"Henry Martin Lower," he replied, bowing his head ever so slightly.

"Alice Mary Fulford," she said, bowing her head in a similarly formal manner, which caused him to laugh.

Alice liked the sound of his laugh, she decided. "Are you enjoying the party, Henry?"

"Yes, quite."

Alice nodded in reply.

Alice waited for Henry to make the next attempt at conversation, but an awkward silence ensued. Alice sipped her drink and then looked around the room.

Henry cleared his throat. "If you don't mind me saying, Alice, a few minutes ago you looked as though you were miles away."

Alice smiled. "Well, I *was*, actually, in a manner of speaking. You see, I was thinking about a recent trip to Bytown."

"Bytown. Ah! And what took you there?"

Henry's eyes were brown, Alice noticed.

"A visit with relatives. My uncle is working on a project there, building one of the new sawmills. I call him my uncle, but technically he's a cousin of sorts. You see, his wife—my Aunt Mary—is my mother's cousin. Their daughter Penelope and I are almost the same age. We were born just one month apart, and so we have always been close."

Henry nodded, taking in this information. "And you went to visit them."

Alice nodded. "Yes. Actually, I was sketching and painting the commerce of Bytown."

"That sounds frightfully interesting." Henry was leaning forward now.

Alice shrugged. "Not really, no. Painting is merely a way for a woman like me to pass the time."

Henry's posture slumped slightly, and he leaned back again and looked down at his shoes.

Alice felt a pang of regret for her somewhat dismissive tone. She needed a way to remedy the situation. She glanced sideways as she said, "Actually, Henry, something interesting *did* happen to me while I was painting in Bytown."

"Oh?" Henry looked up at her again.

"Yes, well, my cousin Penelope and I had quite an adventure. We solved a murder!"

Henry's eyes opened wider and he sat a little taller. "Indeed?"

Alice nodded.

Henry leaned in again and fixed his gaze on her. "Please do tell me about it, Alice. It sounds rather exciting."

Alice frowned as she examined Penelope's sketch. "Are you sure? I didn't see anything that colour by the shore yesterday."

"It was there, I tell you, Alice. Why else would I have put that dab of colour there and made this notation? What does it matter, anyway? It's *my* sketch."

"But that's the thing about red, Penelope. One's eye is drawn to it. I think you should rinse it out. It's incongruous with the rest of the scene."

"I saw it, I tell you. I remember wondering what it was as I put the red dot on the paper to remember. But then, I was distracted when that man fell off the log into the water." Penelope giggled at the memory. "Do you remember the way he kept going back on the log and falling in the water over and over again? I do believe he was showing off for us, Alice."

"Honestly, Penelope, what a thought," Alice scolded her cousin. "Men like that are beneath our station."

"All I'm saying is—"

But Penelope never finished her sentence as, just then, the door to the parlour flung open. The two girls stood up involuntarily as the patriarch of the household strode across the room. He pulled open the cabinet, poured himself some whiskey and then drank it back in one gulp. It was obvious he hadn't noticed them.

"Father?" Penelope said tentatively. "Is everything all right?"

"Penelope!" Percival Rutherford swung around and coughed stiffly. "Oh, and Alice. I didn't realize you were in the room. I—we've had a bit of a shock at the sawmill, I'm afraid."

"What happened?" Penelope walked over to her father, touching him lightly on the arm.

"Our foreman was found dead this morning, floating in the river, down beyond Barrack Hill."

"My goodness!" Penelope said.

"A logging accident?" Alice asked.

"Actually, we suspect foul play."

"Indeed?" the cousins said in unison.

"Well, his skull had a rather brutal gash in it."

"Uncle Percival," Alice said sharply, "you must call the constabulary *at once* and report this."

"A policeman is on his way here now, in fact. I just needed something to steady my nerves before he arrives." He waved his whiskey glass weakly at them. "And the reason I have called the police is that we received a note at the mill today, a threatening note, which inferred that *your* fate would soon be the same as that of my foreman." He rubbed his left temple nervously.

Penelope frowned. "*Our* fate?"

"Yours and Alice's, yes."

"That doesn't make any sense. Why would anyone want to threaten us?"

"I have no idea. But in light of the note, it's likely that the death of my foreman was murder." Penelope's father poured himself another dose of whiskey and gulped it down quickly. "What I can't understand is why someone would want to harm you. It is why I`ve called the police. I just have to find a way to break the news to your mother. You know how anxious she gets when it comes to your safety in this town."

"You two are talking about murder? How fascinating."

Alice and Henry looked up. The woman was staring directly at Henry as she spoke.

"Hello, Elizabeth."

"Everyone! Henry and Alice are talking about a murder over here!" Elizabeth called out to the others as she pulled up a chair and sat down. "Alice, who was murdered, exactly? And why is this the first I am hearing about this?"

Alice paused before replying. Elizabeth was not her favourite acquaintance, and she was reluctant to give the woman any fodder for gossip. "It was a man working at a sawmill being built in Bytown. My uncle is overseeing the construction of the mill, and the dead man worked for him."

"Yes, that's right. You spent the spring season in Bytown, didn't you?" Elizabeth smiled sweetly at Henry while addressing her remarks to Alice. "You were there to do your sketches, weren't you?"

Alice nodded, noting Elizabeth's slightly caustic tone when referring to her art.

At Elizabeth's bidding, a few men and women had wandered over. Henry turned to them and caught them up. "Alice was just telling me that, during her visit to Bytown, a man's body was discovered, following which her uncle received a note saying she and her cousin would be killed next." Henry turned back to Alice. "Do go on, Alice."

"My heavens! Well, Bytown is still a very rough place. I mean, those riots last year." It was only the look on Henry's face that made Elizabeth stop and add, "Yes, *do* tell, Alice."

Alice sighed. She hadn't wanted Elizabeth to know the details of her visit, but there was no way to avoid sharing them with her now.

"*Your daughters will be painting their own deaths soon,*" Penelope read aloud, then handed the paper to Alice, who was seated beside her. "But what does this mean? And what is it you are expected to do exactly, Father?" Penelope asked.

Alice read the paper and then stood up to give the note to the police constable standing beside her uncle. "It doesn't make any sense, Uncle Percival. Neither Penelope nor I know the man who died," she said. "Maybe whoever wrote this is sending a message to you—someone displeased with how you are overseeing the building of the new sawmill for that New England investor, perhaps?"

"Could it be true, Percival?" Alice's Aunt Mary wailed.

Percival Rutherford looked sheepishly at his wife, who was wringing her hands and pacing in front of the window. He cleared his throat and turned to the police constable. "We have no way of knowing what this is about, which is exactly why I summoned the police." Then looking sternly at the two young women, he said, "And it is why the two of you must not leave the house until this whole matter has been sorted out."

"But—do you really think the girls are in danger, Percival?" Mrs. Rutherford asked.

"I'm not sure."

"My cousin will never forgive us if anything were to happen to Alice." Mrs. Rutherford turned to the constable, adding, "My cousin —Alice's mother—is married to the Anglican Bishop of Montreal. He was reluctant to let Alice come visit us to sketch and paint Bytown because he wasn't sure it was safe enough. We assured them it is safe enough for our Penelope, so it would be safe for Alice. They will be most distressed by this turn of events."

The constable stepped forward. "We are posting a police officer at your front step, night and day, just to be sure."

"But this is preposterous," Alice retorted. "Why would someone threaten us? All I've been doing, with Penelope as my companion, is painting scenes of Bytown and its various commercial activities."

"And where, exactly, have you been painting since you arrived, Miss Fulford?" The constable removed a stub of pencil and a small notebook from his pocket. "Perhaps if we knew the locations, we would have some place to start."

"But I've been everywhere—to various parts of the canal works, along the river where various logging activities take place, up at the military barracks and across the river to get a good view of the grist and woollen mills. I've painted the falls east of Barrack Hill, the markets and even the new cathedral being built. I can go fetch my portfolio, and we can look at the back of my sketches, where I make my notes—the date of the sketch and the location."

"Well, that's a good place to start," the constable said crisply. "Would you mind, Miss?"

"No, of course not," Alice replied, "But honestly, Constable, any number of people have seen me painting over the past two weeks. Ask Penelope. She was with me most days, walking me to various locations and occasionally keeping me company while I sketched. Many people stopped to ask what we were doing and to admire my drawings. I never thought anything of it and I doubt I could describe even one of the people I conversed with over the past few weeks. What about you, Penelope?"

"No," her cousin admitted, shaking her head. "They were just everyday people."

"Right, then," said the constable, closing his notebook. "We shall not waste police resources on that line of inquiry. But as we have no way of fully comprehending the nature of this threat, I really must insist that you remain here, at the house, until this matter is resolved."

"I agree." Percival's tone was firm.

"My feelings exactly," his wife added plaintively.

Percival turned to Alice. "I'm sorry, my dear, but as you can see, Bytown is still rather a rough place. We cannot be too careful."

"Wait," Penelope interrupted her father. She turned to the constable. "May I see that note again?"

He handed her the note, and as she read it, Penelope's mouth twisted in concentration. "Perhaps we are coming at this the wrong way."

"What do you mean, Miss?"

"Well, first of all, the note refers to daughters—in the plural. Alice and I do look somewhat alike, so someone could have mistaken us for sisters, especially in the evening dusk. But it can't be anyone who knows our family, Father, because they would know you only have one daughter. No, the person who wrote this note would have seen us at night, and there was only one night I was out painting with Alice, and that was last Tuesday evening for my first sketching lesson."

"Yes, that's right, Uncle Percival," Alice added, seeing the point Penelope was trying to make. "I recall quite clearly that we needed your carriage so we could be back home before dark. It must have been that evening when someone saw us together." She turned to her cousin. "Other than the logger, was there anyone else there along the shore that evening, Penelope?"

"Wait, there were loggers on the river that evening?" Percival asked.

"Yes, Father," Penelope replied. "Well, just one. He was showing off for us, making his log roll faster and faster until he fell in. Then he got back on the log and did it again." She smiled, remembering her amusement at his antics.

"Was it near the new mill that you were sketching?"

"Yes. Actually, no. We were a bit further downriver, where they square the logs and tie them together into rafts."

"This logger, would you know him to see him?"

"I suppose, yes. He had carrot-coloured hair. I remember thinking he must have been one of your Irish workers, Father."

"What was he wearing?" The constable was poised with his pencil and paper to take notes.

Alice spoke up before Penelope could reply. "Blue shirt, grey pants."

"You sound very certain, Miss," the constable noted.

"I'm an artist. I notice details."

"Well, then, it wasn't the foreman, the victim," the constable said, closing his notebook. "When his body was found, he was dressed in dark pants and a red shirt."

"Well, we certainly would have remembered if the logger was wearing red," Penelope spoke up. "You see, Alice and I have been arguing because my sketch showed a red patch near the shore, and she insists that there was nothing red there that evening, but as I told her, why else would I have—oh, my goodness!" Penelope gasped all of a sudden. She stared wide-eyed at the others, but only the police constable seemed to have caught the significance of what Penelope had just said. "You don't suppose—"

"What are you twittering about, Penelope?" Alice asked reproachfully.

"Don't you see? The red that I saw in the water. It was the foreman! It was his body that I saw. Or rather, his red shirt. He had already drowned!" Penelope jumped to her feet. "I shall get my sketch!" She ran from the room.

"Could it be true?" Mary Rutherford gasped.

Alice hesitated. "Penelope does have a frightfully active imagination. I didn't see anything red myself and I do have a keen sense of observation."

"That may be true, my dear. However, the fact remains the foreman was last seen very near the same place you and Penelope were sketching. And his body was later found along the shoreline, past the Rideau Falls. It's quite possible that Penelope *did* spot the body."

Penelope burst into the room, her cheeks flushed. "Here! There!" She thrust the paper in front of the constable, pointing at her rough sketch and the small dot of colour. "Red!" She exclaimed triumphantly, then added, "It was him! The dead foreman! I'm sure of it now. I just didn't realize it at the time!"

They all examined Penelope's sketch, which also showed an awkwardly rendered man on a log. Penelope suddenly jabbed at the figure in the centre of her painting and shrieked, "*He* killed him! The man showing off for us!"

"What?" Alice cried out, incredulous. "How can you say that, Penelope? You have no proof!"

"Don't you see? It's why he was showing off, falling in over and over again. He was trying to distract us! He knew the body was there and he didn't want us to see it."

Alice felt a flush of blood rush into her face as she realized her cousin may have a point. What she was suggesting made sense.

"Good heavens!" Mary Rutherford called out suddenly. "I feel faint!" and then she collapsed onto the window seat.

There was now quite a crowd gathered around Alice.

"Extraordinary!"

"Imagine!"

"Quite the coincidence."

Alice waited until the comments had died down before she continued. "Well, believe it or not, Penelope's theory turned out to be true. The police had been questioning some of the other men at the mill who admitted that the foreman often gambled with his work-mates. He threatened those working under him to gamble more and incur further debts to him. These men needed their jobs and felt trapped. More than one man admitted owing money to the dead man, though none felt the need to provide the police with the exact nature or size of their debts. I dare say, most of them were probably happy the foreman was dead."

Alice paused and smoothed the skirt of her dress. She looked up and saw all eyes were on her, but she turned and directed her next words to Henry. "That proved to be the motive, Henry. The man with the red hair had been cornered by the foreman near the rapids west of Barrack Hill. He was told to pay up or he would be fired. Talk turned to fists, as so often happens with these working men, and the foreman took a fierce punch to the head, which caused him to fall backwards against the rock outcropping, knocking him senseless before tumbling into the water."

"Are you saying the cad just let him drown?"

"Well, the man claims he was about to go after him to fish him out in case he was still alive, but then he looked up and saw us sketching and panicked."

"You hadn't heard them arguing?"

"The roar of the rapids is quite persistent in that area. They were probably around the bend when they had their altercation."

"But why the threatening note to your uncle?"

"To throw suspicion elsewhere. The man with the red hair recognized the carriage as belonging to Uncle Percival, who is overseeing the construction of the new mill. I guess he hoped that my uncle would believe that the death of his foreman was linked to a threat against his family and that the police wouldn't look so closely at the gambling debts owed to the dead man."

"Quite!"

"Did they catch him? The red-haired Irishman?"

Alice nodded soberly. "After Penelope and I identified the man we saw on the river that night among the workers at the mill, he confessed to it all." She turned to look Henry in the eye. "All this to say, Henry, that is how my cousin and I solved a murder."

"Bah!" Elizabeth sputtered. "It sounds more like it was Penelope who solved it, not you."

Alice felt a rush of irritation at this comment but she shrugged it away. Henry seemed more intent on her at the moment than on Elizabeth's remark. "We *both* identified the murderer," Alice said.

"One has to admit, it is quite extraordinary. An artist solves a murder!" Henry exclaimed.

Alice smiled bashfully. She decided then and there that she liked this Henry very much.

"I expect the painting that your cousin made will become famous one day." Henry added.

Alice laughed. "Well, Penelope certainly thinks so. She kept the dot of red in her painting and has given her sketch a fitting title: The Incident in Bytown."

Those who had gathered began to talk amongst themselves again and wander to other parts of the room.

Henry took this opportunity to lean in. "I should like to see some of the sketches that you made while you were in Bytown, Alice, if you would oblige. I've not yet had occasion to travel there."

"I would be happy to show them to you, Henry, if you are interested."

He nodded eagerly and then stood up. "Alice, may I get you

another drink? You must be parched after recounting your adventures."

"Yes, Henry, I am thirsty, now that you mention it. That would be very kind."

As she watched him move through the room, Alice smiled. For the first time in a very long time, she had enjoyed herself at a party.

As she waited for Henry's return, Alice began to compose in her head the letter that she would write tomorrow to her cousin Penelope.

Nancy Pawelek is a retired federal public servant who shares her love of creative writing by leading a program for life writing at Hospice Care Ottawa and facilitating writing workshops at the library in her neighbourhood. She spends her evenings watching crime shows and reading mystery novels. From time to time, she also dabbles in writing mysteries involving crime.

BLIND SPOT

5

KATIE TALLO

THURSDAY 10 A.M.

The limo fills with jasmine perfume. It makes the boy's eyes water. He shuts them tight, and a blood red universe dances across his eyelids. He wishes he could disappear into that red world so he wouldn't have to live in this one where parents and doctors and teachers treat him like he's wrong. Maybe in a red world he'd be right. Maybe draped in red, he'd be invincible like the superheroes in his comic books.

She swivels away from him, looks out the window, talking softly into her phone so he won't hear what she's saying. But he can hear her. His ears are fine. That's not the part of him that's broken.

The doctor says it's a genetic defect. She pauses, listening.

Yes, Henry, of course I asked. Pauses again.

Well then you should have been there instead of at your oh-so-important meeting.

The boy tries to sit taller in his seat so he can see the icy Ottawa River out the window, but he's still too small even though he just turned 12. His mother took away his booster seat.

You're not a baby anymore, darling.

He wonders if she liked him when he was a baby.

The limo turns onto Hillsdale Road and rolls through their Rockcliffe neighbourhood—the fancy part of town where *important people live*—like his parents and ambassadors, politicians and the King's representative—people who expect their houses and children to be perfect.

Didn't your grandfather have something wrong with his eyes? She sighs.

I'm not saying it's your fault, Henry.

The limo pulls through the ornate iron gates and drives up the tree-lined lane leading to the massive red-brick building.

It's gotten worse since his last examination. It's happening so fast.

The limo stops at the steps. The boy unbuckles, grabs his school bag and opens the door.

Oh, by all means, take the call, Henry. He could be going blind for all you care.

Fine. I said, fine. But don't work late tonight. It's parent-teacher interviews.

She hangs up. Doesn't look at the boy. He gets out. No goodbyes. The limo drives away.

The bright winter sun reflects off the snow. The glare is unbearable. The boy shields his thick glasses as the world becomes a haze. He stumbles up the stone steps of the private school. The front doors are locked. There's no point in knocking. They won't come. Classes are already underway. The boy lifts his collar as the bitter wind numbs his ears. He makes his way around the side of the building, boots crunching in the crusted snow.

At the rear, he hurries to the shelter of the alcove that leads to the back doors. As his eyes adjust to the shadows, he sees movement. Others are there. It's Fitz and his friends. They're huddled together sharing a cigarette.

Look who it is, boys. Playing hooky, Beachbum?

Fitz blocks the doors. One of his friends flicks the cigarette at the back of the boy's head. Sparks fly as another yanks the boy's school bag from his shoulder. It falls to the slushy ground. Fitz picks it up just as Mr. Harding pokes his head out one of the doors.

Back inside right now, lads.

Fitz shunts the school bag into the boy's chest as he pushes past. Fitz heads through the door and his minions follow. Mr. Harding stares at the boy.

Don't just stand there, Beacham. Chop, chop.

THURSDAY 3:45 P.M.

Under a dull grey sky, Beacham scurries along the path through the frosted woods behind the schoolyard. His street sits on the far side, and this path is the fastest way home. A blustery wind burns his cheeks. He's halfway through the woods when he hears crunching snow behind him. He should have waited in his hiding spot but he wanted to leave at the end-of-day bell like all the other boys. It was a mistake.

Beacham starts running. He knows who it is. Maybe today he'll get away. The crunching gets closer and closer. He makes another mistake—he looks back, trips and falls on his face, school bag skidding across the snow. He rolls onto his back. Fitz is standing over him. The bigger boy knee drops onto Beacham's chest, knocking the wind out of him. Beacham gulps for air. Fitz fakes like he's going to punch him but instead he stops short and rips Beacham's glasses from his face, tossing them into the snow.

No, I need them. Where are they?

You blind, Beachbum? They're right over there.

Fitz laughs and runs off. Beacham watches as the blur of Fitz is swallowed up by the woods. The boy lies back in the cold hard snow. He decides to stay there. It shouldn't take too long to freeze to death. His mother will probably be relieved that she can spend all her time on the new baby once it arrives. Beacham closes his eyes. A reddish gossamer web floats across his lids like jellyfish tentacles. He feels himself being wrapped in the warm, red web, pulled deeper and deeper.

A twig snaps, the sound pulling him from his web. Beacham opens his eyes and sits up. He looks around but he can't see who's there. He needs his glasses. He scrambles to his knees and crawls around, feeling for them. He finds them and puts them on. Beacham gets to his feet and staggers to his school bag, hoisting it onto his shoulder. Another snap. He spins around. A boy is standing in the woods not 20 feet away. He's about the same age as Beacham but he's not dressed right. Not for winter. His red jacket is thin and tattered. He has no mitts or scarf. He steps out of the woods. The stranger nods in the direction where Fitz ran off.

You know that wanker?

Beacham shrugs. The stranger cups his bare hands to his mouth and blows to warm them. Beacham looks at the holes in the boy's jeans and the dirt on his running shoes.

You poor?

The stranger shrugs. Beacham reaches into his bag and pulls out the rest of the tuna sandwich he didn't eat at lunch. He holds it out. The boy looks at Beacham's thick wool coat.

You rich?

Beacham shrugs. The stranger takes the sandwich.

Name's Murphy.

I'm Beacham.

Murphy eats the sandwich in two bites.

THURSDAY 5:30 P.M.

Beacham sits between his parents at a table across from Miss Kelly.

There have been a few mishaps lately in PE. Getting hit by the ball and such. Some of the other teachers have noticed he's having difficulty focusing. Is there anything going on at home?

Henry clears his throat.

It's his eyes. He's getting new glasses, right Clara?

His parents look at each other. He knows his father is lying. They won't say it out loud, but Beacham knows he's going blind. He's defective. It's in his genes and it's getting worse. No one can stop it. His mother adds her two cents.

He's not been himself lately. You see we're expecting. It's a big change.

She touches her belly. The teacher makes a note then looks at his parents.

Have you thought about enrolling him in an extracurricular activity? Maybe he could make a friend.

Beacham sees red.

I have a friend.

The three adults look at him like they just noticed he's in the room.

His name's Murphy.

The teacher sighs.

We don't have any Murphys enrolled at the school.

THURSDAY 7:30 P.M.

His mother stands by his open bedroom door, hand resting on her belly. His father tucks in his covers and sits on the edge of his bed. He never does that. He's trying to act like a dad.

This Murphy fella. Where'd you meet him?

In Village Green Park.

So, he lives in the neighbourhood?

I don't think he has a house. I think he lives in the park.

His father looks at his mother. They don't believe him. Henry furrows his brow.

A homeless boy?

Beacham rolls over. He doesn't care what his parents think. Murphy is real.

THURSDAY 8:00 P.M.

Beacham sits on the landing and watches his mother through the railing. She's put on red lipstick. She doesn't look like his mother anymore; she looks like Clara. She dims the lights and gives the room a once-over. She straightens the books of photography on the glass coffee table and adjusts the matching white sofas so they're centred below the red painting she bought at an auction at Sotheby's. Clara repositions the rack on the mantel that holds the ornamental dagger Henry brought home from a business trip to Japan. Everything has to be perfect.

She is checking her reflection in the floor-to-ceiling windows when the doorbell rings. Beacham tucks himself into the darkness of the stairwell and watches as the other mothers stream into the living room. Hors d'oeuvres are served. Wine is decanted. Debussy plays on the speakers. The room hums with high-pitched chatter. Someone mentions the parent-teacher interviews. His mother's lip quivers when it's her turn to share.

Glowing reviews from all his teachers. He's in the top percentile of his class.

Rachel Fitzpatrick makes a funny clucking sound. Clara picks up the hors d'oeuvres and offers them around. Rachel takes a leek and Gruyère galette then leans to the mother next to her like she's going to whisper only she doesn't.

Sizable endowments can work wonders with report cards.

Rachel washes down her galette with a gulp of red wine. Clara places the platter gently on the coffee table and lifts her gaze to Rachel.

And young Fitz? Is he doing any better in algebra this semester? You know if he's still struggling, a private tutor can—how did you put it—work wonders.

Rachel's cheeks turn the shade of his mother's red lipstick.

FRIDAY 12:15 P.M.

Beacham didn't see Murphy in the woods that morning. He decides to save half his ham and cheese sandwich just in case he runs into the boy on the way home. The bell rings. Lunch is over. Beacham wraps up the sandwich and steps out of the bathroom stall. Fitz is waiting for him. He forgot to check under the door. Fitz shoves Beacham back onto the toilet. He drops his lunch box. Its contents spill onto the floor. Fitz steps inside the stall and locks the door. He faces Beacham, stepping on the ham and cheese.

You a rat, Beachbum?

Beacham shakes his head.

You told your mum I don't get maths?

I never.

Fitz grabs Beacham by the ears and lifts him to his feet. Beacham winces in pain. Fitz yanks Beacham's glasses off his face and holds them high overhead. Beacham tries to grab them.

Give 'em back.

Fitz tosses the glasses behind Beacham. They splash into the toilet. Fitz laughs.

Oops.

FRIDAY 3:45 P.M.

Beacham sneaks down to the old boiler room in the school's basement. He found the room when he was trying to avoid Fitz at the beginning of term. Ever since, it's been his hideout. The custodians don't use it anymore, not since the school installed a new heating system. A few weeks ago Beacham waited for the nurse to leave then took a blanket, thin mattress and lamp from the infirmary. He set them up in the boiler room and brought his favourite comic from home, *Warriors of Mars*. It's about two boys stranded on the red planet after missing the return trip to earth and their epic battle fighting a giant Martian creature.

Beacham lies on his makeshift bed and disappears into the pages of his comic book while he waits for the coast to clear after school.

FRIDAY 4:45 P.M.

The cold blue woods are quiet and empty but dimming fast. He's almost made it to the other side when a blurry shape appears up ahead at the opening to the street where he lives. He can't tell who it is. His eyes are worse at dusk. Is it Fitz?

Footfalls crunch in the snow. Faster and faster. He's frozen in place. The shape is coming toward him. He unsticks his boots, turns and runs back in the direction of the school. A voice calls out.

Run rat run.

It *is* Fitz. Beacham drops his school bag and runs as hard as he can. His snow boots are heavy, his glasses fog over, but he can't stop. He can hear Fitz panting right behind him. Then Beacham hears a thump. Fitz must have fallen. Beacham doesn't look back. He keeps running until he can't run anymore.

When he finally stops, he slowly turns around. No one is there. But there is something. Slowly, Beacham moves toward it. As he gets closer, he comes upon a stain in the snow. It's blood. A trail of red weaves into the woods and disappears. Beacham spots his school bag. He races for it and runs home.

FRIDAY 7:00 P.M.

Beacham is practicing his scales on the piano, his father is reading the Ottawa Citizen, and his mother is writing in her pregnancy diary when her phone rings.

Rachel? Pause. *Your Fitzy?*

Beacham stops playing.

No, he's not here. Hang on.

She lowers the phone and looks at Beacham.

Arthur, do you know where Colton is?

Beacham shakes his head.

No, he doesn't. Oh, of course we will. Yes, I'll let you know if I hear anything. Bye, bye.

She hangs up.

The Fitzpatrick boy didn't come home from school. I hope he's okay.

Henry looks up from his newspaper.

Never liked that kid.

Henry goes back to reading. His mother turns her attention to the pages of her diary. Beacham is about to start playing again when a movement catches his eye out the window. He scans the yard and spots Murphy standing near the snow-covered trellis at the bottom of the garden. Beacham glances at his parents. Neither of them has noticed. Murphy motions for Beachum to come outside then disappears into the shadows of the pines.

FRIDAY 11:00 P.M.

Flakes of snow cling to Beacham's eyelashes. He crosses the street, pulling his wool coat over his pyjamas. He takes the path into the woods. He comes to the spot where he saw the blood. Everything is snow-covered now. He steps off the path and moves deeper into the woods until he comes to a clearing at the edge of a ravine. There are traces of pink in the fresh snow.

I knew you'd show.

Beacham spins around. Murphy is behind him. Beacham is glad to see his friend.

I brought you something.

Beacham hands him a Tupperware container of leftover Cornish hen and roast potatoes from tonight's dinner.

Wicked.

Murphy dives in, eating with his fingers. Beacham nods to the pink snow.

What happened to Fitz?

Murphy chews as he talks.

Got what was coming to him.

Murphy points to the edge of the ravine.

You killed him?

Murphy licks his fingers.

Wanker was dead already. Hit his head. I tossed him down there.

Why'd you do that?

I was covering for you. I knew they'd think it was you.

Me?

You got motive.

Murphy puts down the empty Tupperware and wipes his greasy fingers in the snow.

Beacham knows he's right.

Thanks. No one's ever done that.

Murphy looks at Beacham.

Done what?

Looked out for me.

SATURDAY 7:30 A.M.

Beacham is up before his parents. He slept like a rock. No bad dreams. No wet bed. He wanders into the empty living room in his pyjamas. He stares up at the red abstract painting on the wall. It looks like the surface of Mars. Beacham glances out the large window. He's surprised to see Murphy standing on the other side. Murphy tosses a snowball at the window. Beacham laughs. He pretends to make a snowball and toss it at Murphy. Murphy holds up his hands to protect himself from the imaginary snowball. They laugh.

Beacham holds up an index finger, telling Murphy to stay put. He crosses the room and picks up the Japanese dagger from the display rack on the mantel. He brings it over and shows it to Murphy. The gold handle of the blade is wrapped in red silk. Murphy mouths *wow*. Beacham stabs at the air with the dagger. It looks like a sword in his small hand. Murphy shakes the snow from a nearby shrub, breaks off a branch and holds it like a dagger.

The boys mirror each other's movements as they joust on either side of the glass. Murphy dodges, Beacham dodges. Beacham dekes, Murphy dekes. Murphy twirls, Beacham twirls. As he spins, Beacham loses his footing and crashes into the grand piano. He drops the dagger, elbow knocking the piano. Before he can catch it, his parents' wedding photo falls to the floor, the glass in the frame shattering.

His parents enter the room.

Beacham looks out the window; Murphy is gone.

MONDAY 9:00 A.M.

The hallways at school are buzzing with whispers as Beacham makes his way to his locker. They must be talking about Fitz's disappearance. Beacham's parents didn't say another word about it all weekend, but they never tell him anything. And he knows Mrs. Fitzpatrick phoned his mother again.

Beacham gets to his locker, turns the combination and opens the door. He removes his coat and hangs it up inside. As he's changing his boots for indoor shoes, he notices a piece of paper on the floor of his locker. He picks it up. It's a note written in red marker.

It says *RUN RAT RUN*.

Beacham drops the note and slams his locker shut. A couple of boys stare at Beacham as the bell rings for first period. The hallway clears in seconds, and Beacham is alone. He leans against his locker waiting for his heart to stop beating so fast. A sound makes him turn. Someone is standing at the far end of the hall. The figure is blurry, but from the size he could swear it's Fitz.

Care to join us, Mr. Beacham?

Mr. Harding is standing in the middle of the hallway, holding his classroom door open. Beacham hurries across the hall not daring to look in Fitz's direction. He takes his seat at the front and glances back to Fitz's desk. It's empty.

A policeman comes to the open doorway. He's there to speak to the class. Mr. Harding lets him in. Sweat drips down Beacham's back. His vision blurs in and out of focus. He feels dizzy. Beacham raises his hand.

I need to go to the toilet.

The class snickers. Mr. Harding motions to the door as the policeman introduces himself.

MONDAY 9:15 A.M.

Beacham is sitting in the stall. He hears the bathroom door open as someone comes in. He lifts his feet and stays very still. He can see their shoes. They're not moving. They're standing at the sink right across from his stall. He holds his breath. Finally, they walk away, and he hears the door close. Beacham waits then slowly comes out of the stall. The room is empty. He looks at the mirror and gasps. Someone has written on it in red marker. One word.

RUN.

He does.

MONDAY 9:45 A.M.

Beacham races down the path through the woods. When he reaches the break in the trees that leads to the clearing, he slows down, catching his breath. He enters the woods and finds Murphy sitting on a log near the edge of the ravine. The boy is warming his hands on a small campfire. Murphy looks up when he hears Beacham coming through the trees.

Ditching?

Beacham nods. He sits next to the boy. Murphy picks up a stick and pokes at the logs. The stick catches fire at one end. He traces the sky with it, and sparks dance like fireflies. Beacham grabs a stick and lights his in the fire. He jumps up and holds out his stick, challenging Murphy to a battle. Murphy jumps up, and they begin a fiery sword-fight, jabbing and clacking sticks as sparks fly. They play fight until they're out of breath. They sit back down, tossing their sticks in the fire. Beacham turns to Murphy.

I saw Fitz.

Murphy looks at him.

On the news?

No, in real life.

You sure it was him?

Looked like him.

Must have been his ghost.

You think?

Had to be.

Murphy lifts the collar of his thin jacket and shivers. Beacham takes his coat off and offers it to Murphy. At first, Murphy doesn't take it. Then he removes his jacket. They swap. Murphy smiles when he feels the warmth of Beacham's coat. Beacham feels sorry for his friend.

Don't you have parents?

Murphy shakes his head.

Got left behind when they took off. They never came back for me.

Beacham feels even worse for him now. Then he gets an idea.

MONDAY 11:30 A.M.

The boiler room is musty but it's warm. Murphy looks around and nods his approval.

Beats sleeping in the woods.

Beacham smiles.

I'll go find you something to eat.

Murphy lays back on the mattress, hands behind his head. Beacham sneaks up to the cafeteria where kitchen staff are prepping lunch. He hides behind some crates and waits for his moment, then ducks into the walk-in fridge. He grabs a bag of dinner rolls and a container of sliced turkey. He moves fast and smart, slipping out of the kitchen without anyone seeing him. He makes it to the bottom of the basement stairwell just as the lunch bell rings.

MONDAY 4:15 P.M.

Beacham hums as he ambles through the woods. He doubts anyone even noticed he skipped classes.

He had spent the rest of the day hanging out with Murphy in the boiler room. They outsmarted everyone. The policeman didn't come to arrest him, and Fitz's ghost never found them. When the end-of-day bell rang, Beacham had waited until the school went quiet before heading home.

Now, as he makes his way along the path, he feels strong and brave. He even feels a little taller. But halfway through the woods, the feeling dissolves when he sees a policeman up ahead. Then another. He squints. He thinks about turning back, but they're sure to see him. He has no choice. Beacham heads towards them. As he gets closer, he sees a third policeman moving through the woods. They must be searching for Fitz's body.

Then he sees his parents. His mother is looking at an object in the policeman's gloved hand. It's the Tupperware container. His father spots him. They rush over.

His mother looks white as the snow.

Arthur, thank God. We've been worried sick.

His father grabs hold of his shoulders.

The school said you left class this morning and never came back.

The policeman comes over. He's not the same one from Mr. Harding's class.

Arthur, tell the officer about your friend.

The policeman looks at Beacham's ratty jacket.

This your boy?

His father nods. The policeman leans closer to Beacham.

You have any idea who's been living in these woods, son?

Beacham shakes his head. His mother touches his arm.

Where's your coat, Arthur?

Beacham swallows.

Someone stole it. Had to grab this one from lost and found.

The policeman stares at Beacham.

You sure there's nothing you can tell me, son?

Beacham glances toward the clearing.

I'm sure.

The policeman looks at his parents.

Appreciate the tip. We'll get this sorted. Call me if he remembers anything else.

The policeman hands his card to his father.

MONDAY 6:30 P.M.

Beacham picks at the coq au vin on his plate. The chicken is bloody at the bone. His mother hasn't touched her food.

Your father and I want to talk to you about something.

Beacham doesn't look up. His father folds his napkin and places it on the table.

I got promoted to the European office. We're moving to Paris.

Beacham looks at his father. A red glow hovers around his father's head.

It's not for a few weeks.

Beacham drops his fork.

This coq is raw.

His mother gags. She puts her hand over her mouth. His father pounds his fist on the table.

We know you took food to that boy. They found a campsite. Is that where you were?

Beacham stares at his father.

He's my friend. You shouldn't have ratted him out to the cops.

His mother reaches for his arm.

He could be dangerous, darling.

Beacham stabs his knife into the bloody chicken. His mother shrinks back.

Arthur!

Beacham runs from the room.

TUESDAY 3:00 A.M.

The sky is blood red. Its echo on the snow makes the whole world look red. Beacham runs down the red path through the red woods. When he gets to the school with its glowing red windows, he finds the doors locked. He uses the butt of his flashlight to smash a basement window. He rakes the broken glass from the sill and crawls inside. The basement is pitch black. The flashlight beam flickers as he stumbles along the hallway, his vision warbling like he's underwater. He enters the boiler room and aims the flashlight at the mattress.

Murphy is sleeping. The boy wakes and holds up a hand to block the beam shining in his face.

The cops were searching the woods.

Murphy sits up and rubs his eyes. Beacham lowers the flashlight and comes closer.

We gotta run, Murphy. I know where we can go. Devon Island.

Where's that?

Way up north in Nunavut. I read about it. Looks just like Mars. No one lives there, so we can have it all to ourselves.

What about your parents?

They don't want me. They're moving to France without me. Listen, I can get money from an ATM and we can run.

It's too late.

It's not. I don't think they found the body yet.

They won't.

Why? Where is it?

Murphy looks at Beacham.

You really that blind, kid?

A red glow clouds the edge of Beacham's peripheral vision.

You know what happened to Fitz.

He stares at Murphy, trying to understand what the boy's saying.

Take a good look around, Beacham. What do you see?

Beacham skims the flashlight across the boiler room. His wool coat lays on the floor next to a half-eaten bag of dinner rolls. His comic book lies open by the lamp. He moves closer to it and shines the light on its pages.

A giant beast chases two boys across the barren terrain of a red planet. In the next frame, the boys draw their swords. They fight the beast in an epic battle, lighting their swords on fire to defeat the hideous creature. In the final frames, a trail of blood streaks the dunes as they drag the dead Martian to the edge of a crater and toss him in.

Beacham drops the flashlight. It goes out. And in the darkness, he sees the truth.

He sees himself in the clearing, by a campfire, dancing alone with a burning stick, grabbing a red jacket from the drama club's costume box, twirling in his living room with the dagger, dropping a note in his locker and writing in red marker on the bathroom mirror. It was all him and him alone.

Beacham gropes on the floor for the flashlight. He finds it, turns it on and aims it at the mattress. There's no one there. There never was.

He killed Fitz.

WEDNESDAY 9:00 A.M.

Beacham sits in a chair, his forehead and chin strapped down. They've restrained him. He can hear voices. It must be some sort of interrogation room. His feet don't touch the floor. He can hear someone tapping on a computer keyboard. Then a chair moves closer to him. The boy keeps his eyes shut tight. He can't remember anything since the boiler room.

Whenever you're ready, lad.

Beacham shuts his eyes tighter. If he says nothing, maybe they'll let him go.

Arthur, just open your eyes and begin with the large letters on the top row.

Wait. Beacham knows that voice. He opens his eyes. He knows this room. This is not an interrogation, and the man talking to him is not a policeman. It's Doctor Felix, his optometrist. The man reaches out and adjusts Beacham's new glasses.

There you are. Now give those lenses a go.

Beacham gazes across the room. There's an eye chart on the far wall. He blinks. He can't believe it. His vision is crystal clear. In that moment, *everything* becomes crystal clear.

Fitz was chasing him through the woods then tripped and hit his head. Beacham dragged him to a clearing and left him there. Later, Fitz woke up and made his way home with a concussion and frostbitten fingers. He'd overheard his mother telling his father the news, but he didn't want to believe it. At school on Monday, Fitz was waiting in the hall while his mother got his homework so he could go home and rest. He wasn't a ghost. Beacham knew this. He knew all of it. But he just wanted to be the hero of his own epic adventure.

Just once.

Go on, darling. You can do it.

Beacham looks over. His mother is sitting next to him. She takes his hand and squeezes it. There's love in her eyes. He was wrong about her too. She would never take off and leave him stranded on a red planet. He *is* wanted.

Beacham looks back at the eye chart. He reads the bottom row, the smallest letters. Because he can now see clearly.

Z O C E F L D P B T

An award-winning Canadian screenwriter and director for more than three decades, Katie Tallo won an international novel contest in 2013 and began writing mystery thrillers. Her debut, Dark August, was an instant national bestseller, NYT Book Review Editor's Choice and Apple Book of the Month, and made The Globe 100. Since then, Katie completed her critically acclaimed Gus Monet trilogy which includes Poison Lilies and Buried Road. She lives in the Wellington West neighbourhood of Ottawa with her husband.

CAFÉ AMORE

6

ADRIENNE STEVENSON

"Why on earth did you hire him?" Deborah wiped a smudge of chocolate mousse off her nose with a corner of her apron, adding to the previous daubs of tomato sauce, baba ghanouj and steak marinade.

"Because I can't afford both a headwaiter and a bouncer," said Sophie. She tilted her head. "Think about it, Deb, we're still recovering from the pandemic. Do you really want to be harassed by former clients? Or worse, blackmailed? People in this town have long memories. Just because we're a supper club now doesn't mean they'll have forgotten what we used to do."

"You haven't had another threatening letter have you?"

Sophie shook her head. "Just the one that was left in the mailbox on the patio. But I need some muscle on staff, just in case."

Deb resumed her critique of the new headwaiter. "He really gets up my nose," she said. "He still acts like a cop. What if he took this job as some kind of cover to get us charged?" She shook her head, as if she still had that long hair she'd fling over one shoulder while providing specialized services upstairs. But her hair was short now, the makeover complete. Surely no former client would recognize her.

Garth had seen better months. The decree absolute in his divorce had been hand-delivered to him the same day he parted company with the Vancouver Police. Ten years of graveyard shifts working drugs and vice on the Downtown Eastside had burned him out, and his frigid ex had cleaned him out. Not only had she spent every penny he made, and more, she had spurned his attempts to inject a little romance in their lives, then taken off with a scheming day trader. He was left jobless, loveless and soured on the west coast. Getting far away from his former life was the only option, and Ottawa sounded about right—something of a backwater, even if it was the national capital. There were quite a few jobs listed, too, but the only one he was able to snag was a position as headwaiter at a recently opened supper club a few blocks from Parliament Hill. The proprietor, Sophie Spiro, interviewed him by video call and told him she really needed someone who could double as a bouncer because sometimes her clientele could get out of hand. When he mentioned he used to be a cop, she offered him the position on the spot, hoping he could start that weekend. At the time, it seemed like a no-brainer to Garth, so he stored most of his possessions, packed a couple of bags and caught the red-eye flight east on the same day.

Café Amore was housed in a renovated red-brick Victorian town-house on Somerset, a street with many such conversions. It seemed a place where he could settle in and take stock of his life. Maybe put some colour back into it, especially the kind that came on paper with the signature of the Governor of the Bank of Canada. Maybe he could get a little romance as well...but no, it was too soon for that.

Right now, though, he was regretting the whole venture. He sat on the sagging couch in his furnished room, head in hands. He had been so focused on escaping his west coast woes that he hadn't reckoned on the people he'd be dealing with in this new job. Sophie was older, maybe mid-fifties, and a bit intimidating—he could handle that. But that snippy chef, Deborah, was a real pain in the ass. He recalled their first meeting and the following days with intense irritation, and not just because she might be cute if she tried.

For a skinny twentysomething, she had done everything possible to make herself unattractive. She sported a pomaded butch haircut, wore baggy cotton shirt and jeans, and if there was a particle of makeup on her shiny face, he couldn't see it. She challenged him on his dress (he didn't own a tuxedo), demeanour (not that he didn't know he was more bouncer than headwaiter material) and knowledge of wine. Granted, he was no sommelier, but he could style it out enough to satisfy most customers.

He'd made the mistake of trying to ingratiate himself in her kitchen and got thrown out on his ear. He overheard her grumbling about him to Sophie. Better do something to smooth things over or he'd soon get fired.

Mise en place done, Deborah had a pot of soup simmering, sauces for the entrees ready and had moved on to the chocolate mousse, a dessert she prided herself on. She'd sent her sous-chef off to the market for fresh asparagus and chanterelles and was about to take a break. Steps sounded at the door, and she looked up.

Damn, it was that Garth. "What do you want?" she asked, frowning.

He held his hands up. "Not guilty, ma'am."

She stood, hands on hips, blocking his entry to her domain.

He peered around her. "What an amazing kitchen! Something smells awfully good."

She snorted. "Is that all you've got?"

"I'm completely sincere. You obviously run a tight shop." He pulled a white handkerchief out of one suit pocket and flapped it at her. "Pretty please?" He drew a posy of paper flowers from the other pocket and brandished it under her nose.

She tried hard not to laugh. "That's beyond silly," she said. "Sit down, you're giving me a crick in my neck." She poured two mugs of coffee and pushed one in his direction. He took a long pull. "You drink it unadulterated, good," she said.

"See, I'm not a total loss." He wiggled his eyebrows at her, earning another laugh.

"Okay. Truce. Just don't wreck anything in here, and we'll get along fine." She looked him up and down. "Your hands and feet are too big to have you clomping around. Something will break for sure."

He batted his lashes. "Is the truce too fresh to try some of that mousse? Asking for a friend…"

Damn, why did the men get all the long lashes? She spooned some into a small dish. "Here."

He tasted it, and a look of pure ecstasy came over his face. Hmm. Maybe there was more to him than she thought. "Enjoy that?"

"I'm your slave forever."

Promises, promises. Flattery was good for something, though. She was starting to like him a little, or at least some part of him, but was going to reserve judgment. Just in case.

Business picked up significantly as the weather improved. Sophie decided to open the patio earlier than usual and set everyone except Deborah and Garth to cleaning and arranging outdoor furniture. She assigned them to work up a special menu for outdoor dining.

"Why don't we go for something offbeat?" asked Garth.

"Like what?" asked Deborah.

"Like…food is like sex, right?"

She stiffened. "Really?"

"Sure. Alluring, enticing, seductive, that kind of thing. And this place is called Café Amore. I was thinking we could reflect that in the menu. Alluring Appetizers, Sizzling Starters, Ecstatic Entrees, Decadent Desserts, Bawdy Beverages—that kind of thing. Head it up as Seductive Suppers."

Deborah gulped. Was he aware of the house's former incarnation? Maybe not. He was new in town. "Um, I think you'll have to run that by Sophie." She turned back to the menu, feeling a bit queasy. "I suppose you'd want to revamp some of the dishes, too? Include foods supposed to be aphrodisiacs?" Damn, she was warming to the idea.

"Sure. How about sexy seafood bisque?"

She capped that with "dream cream pie."

He laughed at that one, and they went back and forth a few more times, getting the giggles over the silly names.

"Sultry sausage," she said.

"Flirtatious flaming figs."

"Ribald mushroom risotto."

"Bodacious baba ghanouj."

"Lewd lamb chops."

"And then there's cock-a-leekie," he said.

She choked on her coffee.

"Hey, are you okay?" He looked concerned.

"I have a feeling Sophie will be less than enthused. But go ahead and ask her."

Much to Deborah's surprise, Sophie loved Garth's ideas.

"He's got a point, Deb," she said in private. "It's a good fit for a place called Café Amore."

"Maybe you should have gone for a different name."

"I'm not ashamed of what we were. Not that I'm anxious to relive the old days, but this sounds like harmless fun. Clever marketing, too."

So, Deborah went along with the plan. She dreamed up twists on her recipes that would fit the patio's menu. Her camaraderie with Garth grew—another surprise—and she unbent enough to laugh over the humorously shaped carrots and eggplants he bought to display at the patio entrance. To titillate the customers' appetites, he claimed.

"You're not just Hulk Junior, are you?" she quipped.

Garth's eyes rolled. "Don't knock yourself out flattering me."

"But seriously," she said, "when you started working here, I figured you had no sense of humour. Or much finesse, either."

"I thought you were pretty grim, too. Prickly."

Deborah supposed she could live with that. She'd been called worse than "prickly" in her lifetime, even by friends.

Shortly after they introduced the new menu, the outdoor waitstaff started to complain about inappropriate touching by some customers. Within a week, a party of very drunk patio diners caused a ruckus, demanding "extra service upstairs" and making a nuisance of themselves. One legless lush in a loud suit even tried to pinch Sophie's derrière, earning himself a spike heel in the instep, at which he screamed blue murder. Garth's experience at handling drunks and junkies came in handy as he bounced the lush and his party out. Hard. They shouted threats, but at least they left.

Sophie was furious. "I don't care who he's related to, he's not welcome here."

"Who is he?" asked Garth.

"Jerry McBean. Black sheep of an old Ottawa family. They're into everything—politics, property development, you name it. He's an uber privileged brat who never knew how to take no for an answer, so we banned him from our old business. Not that the rest of the family aren't shady as hell. His brother runs a restaurant a couple of blocks from here. I wouldn't darken its doors."

When service ended, he went looking for Deborah, who had sent her sous-chef home and was oiling her precious carbon steel knives.

"I hear there was a ruckus outside," she said. "What was that all about?"

"Some rowdy wanting extra service upstairs." He quirked an eyebrow. "Any idea what that's about?"

Deborah flushed. "I suppose they thought they could get something off-menu."

"Like what?"

She turned away. "You must know by now."

Garth thought it over. There had been hints, some more subtle than others. "Like extra dessert? That they could lick off the wait-staff...or you? For a fee?"

She nodded.

"Sophie could have gone a bit farther in rebranding," he said. His tone dripped with scorn. "I mean—Café Amore?"

That hurt. "What about you? How long did you work vice?"

He hesitated, then said, "Ten years. In Vancouver."

"It shows." It was her turn to sneer. "So, you thought you'd see if you could make use of us? Maybe work for a while, then rat us out, claiming we were back to our old, uh, tricks? Get in good with the Ottawa cops and slip back into your proper job?" She pushed her face up as close to his as she could get. "Just so you know, we're totally legit these days. Our business tanked right from the start of the pandemic. But, thanks to the CERB and some savings, I took a crash course in the Algonquin College culinary program and Sophie finished her MBA. No way would either of us go back now."

He raised an eyebrow. "Oh, right, so if the supper club fails, what then?"

She brandished a knife at him. Only a paring knife, but he backed away hastily. "We own the place, you bastard. This is our home. Get out of my kitchen." She advanced a step. "And stay out!"

Deborah's anger was incandescent, aggravated by months of sly digs and outright snubs from chefs at neighbouring restaurants when she did her marketing. She briefly debated with herself about quitting but after a restless night dialed her reactions back. She could never do that to Sophie—she would get on with her own job and have nothing more to do with that Garth.

She became upset all over again when she stumbled on Sophie in the upstairs ladies' room, in tears.

"Sophie, what happened?"

Sophie held out a sheet of paper that had words cut from a magazine pasted to it. "Another poison pen letter, this one threatening our business. And me."

Deborah read the vile phrases in horror.

"Do you have any idea who sent it?"

Sophie shook her head. "Could be a competitor. Or a disgruntled former client. One of those guys who hates the word no." She wiped her face and rose, mouth set. "Time to make use of our ex-cop."

Garth sorted through the menus, separating the patio bill of fare from the dining room table d'hôte. After last week's upset at the patio, things had been quiet. Deborah was still avoiding him.

He looked up as Sophie approached. Her face was unusually pale, her forehead furrowed. She looked a good 10 years older.

"What's wrong?"

She handed him the letters.

"I'm going to need your help," she said. "It may or may not have anything to do with last week's disturbance, but someone's trying to blackmail me. I thought maybe...do you still have police connections?"

"Not here, no." He took the letters and read through them. "So, whoever sent you this thinks they can use your past against you? What if you make it part of your shtick—that this establishment used to be a bordello, but now it's a CERB success story, rebranded as an up-market supper club? We use this moron's threats to our advantage, instead of his...or hers." He grinned. "You can even say you converted me. But I think most of this will involve you—and Deborah —promoting the change in your business as positive. Show you're not embarrassed or afraid of your past." He hesitated. "Better not tell Deborah it was my idea. Anyway, I bet she tells you the same thing."

"It could work," said Sophie, nodding. "I'll have to go over it with her, in any case."

The next morning, Deborah stormed into Sophie's office, waving the latest issue of the Centretown Buzz, their community newspaper. "Those ugly letters you showed me—they're printed in here!"

Sophie rose. "Stay right there." She went to the hall and bellowed, "Garth!"

He took the stairs two at a time and skidded to a stop at her office door.

"We have a problem," said Sophie. Her phone pinged, and she checked her messages. "A serious problem. Three cancellations already."

"Do you know who might be responsible?" he asked.

"Does it matter?" Deborah shook her head in disgust. "After all our hard work..."

Sophie slammed her fist on her desk. "We won't let this bastard ruin us! It's time to accelerate the publicity war. I'll draft some copy for the Ottawa Citizen and for our social media campaign. We need to post on as many platforms as possible. Get the word out."

Business did fall off over the next few days but then began to recover. Regulars returned, bringing friends. Some new customers actually came because of the scandal. For a while it looked like they might have weathered the crisis.

A week later, disaster struck again. Early one morning, Sophie knocked on Deborah's bedroom door. "Do you smell smoke?" she asked.

They descended to the front door and gazed out on the ruin of their patio.

Someone had piled all of the patio furniture in a heap and set it alight. All that remained were metal supports, melted plastic, charred wood and the mailbox. As they were surveying the damage, Garth arrived. "Hells bells, what happened here?" He looked over their shoulders. "Hey, there's something stuck in your mailbox."

It was another poison pen missive, this one gloating over the damage and threatening worse.

"At least the house is unharmed," said Sophie.

"So far," said Garth. "But this has to go to the police. Dealing with a few rowdies is one thing. Arson is another."

At Garth's urging, Sophie filed a complaint with the police and gave them the letters as evidence of harassment and attempted blackmail. They didn't sound optimistic about finding the poison pen, but her confidence was buoyed by having taken action. And they would be sure to follow up on the arson.

Café Amore's patio shut down for restoration, but Sophie and Deborah kept the main restaurant open and posted about their trials on social media. The Centretown Buzz editor called to apologize, the Ottawa Citizen printed Sophie's fiery letter to the editor, and a local TV crew filmed a spot for the six o'clock news. What had seemed to be a total disaster became publicity money couldn't buy. Best of all, a local building supply outlet offered them good terms for replacement patio furniture that their insurance would more than cover. They'd be back at full steam in no time.

"No more threatening letters?" asked Garth.

"Not so far," said Sophie. "I'm hoping the police investigation has put them off."

Reservations flooded in, and soon Sophie told Deborah they were past the worst of it. "You should cut Garth some slack, too," she said. "He was really hot for our success. If it hadn't been for him…"

Deborah looked thoughtful. "I know. He didn't try to make it all about him. I like that in a man."

"So why not give him a break? He's all but panting at your heels. Make him something special."

As the club wasn't open for business on Mondays, Deborah decided that the following Monday evening would be an ideal time to mend fences with Garth. She gave a lot of thought to the menu and imagined him salivating in anticipation of the treats in store. After all, the way to a man's heart was through his stomach. And what a dinner it would be: Orgasmic Oysters, Adults-Only Asparagus & Asiago, Rare Roast Rump of Lamb, Spicy Sweet Potatoes, Decadent Dessert Surprise. And, of course, Cock-a-Leekie Soup.

On Sunday evening just before closing, she dropped an envelope on Garth's station and fled back to the kitchen. The envelope contained a hand-lettered table d'hôte with his name at the top.

The following day, Deborah locked herself in the kitchen. Much banging of pots ensued, with enticing smells seeping throughout the house. Finally, she loaded up the dumbwaiter and transported every-thing upstairs. The table was set in one of the private rooms, a perfect ambience for a special dinner.

After the main meal, she presented a cake coated in gooey white icing. When she cut into it, the inside was dark and moist and gave off an aroma of chocolate and warm figs.

"Did you make that just for me?" Garth asked.

"Don't kid yourself, buddy. It'll feed at least two." She looked at her creation with pride. "That's real marshmallow frosting, too, not out of a box. I don't go all out for just anybody."

"I think this will go well with it," said Garth, producing a magnum of champagne from under the table.

"That had better not be all for you, either," she said. "Would you pop that cork? I don't have a sword handy and I'm not using my good knives."

He did so and filled two flutes, handing her one and lifting the other.

"To Café Amore!" she said.

He winked. "To satisfying appetites!"

She grinned and stuck out her tongue. "You want to go off-menu? Gimme a quiche, big boy."

Aware that Deborah had an early morning of marketing planned for the next day, Garth declined her invitation to spend the night. He didn't rush away though. It was nearly one o'clock when he let himself out the front door.

After locking both deadbolts, he turned towards the street. Movement on the patio caught his attention. Something white fluttered at the mailbox. He heard a scuffling noise on the interlocking pavement, followed by a thud and muffled "shit".

The poison pen! Garth dashed toward the patio and managed to grab the perp before he could get up and away. He called on his training to immobilize the man without doing serious damage—knee in the small of his back and one hand keeping his arm twisted behind. That left Garth a hand free to fish out his cell phone and call 9-1-1. "Police," he said to their query.

He switched on the phone's light to check the perp's face, and just as he tapped the camera icon to record the scene, a siren sounded. Seconds later the police arrived with lights flashing. "Great response time, guys," Garth shouted as the cops got out of the car. They nodded, recognizing a colleague at once, then turned to see what he had caught.

"Well now, isn't that interesting," said one constable. "A McBean. Jerry, isn't it?"

The man twisted his head away. "Get this clown off me. I want to press charges."

"I think it's going to be the other way around, Jerry." He cuffed McBean, "I don't think your cousin the ambulance chaser will be able to get you off this time. Caught in the act, how perfect is that?" He turned to Garth, who had retrieved the note stuck in the mailbox. "This note's got quite a list of threats," Garth said as he handed it to the constable.

Lights came on in the building behind him. Deborah and Sophie appeared at the door.

"Looks like this is our poison pen," Garth called to them. "Might turn out to be the arsonist, too."

"Early days for that," said the constable. He and his partner took a brief statement from Garth, then bundled Jerry into the car. "Come down to the station tomorrow morning and you can sign the write-up." He nodded towards Deborah and Sophie. "Probably best if you all come down, make sure we have all the details."

"I don't care how late it is," said Deborah, hugging Garth. "You're staying!"

"Group hug," said Sophie. "When your bouncer bounces the bad guy, that's Amore!"

Adrienne Stevenson, a retired forensic toxicologist, lives in Ottawa on the traditional unceded territory of the Algonquin Anishnaabeg People. Her work has been widely published in Canada and abroad. Adrienne's publications include a historical novel Mirrors & Smoke (2023), a co-authored poetry chapbook Skipping Stones (2024), several short stories and many poems. She is an avid gardener, voracious reader, amateur genealogist and sometime folk musician.

INTUITION

7

P. R. ISFELD

THE MOON: ILLUSION

The customer across from you seems both nervous and eager. He's never had a tarot card reading before, he says, rounding his shoulders even further under his black sweater with its white ribbed neck. You suspect that's not all he's never done, even though he must be close to 30 and there's nothing wrong with his looks. He needs to ease up on the cheap body spray if he ever does hope to get laid though.

The guy probably had a picture in his mind of what a tarot reader would look like, and you, in your black leather jacket with your freckles and your cherry-pink lip balm, must disappoint him. The Westboro coffee shop won't do much to help his fantasy either, and for a moment you miss the old occult bookstore where you used to work, on the dirty part of Bank Street just down from Parliament Hill, with the elderly owner who claimed to come from 12 generations of witches. Too bad none of them had a spell for Covid protection.

This sucker tells you that knowing you know things about him makes him a little anxious, but then most things do.

"I thought you'd look more witchy," he says, blushing and

lowering his gaze. His chuckle makes you relax a little. Even though you drew the Moon card in your own reading this morning—a warning that things are not as they seem—you know you have what this fellow needs.

You thank the Elementals for their gift of intuition. Without it, no witch is worth her salt.

QUEEN OF SWORDS: A STRONG WOMAN

You can relate to this guy. People make you nervous, too, but this morning over breakfast, you drew the Eight of Pentacles, a reminder to have confidence in your abilities. As long as you focus on your work, all will go well. Between the Elementals and your cold-reading skills, you've got this spoiled little bureaucrat's number.

Your hand hovers over the Witch's Tarot, but something makes you stop. Instead, you pick the Otherkin deck, with its slightly vintage-looking drawings of cute imaginary animals, for this cubicle dweller. Nothing demonic or shadowy for him. No point scaring him off. You shuffle the cards, then ask him to cut them into three piles from his left to his right. You try not to be put off by his doughy little fingers. Sad if those hands end up being the second most memorable things about him. After his virginity, of course.

You stack the deck back up and lay them out in a Celtic Cross spread. A classic. The first card to show where he is, then what covers or crosses him, what crowns or protects him, his foundation, what's passing out, what he brings to the question. He shakes his head when you get to that last one—people always want to argue with the advice on their part in things—but smiles when you get to the environment, the unaccounted for and the outcome.

Like most men his age, he thinks he has skills the people around him aren't ready to see yet, but he's got a lot to learn. He can be strong but also has a tender side that he shows only to the right people.

Then again, don't we all? But you keep that comment to yourself.

Poor guy, he'll get what he wants in the short term, but the woman he desires is not who he thinks she is. She's a queen who takes nothing from nobody, and her sword is razor-sharp.

No guy likes to hear that a woman is going to stick it to him, so you focus his attention away from that and onto the immediate triumph shown by the Six of Wands. He leaves happy, slipping you an extra $50 on the way out. Maybe, he says, you can have a longer session next time? Take a little extra time? Show him your *other* skills?

You mumble something pleasant but suppress a shudder. Granny would have said a chicken had walked across your grave. Great-great-great-great-great Granny would have warned you about a certain kind of inquisitive man.

That $50 goes into the pocket of your jeans before the barista can notice. You don't feel like sharing these days.

SEVEN OF WANDS: A CHALLENGE

Business is good for the rest of the week. A couple more civil servants, a politician even. Word is spreading about your craft. On Friday you decide to treat yourself to a glass of Zinfandel and an order of deep-fried squid at the wine bar next to the café. A well-dressed man at the granite bar keeps glancing over at you, but you clock his Knight of Pentacles energy and focus on the reprint of *The Witching Hour* one of your more interesting clients gave you. It's classic Anne Rice—entertainment dabbling in truth but lacking the certain realism you find on Reddit.

As you finish your chapter and get up to leave, the Knight sneers and says something to the bartender. He's asking why women go out in public if they don't want to be looked at. Good question. You refrain from turning around to learn the answer.

Your Uber's not here yet, so you stand at the curb, noticing a nondescript man sitting in his silver Toyota, pale hands gripping the steering wheel. There's something vaguely familiar about him, but you can't put your finger on it. As you draw the collar of your leather jacket closer to your throat, you can almost feel his eyes sliding over you. He doesn't smile, and the rest of him doesn't move. You tell yourself that it's the April wind making you shiver, even though the sweat running down your armpits says something else.

Enough. Who has time for this kind of crap?

When the Uber arrives, you get into the back. After a few blocks, the silver Toyota appears behind you, so you ask the driver to stop a few blocks from your house. There's not much in that corner of the ByWard Market except for a safe injection site and a convenience store that sells overpriced cigarettes and lottery tickets to the metalheads from the bar across the street.

What a coincidence: the driver of the Toyota must have been feeling lucky too. He appears behind you, lumbering through the narrow aisles of the shop without getting close enough to give you a good look at his face. Not without being obvious, anyway. Maybe you shouldn't be worrying about that. You know you're up to the challenge, whatever it is.

JUDGMENT: UNFINISHED BUSINESS

You trust that intuition, but you've been walking the aisles of the tiny shop for 10 minutes, and the owner is starting to look at you funny. Oddly enough, he's not doing the same to the guy with the doughy hands. Could this be the sad bureaucrat who came into the café the other day? Nah, that guy wouldn't be brave enough to follow you.

You stop by the news rack, but the magazines are too pricey and not that interesting. So you grab a copy of October's *Modern Witchcraft* and a lottery ticket and get the heck out of there. The door chimes sound again right after you exit.

You're not far from home, but you'd rather not lead this guy, whoever he is, to your nest. The lessons of the ancestors rise up in your mind. The light of the moon shines down. It's waning but still bright enough to guide you.

THE MAGICIAN: MANIFESTATION

The washroom of the biker bar across the road should make a decent spot to hide out for a few minutes. It's not the first time you've had to hunker down here to avoid some guy's attention. You are a woman after all, but somehow, you always feel safe in this place. As soon as you step into the room with the death metal posters on the back wall, the pounding of your heart lets up, just a little bit. No way that guy would ever follow you in here. You know it in your bones.

The tattooed bartender nods as you pass him on your way to the back. You walk purposefully, as though there's somebody you know against the far wall, then keep going down the hallway. Nobody seems to notice your flushed face. You open the door to the pee-scented gender-free washroom and lock yourself in. The graffiti on the walls is interesting enough to help get your breathing under control. Somebody cursing a rival. Somebody else begging for their ex to come back. Petty problems.

It's just a panic attack. Just. You've survived them before.

After what feels like forever, but must be around 10 minutes, you wonder if it's safe to leave. Sure it is. You can do this. You know you can.

EIGHT OF SWORDS: FEELING TRAPPED

The metal door clicks shut as you exit into the narrow passage. A large shape looms in front of you, and for a second you freeze. Maybe you should go back into the washroom? Or make a break for the fire exit at the other end of the hall?

You choose the latter. The man comes up behind you and shoves you out the door, making you wonder how big a mistake you've made. When you feel the knife at your throat and land in the back of the hatchback, you know. He reeks of that cheap body spray, making you almost grateful for the dirty hood that blocks out most of your senses. You could reach up and pull it off, but you know better than that.

THE HANGED MAN: PERSPECTIVE

It's been two days since you arrived here, judging from the rhythms of the movements above you and the tiny slivers of life that seep through the door at the top of the stairs. Now you're on an icy cement floor, crouching over some kind of beef stew that might as well be dog food. It might even be dog food. You don't ask questions, you don't talk back, you do what he tells you.

Despite the humiliations he and his teenage sidekick put you through, whatever they want doesn't seem to include your death, at least not yet. It's taken you this long to register that piece of good news and start to take in what's around you. The kid's not very bright; he brought you a fork with your meal on the first day and then got so rattled when you spoke to him that he dropped his tray and forgot to pick the fork back up. That's got to be a major failure in kidnapping terms. You figured one of them would come back for it eventually— keeping touch of metal cutlery seems pretty basic—but it's lain there, tucked just out of sight under the third rickety shelf from the door. Tantalizingly out of reach.

There are books on those shelves, but they're too far away to read the titles, so no clues there. Maybe you should be counting things, steps on the floor above, minutes in captivity, but numerology has never been your thing.

A mere few days ago you were a creative person. You lit candles. You grew herbs. You read tarot. You thought you could read people. You had friends. You were in a book club with people who worked for the prime minister. Now you crap in a bucket in the corner of a dank cellar. You say please and thank you for things you definitely don't want.

At least you're not hanging upside down. Yet.

TEN OF WANDS: OVERBURDENED

The rusty chain that encases your ankle is attached to a metal ring on a pole coming out of the floor. This contraption allows you to do an eight-foot circle around the futon on the ground. The chain clanks every time it touches the ground, and you don't want to draw attention, so you spend most of your waking hours at the end of it, casting circles, walking spells. Three times widdershins, then three more deosil. Or that's what you think anyway, since you can't see the sun. But intention is everything. Banish and then bring. It takes five seconds to make each circle, faster if you run of course, but after you nearly tripped this morning, you don't want to do that. The ring holding your chain to the pole creaks with each pass. It's a sweet sound.

The corners of the room are packed with boxes, piles of old books and papers. Mice rustle around in the detritus. The bucket is as far away as it can be, but it still stinks. You haven't seen the teenager since yesterday, and the man has only come to the basement twice, first to take the full bucket, then to bring back a clean one and some food. He kept his eyes on the floor the whole time, acting as though you don't exist. Maybe he's ashamed of what he did to you that first night? He should be.

But why are you here if he's not interested in you anymore, and besides, who does he think he is? He's no oil painting himself, nondescript, clean shaven, bland. Doughy, just like you thought when he sat in front of you for his reading. Plastic horn-rimmed glasses, an ironed white T-shirt peeking out from under his black cardigan. Dark no-name brand jeans and running shoes. You might not be able to pick him out of a police lineup if he's standing next to someone of similar size, not that you need to worry about that. The way the Ottawa police work these days, they won't be looking for you before Christmas.

You wonder what happened to the kid after the disaster with the fork. You heard them yelling at each other, no mistaking the stress in their voices. The man was barking about not being able to trust the kid to do simple things. Maybe they're starting to realize that they've bitten off more than they can chew. Something's going to give soon.

It's taken you until now to notice that when the man leaves, he closes the door at the top of the stairs but doesn't lock it. You hear the familiar footsteps above, first right over you and then toward the end of the room. A toilet flushes and water runs into pipes along the ceiling. There's more water running, then more footsteps to the other side of the house. Only one set. He's there for a while, then back to the basement door, bringing the bucket and a sandwich wrapped in plastic. It takes him five minutes and 20 seconds today, five minutes and 31 seconds yesterday. The door stays unlocked for another minute.

Those will be your lucky numbers for the rest of your life.

THE STAR: HOPE

The boredom surprises you. You categorize the bugs that fly around the bare lightbulb above you and count the ones that end up in the spiders' webs in the four corners of the room. Flies, beetles, little crawly things you can't name. You gaze at the dust motes like they're clouds and try to scry shapes in them. You remember every guy you ever kissed and wonder if you should have said yes to the others who wanted to kiss you. There might never be another chance. You sing every song from *Little Shop of Horrors* that you can remember, and when that's only three, you cry. You try to make friends with the mice, who have been getting bolder since that first day. Hopefully none of them carry hantavirus.

It takes several attempts, but you manage to stretch far enough to knock over one of the boxes and pull out the paper inside. Treasury Board policy documents, ugh. Then what catches your eye is worse than porn—a pentagram, poorly drawn cloaked figures and images of goat heads. There are numbers and lists written in Google-translate Latin. You look at the Walmart satanism, printed off the internet, marked up with red and black markers. So embarrassing.

After that you mostly meditate and feel the Elementals close to you. When the man comes downstairs and tosses your tarot cards on the floor before he leaves, it's clear he underestimates you. When you draw the Star, you feel a surge of something in your chest. Hope. It hurts.

But it's going to hurt him more than it hurts you.

JUSTICE: COSMIC FAIRNESS

Your stomach gets it before your mind does: the energy in the house has shifted. Flies buzz around the lightbulb, and every so often one of them bounces off and lands on your futon. The mice have quietened down. Someone's moving furniture and other heavy things across the floor upstairs.

The metal ring is almost gone, worn down by all your pacing, but there is still the issue of the iron shackle around your ankle, not to mention the chain itself. When the ring finally breaks, you collapse on the floor and weep for joy. Then you claw the fork out from under the shelf where it's been waiting since the boy dropped it.

The man brings your food and doesn't bother to look around; it's clear he thinks you're not going to put up a fight. The lack of respect galls you. It's all you can do not to stab him then and there, even though he looks you in the eye for the first time since you met him. When he tells you he's coming back for his reading, you know it's now or never. It's all you can do to stay on the futon until he leaves.

Every hair on your body is standing on end. Your heart pounds against your ribcage, and your breath rasps through your throat. You reach the steps, cradling the chain in front of you. Five minutes and 20 seconds. You're a feather, flitting weightlessly above the stairs. When you get to the top of the staircase, the water is running.

Then, a sharp grunt. And a flash of pain.

The door opens. A bright light floods your vision.

You're on the futon again, your hair matted with blood. On unsteady legs, you manage to stand up. You realize the stairs are far, but your chain is still loose, and the fork is still deep in your pocket. When you hear footsteps heading towards the basement door, you lie back and feign unconsciousness.

Seconds later, the man is kneeling beside you, then dragging you onto the concrete.

"Thou shalt not suffer a witch to live," he whispers.

You want to tell him not to worry about that, he'll soon have better things to suffer, but you manage to stay quiet. When you peek through your eyelashes, you see him opening a box and taking out white chalk and candles. He stands above you and begins to chant. Some BS, probably Babylonian, whose meaning he doesn't even know. Ridiculous.

You raise your legs and kick him in the balls, hard, using the shackle to your advantage. He bends over in pain, but before you can get up, he's on you again, pinning your wrists to the ground. You get him in the stomach with both feet and all your strength. He falls back, but he recovers quickly. In a split second, he's on top of you again, pinning your shoulders to the ground, swearing, ordering you to stay down.

His forcefulness almost makes you respect him. But he underestimated you too much to search you, so you reach for the metal handle of the fork in your pocket. You bring your knee up to his groin hard enough to make him loosen his grip for a second, then you jam the metal prongs into his neck. It sinks into his flesh like a piece of lean pork.

"Suffer *that*," you whisper.

Now he's looking at you like he sees you, really sees you, and this time, you don't flinch. You twist the handle, and he jerks sideways, off your body. He pulls it out of his neck, and dark blood spurts out. He staggers to the stairway and fumbles with the doorhandle at the top. You follow him and yank on the back of his shirt, so he loses his balance and tumbles back down the stairs. It takes a while for him to choke, but you enjoy the wait. You close the door and latch it behind you. Ahead of you is a long hallway, and there's a light at the end of it.

He's not suffering anything anymore.

Your intuition is clear.

P. R. Isfeld has been writing fiction for several years, partly as a creative refuge from the bureaucracy associated with her foreign service career. Her short story "Intuition" won Second Prize in the 2024 Audrey Jessup Short Story Contest, and her manuscript "Captives" was shortlisted for the Crime Writers of Canada Award for Best Unpublished Manuscript in 2022.

COLD SHOULDER

8

MELISSA YI

E dward Neff had discovered the perfect property and the perfect woman, followed by two flaws.

The property, a timeless two-storey brick home with an extensive garden in Manotick, a rural area in the south part of Ottawa, had come first. On the first floor Edward could read in his library or press a button to start a fire in the living room. In the back-yard he could tend to his bonsai in the greenhouse, take a dip in a heated saltwater pool or roast marshmallows in a fire pit. His house-keeper, Mrs. Hohenwart, oversaw the staff keeping the five-bedroom house spotless, from its vaulted skylight and meditation room on the second floor to the workout equipment and cold storage area in the basement.

Then came the perfect woman. Edward had rediscovered her the previous week, at the beginning of August. He and Renée Morton had once attended middle school together in Orleans. She had become even more beautiful in the intervening years. Unfortunately, she had also acquired two liabilities.

The liabilities spoke. In fact, they yelled, they swore and screamed.

Therefore, Edward would have to discourage the two liabilities from his property as gracefully as possible, starting with supper served at a table large enough for ten, under a crystal chandelier.

Edward, Renée and her two liab—ahem, *children*—gathered around the silver platter where Mrs. Hohenwart had artistically arranged a raw slab of beef.

"What is this?" asked Renée, covering her nose from the scent of blood. She still looked elegant in a blue dress and matching heels with her hair swept into a chignon and makeup expertly applied.

The blood pooled beneath the beef and began to run to the edge of the platter. Edward felt his cheeks flush as he said, "I would call this an idiom brought to life."

Renée's 11-year-old daughter, Portia, interrupted him, as impatient at the table as she was on the football field. "Mom, it's raw. That's freakin' gross."

"Why's it all red?" asked Lyle, Renée's five-year-old son, shrinking into his green velvet chair near the china cabinet.

Portia flicked her brother's arm. "Because it's raw, stupid head."

"But why is it raw?"

Edward cleared his throat. "We believe this may have started as a custom in medieval England when they would first greet guests with a warm meal. However, they would serve a cold shoulder of beef, or perhaps mutton, once guests had, er, overstayed—"

Portia burst out laughing. "A cold beef shoulder? Mom's a vegetarian!"

"Edward knows that." Renée touched his shoulder, her cool fingertips pressing through his linen dress shirt. For a moment Edward's resolve faltered. Her eyes reminded him of his glory-of-the-snow flowers in springtime. He and Renée had grown up in Yorkshire, England, riding bicycles and reading Enid Blyton together. They'd stayed pen pals after her family moved to Rockliffe Park. His diplomat parents were later assigned to Ottawa.

When Renée had separated from her husband last week, Edward had naturally offered to help. Children could always go to summer school, he had assumed.

"What the hell?" Portia texted a picture of the beef shoulder to her friends, making Edward twitch uncomfortably.

"You shouldn't say the H word," said Lyle, sticking his thumb in his mouth.

Portia's braces flashed at her brother. "You shouldn't suck your thumb. You're way too old. I'm gonna cut it off with Mrs. Hohenwart's meat cleaver!"

Lyle screamed loud enough to rattle the crystals in the chandelier and frighten Céline Dion. Then the boy upset his water glass in his lap, ice cubes bouncing onto the floor while Edward sucked in his breath.

Renée leapt to daub the liquid up with the Irish linen napkin that had been embroidered by Edward's great-aunt Lucille. "I'm so sorry, Edward. At least the crystal isn't broken."

"Quite all right," said Edward. He rang for Mrs. Hohenwart, using a Victorian sterling silver table bell in the shape of a wizard, with the figure's hinged head attached to a clapper. Then he collected the glass, replaced it on the table and gestured back at the cold shoulder. "As I was saying..."

Portia snorted at her brother. "Now it looks like you peed yourself."

Edward felt sympathetic toward Lyle until the boy countered, "I'm gonna pee on you next!"

"Freak!" Portia pushed her chair away from the table.

"I'm gonna break into your room and pee all over your clothes. You'll never be able to get the smell out."

"Mom!"

Renée crossed her arms. "Both of you, be quiet. Portia, go to your room."

"Why?" Portia shoved her newly reupholstered chair, knocking it onto its back.

Edward flinched and rang again for Mrs. Hohenwart. The table bell, created by John Septimus Beresford, existed for 140 years, about the same amount of time it took to rouse Mrs. Hohenwart who seemed to go deaf whenever he invited lady friends to stay. He raised his voice to Renée. "I'm sure you've noticed that we continue to use the idiom today..."

"Not exactly." Renée pressed her hand on Lyle's knee as her son tried to clamber away. "Sit *down*," she hissed.

"Mom, I'm all wet!"

"Don't let him go! He'll piss all over my stuff!" Portia called over her shoulder.

Edward set Portia's chair back on its teak legs. He could smell his perspiration underneath his cologne and aftershave. "A shoulder cut of beef or mutton was the most inexpensive portion of meat. First the guests would receive it for dinner, and then the next day, the same shoulder would be served cold."

Renée raised her delicately arched eyebrows, and for a second, he thought she understood. Then she stood up. "Edward, I'm fascinated by what you have to say, but Lyle's shaking. That was ice water. Can we talk after I get him cleaned up and find them something to eat?"

Edward stood, too, dropping his napkin on the table. "Absolutely. It was lovely having you. Do you need help taking your cases to the car?"

Renée stared at him. "We don't need suitcases for Taco Bell."

Edward sank into his chair and glanced furtively at the beef shoulder. "Yes, well, I thought perhaps you understood that the beef shoulder has a history of signalling to guests that they had, er, outstayed their—"

"I want a chicken soft taco!" Portia yelled from the front hall, already clomping her shoes on his terrazzo floors.

"Me too! Me too!" Lyle raced after her, tripping on his own socks. The china cabinet reverberated with the impact from the boy's fist. The cabinet withstood the treatment, but Lyle howled.

Mrs. Hohenwart thrust her jowls into the dining room. She said nothing, but her silence spoke an encyclopedia's worth of disapproval.

Edward winced.

Renée folded Lyle in her arms and kissed the top of his head. "Edward, can you tell me afterward? I promise I'll make it up to you."

Edward said, "Er, no need. Please, if I could assist you in gathering your things—"

"We're fine. We've got everything we need right here. You're the best, OK Eddie?" Renée hefted Lyle onto her hip and made her way to the door.

Edward covered his face with the napkin.

"Oh, and Eddie?" Renée spun her son around to smile at him.

Edward pulled the napkin aside and peered at her. At last, she understood. She and her brood would depart in the morning. "Yes, Renée?"

"You go ahead and eat that. We don't need any beef shoulder. Thanks, though. You're one in a million!" Renée escaped to the front door. "Portia, take off my wrap. You've got one of your own. Lyle, how many times do I have to tell you, Edward doesn't like us wearing shoes inside!"

Edward uttered a small moan.

Forty hours later shortly before lunch, Portia slammed her room door and shouted down the second-floor hallway, "It stinks in here! I can't stand it."

Edward emerged from his meditation room and pretended not to notice the stench. Perhaps he had been too erudite with his first attempt. Not everyone enjoyed the derivation of idioms. A comparative literature professor, he sometimes forgot how to communicate effectively, particularly with people significantly under the age of majority.

Edward could not wait to reclaim the room's carved mahogany Chinese bed, now dotted with spilled nail polish, and the scarlet drapes Portia had literally tied in knots.

"Edward, have you been cooking again?" Renée peeked out of the sunflower room on Portia's right before she wrinkled her nose and slid her arm through his. "You should leave that to Mrs. Hohenwart and your staff, you know that."

Edward swallowed. Her skin felt as smooth as a bamboo reed. "No, I haven't been cooking." Plan B hadn't required any heating or preparation. He'd simply allowed nature to take its course.

"Pee-YEW!" Lyle burst out of the aquatic-themed room on Portia's left, holding his nose. "This is nasty!"

Renée sniffed around the threshold of Portia's bedroom. "Is Mrs. Hohenwart not cleaning in here? What's going on?"

"Yesterday was her day off," said Edward. Otherwise, he'd never have gotten away with it. As it was, he'd kept his item stewing in the garden house and had only brought it in that morning while Portia was steaming up the bathroom with one of her interminable showers. "I can see your family's not comfortable here. Perhaps you'd feel more at home in a hotel or a bed and breakfast. You know that old chestnut: after three days, guests—"

"It's fine," said Renée, shooting her children a look. "It'll do us good to clean up around here. We've been spoiled by you and Mrs. Hohenwart. It's my day off, too, so the kids and I will start in here."

"But Mom, you promised we'd go shopping!" Portia protested.

"After," said Renée, patting Edward's arm. "It's time for us to contribute here. You were so good, taking us in after my ex-husband..."

"No, no," said Edward. "I'd rather you found a better place for yourselves. Go and enjoy your shopping. I'll see you later." *And your children never.*

Renée strode the room's perimeter, her head angled upward. "I have a good nose. I can pick up perfume at 20 feet, and at 10 feet I can tell you what brand—aha!" She crouched under the bed. "It's coming from under here. Lyle, get under here!"

"Better you than me," said Portia.

"You too, Miss Smarty Panties. I raised you better than this."

To Edward's amazement the two children did crawl under the bed. Lyle went first, eager to prove his mettle, while Portia moaned and stuck her head under the frame.

"Mom, there's something under here!" shouted Lyle. "On the bed frame!"

"Get it out, then!"

"Let me out first!" Portia scrambled backward and hit her head on the edge of the frame. "Ouch!"

Edward watched, mute, as Lyle backed out from under the bed, dragging the tinfoil-wrapped item along his hardwood floor. Lyle ripped the foil open to reveal the flounder. It seemed to stare at them with the shrunken remains of its two eyes. The rest of its slimy body had begun to cave in.

"What on earth? Did you kids do this?" Renée clapped a hand to her mouth.

"No way, Mom!" said Lyle.

"Like I'd touch that," said Portia, who had her nose firmly pinched.

Renée turned to Edward. "I don't understand it. Why would someone put a fish under someone's bed? Is it some sort of weird German custom of Mrs. Hohenwart's?"

Edward coughed. "She is Austrian."

"Could you get rid of it? We're going to be sick." Renée held out the flounder at arm's length, nearly nudging Edward in the belly with it.

He took a step back. "Er, are you familiar with the saying about guests and fish?"

"You mean that thing about serving fish on Fridays?" Renée choked out.

Portia shouted, "Mom, I'm gonna hurl! Why are you just standing there with it?"

Despite himself, Edward felt compelled to explain. "No, the reason Catholics abstain from meat on Fridays—"

"Moooom, it reeks! You might like the stench, but I don't!" Portia stormed out of the room.

At last, something was going according to plan. "I apologize. I think you'll have to find alternative accommodations. You know Benjamin Franklin's saying about how guests and fish smell after three days." Edward coughed again.

Renée rushed to her own room, tossed open the balcony door and dropped the flounder, tinfoil wrapping and all, onto Edward's prized lilies. Still gasping for breath, she ducked into the adjoining bathroom to wash her hands. "Oh, don't worry about it. A bit of fresh air and elbow grease and we'll be all right. Portia, get back in here with some bleach. Lyle, you find a mop and bucket."

That night Edward tried to broach the subject while Renée's offspring stampeded his garden on the pretence of playing baseball. At least the children had marked bases around the salt pool and firepit, and they were staying back from the greenhouse next to the house.

Renée spoke first, her eyes on the cattails bordering his backyard. "I want to thank you for letting us stay with you. I know it hasn't been easy." Renée leaned forward. Her sweet breath reminded him of calendula, a herb the Egyptians used for rejuvenation.

"No, it hasn't." Edward felt drawn to her despite her children.

Renée gazed at Portia, who flung the baseball bat into the firepit after striking out. "I know they need more boundaries. I blame myself and Richard for fighting so much. They don't know what's right. I'll try and raise them better now."

Edward nodded. He could appreciate the challenge of rearing children.

Lyle's scream broke across the air. "That was a foul!"

"No, it wasn't. We said the baseline was from that mound to the pool!"

Renée sighed and glanced down at her own meticulous nails. "I'll leave them a minute to resolve their own problems."

Lyle had turned puce. "MoOOOOOOM! She called me a dipwad!"

"MoOOOOOOM! He's cheating!"

"They're bored," Renée continued. "I took them away from their friends over the summer, but we had to get away from Richard, and I couldn't afford to pay for rent after he froze our bank account. You're a godsend."

Edward leaned toward her. He appreciated acting as her knight in shining armour, even if the damsel's children had become extremely distressing. The girl had ripped up some cattails from the edge of his property to beat on the boy, and the boy was yowling—

Renée stood. "Excuse me," she said as the boy hurled the ball at his sister. Although he had a surprisingly good arm for a five-year-old, his aim was terrible, and the ball whipped toward Mrs. Hohenwart who had come out of the house to beat the carpets.

She ducked with impressive speed for a stout woman.

The ball smashed through a window of Edward's greenhouse.

Edward raced toward the greenhouse. He was horrified to see his yamadori bonsai, over 40 years old, knocked clear out of its pot.

Edward couldn't speak for a moment.

Mrs. Hohenwart joined him first. She said only four words. "They have to go."

Renée bore down on them, dragging a sulky Portia and a white-faced Lyle. Edward replied, *sotto voce*, "I see no alternative. Prepare the nuclear option tonight."

"Yes sir," said Mrs. Hohenwart.

Four hours later, ensconced in a green velvet chair, Renée sniffed the bowl of soup Mrs. Hohenwart had placed in front of her before she reached for her silver spoon. "Cream of broccoli? That sounds delectable."

"Says you," muttered Portia.

Renée's voice carried a hint of steel. "Portia, you mean thank you."

Portia muttered, "...you."

Edward wasn't entirely sure about the first syllable, but since Renée continued smiling, he let it go and took a sip of soup. "The chef and Mrs. Hohenwart have outdone themselves."

Renée waited until the housekeeper returned to refill their water glasses. "Mrs. Hohenwart, there's no chicken broth or anything in here, is there? Even the powdered kind?"

Mrs. Hohenwart topped up Edward's water with a tinkle of ice cubes. "No powder. I never use powder."

"She makes everything from scratch. That's why my mother hired her 20 years ago." Edward nodded respectfully at Mrs. Hohenwart.

"I like it," said Lyle, slurping up the last from his bowl and banging the porcelain on the table. "Can I have more?"

"Please, may I have some more?" prompted Renée.

"Please. May I?" the boy asked.

Mrs. Hohenwart whisked away Lyle's bowl.

Portia groaned. "I'd rather have Campbell's."

Lyle snatched her leftovers. Portia slapped his wrist, nearly upturning the bowl.

"Lyle, wait for Mrs. Hohenwart to serve you again." Renée sipped soup from her own spoon. "Oh, this is wonderful. Is that butter as well as cream? That always helps. Not with the waistline, of course." Edward's glance dropped to Renée's slender figure, much of it draped under the tablecloth.

Lyle devoured his second serving. Edward watched him slurp and spill stray soup not only on the saucer but on the tablecloth and his slacks. Surely if he liked it so much, he could take some care with it.

Edward waited for Renée to admonish her son. Instead, she asked Mrs. Hohenwart for her secret.

"Beef shoulder," said Mrs. Hohenwart.

Renée reached for her throat. "But I asked you—"

"No chicken. No powder."

Renée rose to her feet. "I haven't had meat in 15 years. It makes me sick."

"Mrs. Hohenwart," began Edward, but Renée had dashed out of the room, leaving her napkin crumpled on the floor.

The following morning Renée, her children and their suitcases stood between the two lions on his front doorstep. "I guess this is goodbye, Edward."

Portia said, "This sucks." Then she turned on her heel and slouched over to the car.

Lyle looked up at Edward. "Are we gonna see you again?"

Edward hesitated. He exchanged a look with Renée. Her smile strained as she spoke. "Maybe, Lyle. Whitby is pretty far from Manotick. But we can write and message him, right?"

"Right," said Lyle, looking away before he followed his sister to the car.

Neither child seemed to notice the suitcases at Renée's feet. She held out her hand to Edward. "I know we were a trial. Thank you for taking us in."

So many words hovered on Edward's lips. He wished Renée herself could stay.

Renée didn't wait for him to speak. "I'll miss you while I'm at my aunt's. I guess it's for the best. I want to settle somewhere where the kids can go to school."

"There are perfectly adequate schools within five miles from here," Edward found himself saying.

She touched his arm, and he felt himself leaning toward her smooth skin. "That's sweet. I'll write to you," she said.

Mrs. Hohenwart cleared her throat and hefted the two suitcases.

"Well, goodbye," said Renée, kissing Edward on the cheek. While he waved farewell, he thought he smelled night-blooming jasmine.

That night, after his favourite dinner of steak and fresh asparagus at the table for ten, Edward turned the page of his latest journal and wondered why he felt lacking. Life was exactly as he had arranged it, and yet—

"Glass of port, sir?" asked Mrs. Hohenwart from the doorway.

"Mrs. Hohenwart, thank you for the beef shoulder soup. It served its purpose."

The housekeeper's expression didn't change. "I also fed her some information, sir."

Edward set his journal beside his plate. "That I was impoverished?"

"Overextended and about to have your home repossessed, sir."

Edward shook his head. Renée had seemed so genuine, and yet she'd fled at a single lie without verifying it. Perhaps it was best not to remain in contact, then.

Mrs. Hohenwart carried in a tray with a glass of port and chocolate-covered biscuits. As the port rolled down his throat, Edward considered the fact that, following the sad demise of his beloved parents, only Mrs. Hohenwart had stayed by his side.

Edward's few female visitors never remained. Last year he'd taken Anne to the hospital for a bad stomach flu. She'd blamed Mrs. Hohenwart's marzipan and refused to return, even for her luggage. The year previous Ursula had claimed that rampant cat hair and smoke had triggered her allergies, even though Edward had assured her his family had never kept pets or lit a single cigar.

The feminine mind remained a mystery incompatible with his home. Edward set down his glass with a clink on the mahogany table and gazed across the room at the housekeeper ever-present in the arched doorway.

Had Edward been the proverbial blind man, unable to see the sturdy, loyal edelweiss before him? He'd failed to compliment the one woman who continually made his palatial house and garden a gracious home.

"Mrs. Hohenwart, would you do me the honour of joining me for port and cookies?" Edward pushed aside his journal on wills and estates with hardly a glance at the table of contents. For the first time, it occurred to him that he should make a provision in his will for his most loyal servant.

Mrs. Hohenwart followed his eye to the journal, and for the first time, she smiled. "Of course, sir."

Melissa Yi is an emergency doctor who writes every spare minute, mostly about Hope Sze, a medical doctor who solves murders. Her latest, Killing Me Slothly, confronts the sin of sloth and the supernatural. Hope's secret

younger cousin, Edan, takes on The Red Rock Killer, which was named a finalist for the Crime Writers of Canada's Best Juvenile/YA Novel Award. Melissa writes all genres, sometimes under the name Melissa Yuan-Innes.

THE SUCCESS STORY

9

BRENDA CHAPMAN

Ava set a plate of fried eggs and bacon in front of Max and stepped back to look out the kitchen window. She'd remember this June day as the last decent one before Max's brother, Leon, newly released on parole from the Joyceville penitentiary, darkened their Westboro door.

"Why does he need to come here?" she'd asked Max when he first broke the news. "Surely, he has a friend or somebody else who can put him up until he gets a job." *And good luck with that*, she thought. His criminal record would make the guy virtually unemployable.

"He's my brother, and I feel a certain responsibility."

"Leon's lucky to have you in his corner, but this really isn't a good time." She turned sideways so Max could see the swell of her belly in case he needed reminding that a baby would be arriving soon.

"He'll be gone before you change the first diaper. It's just till he gets on his feet."

"Promise me."

Max held up a hand and made an X across his chest. "Cross my heart and hope to die."

"Jeezus, don't say that."

Max left for his lawyer job on Parliament Hill, and Ava cleaned up the kitchen. She'd stopped work at the pub the week before and still wasn't used to having an entire day stretching out in front of her with endless possibility. Only three weeks until the baby's arrival, so she planned to make the best of these last hours of freedom. Lunch with a girlfriend at Petit Bill's and then a facial and pedi at Renu Spa. She'd happily put Leon out of her mind for the afternoon.

The next day dawned cloudy and wet to match Ava's mood. She waited in bed until Max finished his shower, put on his grey suit and went downstairs to make coffee. He was supposed to take the day off to be home when Leon arrived, but a scandal brewing in the PMO meant Max was needed. He'd worked hard to become indispensable to the new prime minister, telling her that this was an important stepping stone before he himself ran in the next election. "How will it feel to be married to a member of Parliament?" he'd asked, dancing her around the kitchen.

Ava got dressed in her pregnancy jeans and smock top and pulled her hair back with an elastic. She glared at her oversized reflection in the floor-to-ceiling mirror before clumping downstairs to join him in the kitchen.

Max looked up from his phone. "I made a pot of herbal tea for you."

"Great." He must be feeling guilty. She poured a cup and sat across from him at the table.

"Don't worry about cooking breakfast. I'll pick up something on my way in."

Really guilty. "What time is your brother supposed to show up?"

"I'm guessing mid-afternoon. I'll try to get away early so you don't need to entertain him for long."

"You promised me—"

"And I'm sorry, but CTV got its hands on a story about one of the backbenchers and a prostitute that I've been tasked with getting quashed."

"Well, I hope you're taking tomorrow off."

"I'll try my damnedest."

Max had no sooner pulled out of the driveway than the front doorbell rang. Ava picked up a tea towel to dry her hands on the way down the hall. The man standing on the top step looked vaguely familiar. "Can I help you?" she asked through the screen door.

"You must be Max's wife, Ava. I'm Leon. Sorry to get here so early."

Ava blinked. Leon looked nothing like the thug she'd seen in photos. But then, the latest pictures Max had of the two of them had been taken at least six years ago. This new, improved Leon had cut his shoulder-length brown hair and shaved off his beard, no longer appearing like a hardened biker. He was dressed in faded jeans, a black leather jacket and work boots but otherwise could pass for a man with a government job. Still, a shiver of unease travelled up her spine. She inwardly cursed Max for putting her in this position. She swung the door open. "Come in. We've been expecting you."

"Thanks, Ava. I appreciate your hospitality."

He dropped his duffle bag on the floor, took off his boots and hung up his jacket on the coat rack before following her into the living room. He glanced around and said, "Nice place. Max at work?"

"There was another emergency that only he can fix." Ava smiled, not wanting him to think she was being critical. "He's going to try to get off early."

Leon grinned back. He was standing too close to her, near enough that she smelled a musky scent coming off his skin. When she turned her head, he was watching her with the same eyes as Max's, only wider apart and darker blue. *Hypnotising like a cobra.* She took a step back.

"Would you like to see your bedroom?" *God, what was she think-ing?* "It's upstairs, last room on the left. You can bring your bag and freshen up while I make some coffee."

"Yeah, that sounds good."

She waited until his footsteps disappeared up the stairs before resting her hands on the kitchen counter and bending over to take deep breaths. This man scared and excited her at the same time. He was a rougher, leaner version of Max, and her attraction to him had come out of nowhere. Pregnancy hormones had to be responsible somehow. *Would you like to see your bedroom? Good God.* She straightened and opened the cupboard over her head. *Get a grip,* she ordered herself before reaching with a shaking hand for the coffee container.

Leon left for a walk around the neighbourhood after Ava fed him a sandwich to go with the coffee. When he returned three hours later, Max was still not home, and she'd drifted into a dream on the lounger in the backyard. She awoke to find Leon sitting in the chair next to her reading a paperback. He'd changed into shorts and a black T-shirt that showed off two armfuls of tattoos. Aviator sunglasses concealed his eyes, but she had the sense he'd been watching her sleep. She was again aware of his coiled energy, and the idea crossed her mind that it might be dangerous to be alone with him.

"You looked so peaceful," he said. "Do you know if it's a boy or a girl?"

She put a hand on her stomach and shook her head. "I like surprises. Can I get you anything?"

"I was about to ask you that."

"No, I'm fine." She looked around the small yard and thought about him living in a jail cell. "What was it like being locked up?" She blushed as soon as the words were out of her mouth but didn't regret asking. There was a need to address the elephant, to face her fear.

He appeared to focus his gaze on the tomato plants she'd arranged in pots at the edge of the bricked patio. "It wasn't like in the movies. I didn't spend much time in a cell. You get used to the routine after a while." His voice dropped. "It's not as if you're given a choice."

He didn't appear upset by her question, so she pressed on. "Do you ever...do you ever think about the boy who died that night?"

"Every morning when I wake up and he doesn't."

"The other guy in your car—"

"Grayson Rivera."

"Yeah, Grayson. He used to come around when you were on trial, but he hasn't since you were found guilty of...well."

"You can say it. Guilty of killing someone while driving impaired and speeding on the Parkway. I guess he wants to put distance between me and what happened. I know I would in his shoes."

"There you are!"

They both startled and turned to see Max stepping through the sliding patio door. Leon stood and they shook hands. Max dragged over another lawn chair and sat knee to knee with his brother. Ava felt left out but tried not to let this ruin the moment.

"I'm glad you're here. I'll do anything I can to help you get back on your feet."

"I appreciate that."

They stared at each other without flinching for a long moment until Max looked over at Ava. "What ya got cookin, good lookin?"

"I thought we could eat out tonight."

"It's been a long day," he glanced back at Leon, "but what the hell? We need to celebrate. Italian okay?"

"Sure. Anything."

"Great. Ava, why don't you make a reservation at Café Mio while I have a quick shower?"

Leon stayed with them a full month. Ava delivered the baby two weeks early, and he made himself scarce whenever Max was home, which wasn't all that often with Parliament in session. She had the feeling Max was avoiding his brother, arriving home after dinner most nights in a closed-off mood, not interacting with Leon for more than a few minutes. When Coco was three weeks old, Leon announced that he'd found a construction job and a studio apartment above a shop on Wellington Street, a 40-minute walk from their house. He'd be leaving by the weekend. Ava was surprised to realize he'd become good company with Max working the crazy, overtime hours. At some point, she'd stopped seeing Leon as an ex-con screw-up, though she still didn't trust him very far. She worried the days ahead with only Coco for company would be long and lonely. He seemed to sense her distress the evening he returned for his things as he stood in the doorway with his duffle bag.

"I won't be far if you need anything. You know, diapers or pickles and ice cream at midnight. I may not be allowed to drive, but I can walk and remember how to take a bus."

"I've outgrown that particular combination, but thanks I'm sure."

Max came up from behind and put a hand on Leon's shoulder. "All set?"

"Let's do it."

They'd given Leon a chair, small table and carton of dishes and cutlery that filled the trunk and back seat of the car. He waved from the front passenger seat as Max backed out of the driveway. After they were gone, Ava fed and changed the baby and lay down for a nap. When she opened her eyes again, the room was completely dark except for the moonlight streaming across the bed. Coco might actually sleep through the night for the second time ever and keep her from going insane.

Max's car pulled into the driveway as she padded down the stairs to get a glass of water. She greeted him at the door with a hug, drawing back at the smell of perfume on his skin.

"Sorry I'm so late. Leon and I had a few beer at the Wood after we got everything into his apartment. Shelly was working."

That would explain the perfume. Shelly was known to be a big hugger at the pub. "I thought Leon wasn't supposed to drink."

"Well, not drink and drive at any rate." He laughed. "Actually, doing either one could land him in trouble with his parole officer. Leon drank ginger ale if you want an exact retelling."

Max followed her into the kitchen. "I need to go on a business trip this weekend to Toronto. Sorry I didn't tell you earlier, babe, but I just found out today." His eyes met hers for a moment before he opened the freezer and popped a couple of ice cubes into a tumbler. He'd begun drinking Scotch before bed to help him sleep.

"You and Leon don't seem all that happy with each other." Ava poured water from the tap into a glass before leaning against the counter to watch him.

Max shrugged. "He's jealous of my success, and I pity him. He senses it."

"You barely spent any time with him at all."

Max paused with the glass halfway to his mouth. "We have nothing in common, and honestly, I didn't want him getting too comfortable and thinking he could just stay with us forever. He's always liked taking risks, finding ways to get what he wants and not caring about the impact on anybody else. I'm glad he's out of our house and I hope that he stays away. Coco doesn't need her uncle's bad influence. With the biker lifestyle he was living, it was only a matter of time before he killed somebody. I don't doubt he'll do it again."

"He seemed fine when he was here." She thought about all the times he'd shooed her out of the kitchen to do the dishes, rocked Coco when she was crying, gone grocery shopping while she slept.

"My little brother can become whatever you want him to be. The shame is that it never lasts."

Max crossed the floor and wrapped her in his arms. "Trust me on this one, Ava. Don't invite Leon over or think he'll even want to be asked. He'll settle back into his old skin now that he's back on his own."

Coco turned six months old when Ava confronted Max about the affair he'd been having with an intern at his office. After a round of denials, he swore up and down that it was over, that Ava was the only one he'd ever loved. Through her anger and hurt bubbled a feeling of relief. She hadn't been happy for a while, not with his long work days (that she now knew hadn't all been spent in the office) or his scattered interest in her and Coco. Her love for Max had been slipping away for months, and it was only now that she could face the inevitable.

"I want you to leave," she said.

"I won't let you or Coco go without a fight," were his parting words before he walked out the door.

She cried most of the night but awoke with fresh resolve. She needed to figure out how to successfully separate from a husband who'd become the sole breadwinner. She still hadn't returned to work. Even the bank account was in his name. How had she let herself get so dependent?

At first, Max remained reasonable. He paid the bills and gave her money for food. He asked to see Coco only on Sundays. Ava squirrelled away as much money as she could, eating little and forgoing trips to the hairdresser or meals out. Still, she hadn't saved much when she finally approached a divorce lawyer four months later. Greta Havers agreed to take her on with a small retainer and the promise of a cut from the settlement.

Ava had just put Coco down for her nap when Greta phoned. "Max is asking for full custody and will pay you half of the house's value when he bought it, which amounts to $400,000. He claims that there was only $50,000 in the bank account when you forced him out of the house and agrees to give you $25,000. He further states that you were only married two years and can return to work, so there will be no further compensation. He said that $425,000 more than pays for how long you were together, considering how little income you earned before and during that time."

"Full custody? Never."

"His lawyer said that if you don't agree to the terms, Max will have no choice but to play hardball."

"What does that mean?"

"I have no idea, but I imagine he'll fight you on half the house."

"He was the one who cheated."

"Sadly, that won't matter."

"He can keep all his precious money if he leaves Coco with me."

"Let me see what I can do."

Greta couldn't do much as it turned out. Ava and Coco moved to a bachelor apartment in an ugly building downtown, and Ava got some shifts at the Wood. Another single mom with a two-year old girl in the building agreed to take Coco whenever Ava went to work. She didn't charge a lot and she was kind and competent. Ava never felt anxious leaving her daughter in her care.

The divorce negotiations stalled. Max refused to budge on full custody; Ava began to despair. He was rich and connected, a lawyer working for the prime minister. She was a stay-at-home mom with a high school education who'd worked as a server in a neighbourhood pub. She worried Greta would weigh the odds and give up.

It was a busy Saturday night at the Wood as customers filled the seats to watch the Ottawa Senators game on TV. Ava was alone, pouring drinks and waiting tables. She'd finished serving a group of regulars when she looked toward the door. Leon was sitting at the end of the bar watching her walk toward him. She hadn't seen him since he moved out of their house nine months earlier. His hair had grown almost to his shoulders and the beard was back. The look suited him somehow. She slipped behind the counter and walked its length to stop in front of him.

"What can I get you?"

"I didn't know you worked here."

"It seems I do."

"And I can see that. Soda and lime would be great."

She got busy and didn't have a chance to speak with him again until near closing. Most of the regulars had gone home, but he stayed. "How's Coco?" he asked.

"Good. She's getting used to the babysitter. I'm going to get her now."

"Where's Max?"

She stared at him, trying to gauge his meaning. "We split up. Coco and I are living downtown."

"No shit."

"I thought he would have told you." She'd actually believed Max had sent Leon to strong arm her into submission but could see now that he was surprised by the news. "He's fighting for full custody and isn't planning to pay alimony. We're only speaking through our lawyers at the moment."

"I'm sorry."

"Not your problem. Say, what about you? How's the job going?"

"Good. I'm site foreman, working my way up."

"You never came to visit."

"Seemed better that way. I honestly appreciated you putting me up for that month."

"Did you and Max come here for drinks the night he moved you into the apartment?"

Leon's hand stilled on the counter. His eyes darkened, and she wondered what was going on inside his head. "Is that what Max told you?"

"Yeah, but I always wondered." She thought of the perfume smell on his clothes. "I suspected he was having an affair. My lawyer says that doesn't matter. She hasn't done much for me to be honest."

Leon slid off the stool and zipped up his leather jacket. "Max's never going to let you have Coco, you must know that. He'll run circles around your lawyer."

"I don't know how to stop him."

Leon stared at her without saying anything. Somebody called for her, and the next time she looked his way, he was gone.

Ava set Coco on the floor with a wooden puzzle when her cell phone rang. Greta was the only one who called her, usually with bad news. Ava hadn't worked in three days, and her cupboard was bare, so things couldn't get much worse. She swiped up.

"You're never going to believe this." Greta didn't wait for her to respond. "Max is giving you full custody and all the money he first offered, plus he'll pay child support."

"What's the catch?"

"There isn't one. In all my years as a divorce lawyer, I've never witnessed such an about-face. Break out the champagne, girl. Be at my office tomorrow at 10 a.m. sharp to get things wrapped up."

Ava lowered the phone and tears rolled down her cheeks as she scooped up Coco and spun her around the apartment. Coco held onto Ava's hair and shrieked in delight. Ava kissed her face all over and squeezed her tight. "I'm not going to lose you. Your daddy saw the light."

Still, she spent a restless night, worried that Max would change his mind. In the morning, she dressed with care, putting Coco in her stroller and walking the 12 blocks to Greta's law office on O'Connor. Max and his lawyer arrived with papers, and they sat in the conference room to finalize the details. Max stopped Ava in the hall on her way out.

"I'm sorry about how this went down. I never meant to hurt you, but I know that I did. I wanted to make this right and to tell you I'm sorry for being such an idiot."

"That means a lot." She glimpsed the man she'd once loved, and this gave a measure of peace.

"I just got scared. All the responsibility...no excuses, but I lost my way for a bit. I hope we can be friends."

"Of course. I'd like that."

Ava left the office a free woman with her baby and enough money to live comfortably for quite some time. She could afford to move into the Hintonburg neighbourhood to be closer to work. She would enrol at Algonquin College and take the business course she'd put off when Max came into her life. She wouldn't need to move in with her parents or ask for a handout.

She spent the rest of the morning with Coco in the park and brought her back to the apartment in time for lunch and a nap. Before getting ready for the late afternoon shift, she looked online for a new apartment and set up a couple of viewings for the next day.

Ava and Coco ran into Leon at the Wellington Butchery the week before Thanksgiving. Coco had celebrated her second birthday that summer. Ava thought back to the last time she'd seen Leon; that was over a year ago when he had stopped by the Wood during her shift.

His eyes lit up at the sight of them. "You're both looking great," he said.

"And you as well." His hair had grown past his shoulders, and his jeans and black leather jacket looked well worn.

They strolled down Wellington Street together. The sun warmed them; it had been a hotter than usual October. They stopped at a red light and Ava smiled at him. "I'm in a good place now. Max stopped being a dick and gave me custody. He doesn't spend much time with Coco, but she's thriving. I'm dating a good man who has a three-year-old daughter, and he's become like a dad to her."

"I don't see much of Max either. He's still working on the Hill, making a name for himself."

She laughed. "I wondered after you stopped by the bar that time if you'd threatened him because he made an about-face on custody a week later. Ridiculous, I know."

"He owed me."

"What do you mean?"

Leon angled sideways to face her. "Max was the one driving the car that killed that kid. I took the fall."

"But Max wasn't in the car."

"Yeah, he was, but he ran off before the cops arrived because the scandal would have ruined his career. Grayson knew the truth and wanted to come clean, but Max paid him off. After I saw you at the Wood that night, I reminded Max that the media would love to hear what really happened that night on the Parkway."

"But that's crazy. You did time for a crime you didn't commit. Why?"

Leon shrugged. "I didn't have much going on. Max would have lost everything, and let's face it, he's the successful one in our family."

The light turned green and they crossed the intersection. "He warned me to stay away from you and Coco that night he drove me to my new apartment." Leon paused. "We never went for drinks after."

Ava had long accepted that Max was a cheating louse, but this confirmed it in spades. A surge of anger mixed with her regret. She'd put stock in all the wrong things. But it didn't have to stay that way.

"Say, would you come for dinner Friday night? I'd like Coco to get to know her uncle Leon, and I've missed having you around."

"I'm not the best role—"

"Hand over your phone." She typed her address and cell number in his contacts and said as she handed it back to him, "6:30 and I won't take no."

"Well if you put it that way." He smiled. "What can I bring?"

"Nothing. You are enough." She opened her arms and wrapped them around his shoulders. "I can see now that you're the brother who's always been enough."

Brenda Chapman is an Ottawa crime fiction writer with over 25 published novels, including the lauded Stonechild and Rouleau police procedurals and the Hunter and Tate mysteries; in addition, her short stories have been published in several notable anthologies and magazines. Brenda held careers as a teacher and a senior communications advisor before pursuing full-time writing.

THE ROARING LION

10

GARY COFFIN

Orson Carver gazed at the picture hanging in Ottawa's Chateau Laurier hotel. He'd seen it many times online, but the pixels on his screen didn't do it justice. Now, though, he was seeing the photo as it was meant to be seen. It was the lighting. Exquisite. The way the shadows emphasized Churchill's furrowed brow, the grim set of his mouth. Yousuf Karsh's photo of Britain's World War II leader seemed to boil the man down to his very essence. The single cocked eye dared anyone to cross him.

"Impressive isn't it?" A languid voice from behind.

Carver turned away from the photo reluctantly. A woman had sidled up beside him. Tall, tailored suit, hair pulled back but not harshly. Poised and polished.

"It is," he replied. "Carver," he held out his hand.

She took it. Not quite a handshake, more a graceful brush of her fingers across his. "Tara Moretti."

"Pleased to meet you."

"Your first time?" she asked.

His smile curled. "Yeah. You?"

She shook her head. "I've seen it many times. And it never fails to impress."

Carver's eyebrow arched.

"I work for Peabody's," she explained. "We hold the insurance on all the art in Fairmont hotels."

"So, you were involved in its recovery?"

"I was. I went to Italy to retrieve it."

"Lucky you." He turned back to the picture.

"Are you here for the grand unveiling Friday?" she asked.

"Not intentionally. I'm in town for a security conference across the street and am staying here."

"Security?"

"I'm a private investigator."

"Sounds exciting."

He shrugged. "Not really. Taking down criminal masterminds, saving the world kind of stuff. It gets old pretty quickly."

She laughed and turned her attention back to the picture. "Did you know that just before Karsh took the shot, he snatched the cigar out of Churchill's mouth? And it's that flash of annoyance on Churchill's face that makes the photo so unforgettable."

"I hadn't heard that."

"It might be just lore but it makes a great story."

"It does. Before you got here, I was looking for a signature but I don't see one."

"He did sign. It's just hard to see." She pulled out her phone, put it on flashlight mode and lit up the bottom right corner. "There it is. As usual, he signed in black ink. It's hard to see against the dark background."

Carver leaned forward for a better look. His eyes squinted.

"Something wrong?" A voice from behind.

They both turned to the voice. A dapper man in a mauve suit jacket and polka-dot bow tie, much like the one Churchill wore in the photo, had moved in behind them. Carver suppressed an urge to wipe the man's pencil mustache with his thumb, like a smudge of dirt.

"Oh. Evening Cecil," she said.

"Tara." He nodded politely.

"This is Mr. Carver. He's a private investigator." As if being a PI was notable. "Mr. Carver, meet Cecil Deschambeau. And to answer your question Cecil, no. Nothing wrong. I was just showing Mr. Carver where Karsh signed the picture." She turned to Carver. "Cecil authenticated the picture after I brought it back home."

"You work for Peabody's?" Carver asked.

He scoffed, "No. I am an independent photographic forensics analyst."

"Photographic forensics analyst? Sounds interesting."

"I've authenticated photographs from across the globe. Anything from daguerreotypes, to tintypes, to magnificent gelatin silver prints like this one."

"Can I ask how you authenticated The Roaring Lion?" Carver brought a hand up to chest level to quell any notions of wrongdoing, "I'm not suggesting anything is wrong; it's a field that's always fascinated me."

Deschambeau straightened up and cleared his throat before speaking. "Where others lose themselves in the image, I delve beneath the surface. Is the paper itself authentic to the time period? Was it printed using gelatin silver print? Is the resolution of the image razor-sharp? Is the signature authentic?

"But above all, my most valuable tool is myself. I've examined so many works, pored over so many forgeries and masterpieces, that I've developed what I can only call a sixth sense. My mind absorbs the full weight of a picture: the texture, the tones, the imperfections and many others too subtle to name. And from that," he held a finger up to underscore his point, "I will know."

He met Carver's eyes with the certainty of a man who's never doubted himself. "It's a gift."

Carver glanced over at Tara. Her eyes had glazed over.

"That's impressive," said Carver. "How would you tell that this isn't a digital copy?"

He shook his head. "Digital scanning has made impressive strides, but there are still telltale signs an experienced eye wouldn't miss. Original prints from negatives have a natural, irregular grain baked into the emulsion, something a scan can't replicate. But the pixels are the biggest giveaway. No matter how high-end the printer, digital reproductions are built on pixels, not chemistry. And pixels have edges. Emulsions don't."

"What about negatives. Can they be copied?"

"Of course, but an expert like myself can tell the difference; the copy won't be as crisp and the colour not quite as sharp."

"Very interesting. We were just checking out the signature. Did you also authenticate that?"

"I can," he said, "but in practice, I usually leave that to the specialists."

Tara stepped in. "In this case, we didn't bring one in. The authenticity of the photo was obvious, and we have over a dozen signed Karsh photos on site, so a simple comparison was more than enough."

The sound of a man's voice calling out brought their attention to the desk at the front of the room.

"They're about to start planning," said Tara. She gave Carver a thin smile. "I'll be here till Friday, hope to see you later."

"Likewise," he replied.

"I guess he needs me, too," sighed Cecil in a faux lament before he left.

Carver looked around to see a young woman, Beryl Adams, standing behind him. She had short black hair chopped haphazardly into sprouts, and the row of bejeweled studs over her right eye ran down to her cheek bone. "Hey partner," he said. "How long have you been standing there?"

"Long enough to hear Sir Talks-a-Lot, the Baron of Blowhard."

Carver laughed. "Self-confidence is not his problem."

"I think shutting the hell up is his problem."

She turned her back so she could speak without anyone hearing. "I saw you salivating over Miss Perfect when she bent down to run her flashlight across the picture."

"I wasn't salivating. I uh...I thought I dropped something."

"Dropped something, yeah right. It was probably drool off your lip."

"Enough about me. I need to check something out. Stand behind me while I look at this signature again."

She moved. Carver enabled his phone flashlight and took a video of the signature. "Thanks," he said when finished. He stood and reviewed what he recorded.

"What?" She'd seen that look on his face before.

He leaned toward her and whispered. "I think Karsh's signature is forged."

"Get out of town!" she whispered back.

"It's true."

"Show me."

He held the recorded scan of the signature up and gave it maximum magnification.

"See the colour?"

"Yeah, black."

"And that's the problem. Inks, especially dye-based inks like this, oxidize over the decades. Black ink will shift to grey. We don't see that here. And notice how crisp it is. It looks like the ink is sitting on top of the paper, which it would if it were fresh. The ink hasn't yet saturated into the paper. I'm convinced this signature is recent."

"So... All of a sudden you're, like, "the Ink Guru?""

"When I was with the police, I often worked with the document examination unit. They taught me a lot about forgery."

Beryl, still skeptical, leaned into him. "Okay Ink Man, so you're saying that the picture that was brought all the way over from Italy and verified by the human gasbag, who is, by his own admission, an expert in such things, is a fake."

"I don't know if the picture is a fake. Cecil Deschambeau said he authenticated the picture, so we should accept that it is the real thing. But that begs the question. Why would someone forge Karsh's signature on a valid copy of the picture?"

"Maybe Karsh forgot to sign it back in the day, so they got him to sign."

"Yousef Karsh died more than 20 years ago."

"Okay. Strike that thought. I'm sure you have a theory. Let's hear it."

"I have no theory."

"But you must have an inkling of a concept of a theory?"

"Not yet. We know that the original Roaring Lion was signed by Karsh and gifted to this very hotel where it was displayed for many years. Based on Cecil's analysis, I'm assuming that the photo that now hangs is an authentic Karsh photo from his negative, but the signature is forged." He met Beryl's dubious look. "I don't see any other possibility," he said. "But why would anyone do that? What do they gain?"

"Maybe someone wanted to keep the original? It'd be worth a lot more than any of the subsequent copies."

He shook his head. "I don't buy it. Sure, the original print is worth a lot more than the other copies, but a great deal of that value hinges on it being the most famous copy, the one the world knows about."

"Then you got me Sherlock."

"Let's put that question on hold and ask, who? Who could have done it?"

"It could be your new bestie Tara. She said she brought the picture back from Italy. Plenty of chances to swap it out. Or maybe it's the walking noise in a bowtie, Cecil Deschambeau. He's the one who authenticated it; he had the access needed for a switcheroo."

Carver nodded slowly. "They are suspects, no doubt. But I can't wrap my head around a motive. What about the guy who actually stole the original? He definitely had the chance to make the swap. I suppose the same as the person who bought it from him. But again... why?"

Beryl watched him slip into the familiar trance. The mystery had hooked him, and now he was caught. There was no pulling him back until he had the answers. A few minutes later he snapped out of his reverie. "Here's what we're going to do," he said as he lifted his index finger.

"Hold on, Speedy," Beryl interrupted. "Before you go making all kinds of plans, remember that I want to visit Medusa's Gallery tomorrow morning."

"The tattoo shop?"

"It's called skin art."

He gave her a 'whatever' look. "There should be plenty of time for that. I'm going to send the video of Karsh's signature to a friend of mine and ask him to confirm that the signature is recent. Let's put Tara and Cecil on the back burner for now; they aren't going anywhere. But I'd like to get more info on the thief. I'll see what I can find out about him, and in the meantime, could you dig up some information on the purchaser?"

"Sure. I'll go upstairs now to start," she said.

The next day, Carver woke early. He made coffee and settled down on the couch to read his email.

His buddy on the police force had replied to last night's question about the signature. As expected, he confirmed the signature was recent.

Carver then turned his attention to the thief. He'd been charged with a variety of crimes ranging from mischief to theft. He wondered why someone would steal a photo and sell it for a fraction of its value on an online platform that could easily be traced. There didn't seem to be any upside to it. He found a short bio published by the Ottawa Citizen shortly after the thief was charged. He then browsed through the thief's extensive social media pages before jumping in the shower and heading down for breakfast.

Beryl was already in the restaurant when he arrived.

"Morning Boss."

"Morning. Sleep well?"

"Yeah, if by sleep well you mean staring at the ceiling in a strange room."

Carver ordered another coffee from a server walking by. "Did you have time to get some info on the lawyer?"

"Of course."

"Good, I'll go first. First of all, my buddy on the force confirmed the signature is recent." He paused and looked at Beryl.

"You waiting for a pat on the back? Tell me about the thief," she said.

He waved her off. "He lived in a small town in Ontario. He had been very active on social media up until he was charged, and nothing since. But his social media history has plenty of photos and related info. He spent 12 years as a British military policeman and was even stationed for four years in the British embassy in Rome. It looks like he left for Canada after that but no further details given."

"Good job, Bossman. I checked out some online sources, too. The lawyer has an established practice in Italy, well-known, well-regarded. She bought the picture in May 2022 through an online auction and paid £5,292. At the time, I didn't think her social media had anything useful, but I saw a few photos of her with the British ambassador in Rome."

"That's interesting. Both of them at the embassy. Maybe it's coincidence, but you already—"

She held up her hand. "Don't say it. 'There's no such thing as a coincidence.'"

He grinned. "You're catching on. So, where do we go from here?"

Their conversation was interrupted by a server. They ordered breakfast, talked strategy, made small talk and then went upstairs to get ready for their day.

"That was seven hours of my life I'll never get back," Beryl said as she walked out of the conference centre.

"I have to agree with you," Carver said. "The conference isn't what I thought it was going to be."

After dodging vehicles and other pedestrians, they walked up the stone steps to their hotel's main entrance to enter a world of marble, limestone and the scent of polished wood. It was Old World elegance at its finest.

"I'm going to hang out in the mezzanine. See what I can find out," Carver said.

Beryl's eyebrows arched, "Find out? Like Tara's room number?"

He rolled his eyes and left for the mezzanine. Clusters of patrons loitered in quiet conversation, sipping tea and exchanging polite nods. He made a beeline for the photograph, once again pausing to admire the weight Karsh had captured in Churchill's expression. After a moment he let his eyes wander through the room until they landed on a familiar face. She stood among a half-dozen guests, a bottle of water in hand, laughing politely, playing her role.

Their eyes met, and she bobbed her chin toward Carver, excused herself from her clients and sauntered over.

"Tara," he said as she approached.

She smiled. "How was your conference?"

"Riveting. The most interesting parts made me wish for dental surgery."

"That bad?"

"Yeah."

"What brings you back down here tonight?"

"Well, my options were reruns of Gilligan's Island in my room or engaging conversation down here."

She lifted her bottle in a mock toast. "Lucky me. Go ahead, engage."

"During my zone-outs in the conference today, I thought about you going to Italy to retrieve the picture. That must have been quite a chore. I'll assume the picture was heavily packaged and must have been difficult to handle."

"Perhaps I overstated my role. The buyer had the picture packaged in a wood frame and gave it to the police who brought it to

Rome. So I flew to Rome and picked it up there. And when I say pick it up, I don't mean physically. I arranged for the courier and made sure it was on its way back to the hotel."

"When did Cecil authenticate it?"

"After it arrived. It was kept in a locked room until he showed up."

"Who had access to that room?"

Her eyes narrowed. "What's with the third degree? You sound like you're working a case."

Carver raised his hands in mock surrender. "Apologies. Force of habit. I'm an investigator. It's not something I can turn off."

"No worries," she said, then leaned in. "You should know, when the hotel realized the photo had been stolen, they did a full security overhaul. The picture's been locked down tighter than Fort Knox since it arrived."

"Good to know." He looked around. "I don't get it. You said the official unveiling was Friday, yet here we are, standing next to The Roaring Lion, along with dozens of your friends and clients, admiring a picture that has yet to be officially unveiled."

She nodded. "Politics. The hotel wants the prime minister and British ambassador for the unveiling, and Friday's the earliest. But there's no real reason not to hang it now. Fairmont was humiliated; they don't want it hidden any longer than they have to."

They traded light banter for a couple of hours until the patrons started to drift out.

"Looks like your clients are leaving," Carver said. "What do you say we head to the lounge for a drink?"

Tara was about to say something, then thought better of it. "Can I take a rain check on that? I've got some work that's due in the morning."

"Rain check accepted." They said their goodbyes. Carver lingered and watched her cross the lobby and disappear behind the elevator doors.

He went up to his room, stretched out on the bed, a half-smile on his lips as he thought about Tara. But it didn't last. The itch in his brain returned—the one that had nagged at him all day.

Something about the picture gnawed at him, a loose thread he couldn't see but felt just the same. He let his thoughts unravel, stripped away the noise, sifted through every detail he'd gathered over the past couple of days. Facts fell into place, one by one, until only the essentials remained.

The newly hung picture was a valid copy, made from the original negative. Deschambeau had authenticated it, and Carver believed him. The signature was only recently applied. It looked like the other Yousuf Karsh signatures in the hotel, but Carver knew skilled forgers can be had for a price.

In the gap between its disappearance and return, the original had been swapped out for the picture that now hung in the hotel. Tara didn't do it. Deschambeau didn't do it. That leaves the thief or the lawyer, both of whom had connections to the British embassy, or someone involved in its transportation. The thief seems to have disappeared after he was charged. Why?

And finally, he wondered why anyone would steal it in the first place. There was no money in it for them. And it was likely they'd eventually be caught.

It didn't sit right with Carver. The theft was illogical. Something bigger was in play. He couldn't see it yet, but he felt it. He lay still for a long time. Then sleep came, uneasy and thin.

When he woke, his head was thick. Dreams had been black and white, his mind hard at work. He'd turned over every scrap of evidence. By morning, he had something. An idea. It didn't make sense, not fully. But everything he knew fit.

He texted Beryl, showered and went down for breakfast. Like yesterday, she was already there.

"Morning," he said.

"Morning," she replied, an amused smile on her face. She arched her eyebrows. "Late night?"

"It's not what you think."

"You have no idea what I think."

"True. But in this case whatever you were thinking is wrong." He leaned across the table, "I may have figured it out."

"What? How to please a woman?"

His face twisted. "No. The photo of Churchill hanging in the hotel has been altered. Or rather, I think the original Karsh negative has been altered."

She shrugged. "Tell me then, Maven, why? Why would anyone need to swap out the original photo with an altered copy."

"I don't know, yet. That's my task for today."

"What about the conference?"

"You're on your own. And don't balk. You're new to the PI game and you need to learn the ropes no matter how boring you think it is."

"What are you going to do?"

"I'm going to track down an old copy of The Roaring Lion. If I see differences with the one in this hotel, I'll know I have something."

Carver went back to his room and powered up his laptop.

After a full day of investigating, Carver slumped down in the armchair. A ping from his phone roused him.

Beryl: "I'm hungry. Meet for supper downstairs?"

Carver: "On my way."

Carver freshened up, went downstairs and requested a table at the back, away from the other clients. Beryl joined him soon after.

"How was the conference?" he asked.

"What do you think?"

"Enough said."

"And you?"

He took a deep breath. "The Roaring Lion negative was supposed to be kept at the Library and Archives Canada Preservation Storage Facility along with all the other Yousuf Karsh negatives. I called to arrange a viewing, and they said it was no longer available. It took a bit of sweet talking to get the administrator to tell me that some kind of back-door deal was made a few years ago between the Canadian and British governments. And that the British government now has that negative."

The studs above Beryl's eye arched.

"Undeterred, I found a number of online vendors who sell high quality digital copies of Karsh's work, but after speaking to a couple of them, their digital copies are all new, not more than two years old." He leaned across the table, "I think someone in the British government is systematically replacing all the old printed and digital versions with a new, altered version."

"Interesting," she muttered.

"So, I went back to the only place I could think of that might have a quality original image, *Life* magazine. The Roaring Lion was on the cover of *Life* in May 1945. I downloaded it and compared it against one of the newer digital copies."

"And..."

"It might be nothing, but the only difference I found is a piece of paper, maybe a booklet or something similar, that is peeking out of Churchill's jacket pocket. The newer version is pure white; the original looks like it's crinkled and has a yellowish smudge, like it was indented and stained."

"That's all you have? A tea stain on a piece of paper?"

He shrugged. "It might be meaningful."

"I think I can read the tea leaves already. They say, 'Sorry mate. You'll get no answers here.'"

"Before you dismiss it, I need your expertise. I'll send you an image of that wrinkled paper from the *Life* cover. See if you can work your magic to make sense of it."

"Send it to me."

"Can you do it now?"

"I'm about to eat!"

"Tell me what you want, and I'll bring it up to your room."

Carver, carrying Beryl's takeout meal, pushed her door open and went inside.

"Well?"

"You were right. It's grainy but it looks like a booklet that had a seal pressed into it, like a wax seal with an emblem on it."

"What's the emblem?"

"I was only able to get about half of it. It looks like a portion of an Asian pictogram character."

Carver leaned in to look closely at the screen. The image showed three short vertical squiggles in the top left and a boxy symbol, like a four-pane window, underneath, balanced on a stick. The rest was not recognizable.

"Any ideas?" he asked.

"I think we need to ask an expert."

"Why don't we ask an Asian tourist. There's plenty in this part of town. Send me the image and we'll take to the streets."

Ten minutes later Carver got a text from Beryl. Got it. Meet me upstairs."

Carver went to Beryl's room. "What do you have?"

"An elderly Asian man told me it's a Japanese Kanji character. And though it's impossible to know exactly what it is, he says he thinks it is a symbol for battle or war."

Carver stretched his neck and rubbed his chin. He turned toward Beryl, who was sitting at her desk in front of her laptop. "How smart are search engines? Is it possible to search for that symbol?"

"We can try using AI. In theory, AI has analyzed all the images it ingests from the internet and translated them into something understandable."

"Let's try it. Use the Kanji symbol for war."

She found the complete Kanji symbol, queried the AI interface and uploaded the symbol when prompted. The AI interface chugged along and eventually timed out with an error message.

"I think that's too broad a question for our limited AI access. We need to narrow it down."

Carver thought for a second, "The British government only

started scrubbing old images in the past few years. Let's narrow it down to say, any images with that symbol, uploaded in the past four years, and also limit it to Japanese websites."

Beryl formed the new query and let it rip. A few minutes later the screen filled with a list of websites. She started at the top. When she got to the 15th website, they saw an image of four older Japanese men posing beside a long boardroom table, muted smiles on their faces, as if they had no interest in posing for that photo. The translated caption said: Admirals Yamamoto, Nagumo, Yamaguchi and Commander Fuchida at a planning session. August 13, 1941. (As part of the Japanese historical archive released to the public in June 2021.)

It was what sat on the table that caught Carver's eye—four places set, each with a booklet in front. The top edge of the booklet looked similar to the one in Churchill's pocket and had the Kanji symbol for war embossed in the wax that sealed the booklet.

"Wow," is all Carver could muster.

"It's the same booklet," Beryl said.

Carver now gazed out the window, thoughts reeling. Beryl waited him out.

He eventually turned back to her, a serious twist to his mouth. "I want you to delete everything you've done on The Roaring Lion. And delete your AI account and all the queries you've made. We are never to speak about this to anyone."

The colour drained from Beryl's face, her eyebrows knitted. "Why?"

"How well do you remember your World War II history?"

"Refresh my memory."

Carver took a breath. "Europe was burning in '41. Hitler had taken most of the continent. London was bombed every night; food was scarce and spirits low. The only hope came through the radio when Churchill spoke. He knew they were in trouble and needed the Americans in the war. Roosevelt listened but didn't move. He said it wasn't their fight. That all changed on December 7 when Japan hit Pearl Harbor. That was it. The U.S. was in the war, and they came in with guns blazing; factories were built, soldiers mobilized and weapons produced. Without the Americans, Hitler might have had it all."

"Great history lesson."

"The Roaring Lion photo was taken on December 30, 1941, just four weeks after Pearl Harbor. The booklet in Churchill's pocket looks very much like the booklets in the photo of the Japanese planning session."

"How did he get a booklet?"

"We'll never know. And it doesn't really matter. What's important here is the perception, not proof. What do you think would happen if someone in The White House thought Churchill knew about Pearl Harbor before the attack? That he let it happen to push the U.S. into the war?"

"Shit. It might start World War III." She looked pensive, like she was chewing on something. "So... the theft was bogus?"

Carver nodded. "That's right. The whole thing was a ruse to replace the copy that hangs in the hotel. And that's why we won't tell anyone. Ever."

Carver and Beryl slung their bags over their shoulders and stepped out of their rooms for the last time. The week felt like a write-off to Carver. The conference was a bust, and a mystery that had stirred something in him was pushed back into the dark. That's how it went sometimes. Not every itch got scratched.

They crossed the hotel lobby, quiet with just the soft shuffle of travellers heading for the exit. A familiar voice broke the mood. "Off to save the free world again, Carver?"

There she was, posing like she could sell you an insurance policy and make you enjoy it.

"Already saved the world once today," he said. "Now I'm clocking out."

"We never did go for that drink."

He took a business card out of his pocket and handed it to her. "I know a place with cheap wine and good music," he said.

She took the card, her fingers brushing his, lingering just enough. "I might surprise you."

"I hope you do."

Gary Coffin writes genre fiction with a focus on crime, crafting gritty noirish mysteries set in Montreal where the line between hero and villain often blur. Originally from just south of Montreal, Gary now lives in Rockland, a quiet community near Ottawa.

SHOOT

11

JOE ITALIANO

Ben Matheson ran his fingers through his thinning grey hair, donned an Ottawa Senators baseball cap to reduce the afternoon sun's glare and, holding his AR-15, lay prone on the grass at the Connaught Range and Primary Training Centre in Ottawa's west end. Heart racing, Ben aimed his assault rifle at his target 300 metres away. He accounted for the breeze blowing left to right off Shirleys Bay and over the berm, which was the distance of a football field beyond his target; the wind's direction and speed would influence his last shot's trajectory. His first four had hit dead centre; the law limited magazine capacity of semi-automatic rifles to five.

His eyes blurred; they often did at his age. He blinked until they cleared. An ant tickled his wrist. His heart beat faster. Hands steady, Ben held his breath. *Shoot.* He squeezed the trigger and absorbed the recoil.

Seated on a lifeguard-style stand behind Ben, the range officer and scorekeeper for the gun club's 2025 competition, a man bundled in a red tuque and charcoal grey coat, collar up against autumn's wind, lowered his binoculars. "Hit: inner circle. Five for five. We have a winner."

Ben exhaled, smiled, flicked away the ant and stood as his heartbeat slowed. He had won for a third consecutive year. Ben had joined the club decades ago following a tour in the armed forces and his decision to not become a sniper; the thought of shooting people revolted him.

Nearby, Ben's son, Todd, holding another AR-15, nodded. The other competitors gathered around Ben and congratulated him.

A lean white-haired member, also a senior, said, "When shooting, I picture politicians. Improves my concentration. Damn buggers want to take my guns next year. Well, over my dead body, or theirs, for the little time I got left."

Ben shook his head. "Clyde, you're kidding, right?" Ben knew that doctors had diagnosed Clyde with terminal cancer. He had about six months to live.

"The only way to stop the nonsense is to shoot them all." Clyde grinned and held up an AR-15. "Baby goes back into the clubhouse, for now."

A woman asked Ben, "Did we raise much for the food bank? Great idea you had."

"Yep, $800. I'll drop it off at Bronson Street before going home."

Those who had gathered around cheered.

Ben smiled. "What happens when two guns fall in love?" He looked from person to person as they shook their heads. "They bang."

Everyone laughed as they headed to their cars in the dirt and gravel parking lot. Clyde followed.

Todd shook his head. "I came second again. Why?" he asked his father. "You taught me everything I know."

"I never taught you everything I know." Ben laughed. "You need more practice; that's all, son. Say, what do you call a sheep with a machine gun?"

"What?"

"Lambo."

"Ooohh." Todd shook his bowed head. "That's bad."

Ben smiled. "You've no sense of humour. That's why Mom tried to trade you for Jenn when you first met the greatest daughter-in-law ever. Too bad her mom refused."

Todd laughed and the two entered the clubhouse.

Seated on separate benches before an unlit fireplace, a refrigerator behind them, they cleaned their rifles and removed the firing pins. Ben collected the firearms, ammunition and firing pins for storage in an adjoining room's vaults. As club president, he controlled the three safes.

Now taking the $800 from a donation box by the entrance, Ben hung his Senators cap on a hat rack, set the alarms and joined Todd in Ben's silver Toyota Corolla. They drove past range control, turned left at Malabar Boulevard and headed for Rifle Road. The sight of the rappel tower for training army cadets in rope-assisted ascent and descent caused Ben, as always, to shake his head in wonder. He still marvelled that it had been a part of his life at one time.

An hour and a cash drop later, Ben parked beside a blue Chevy Cavalier in the driveway of his bungalow. Heavy metal music blared from the bungalow across the street, a house fronting a large treed area. Yellow, green, red and orange leaves galore covered the ground and the roof.

Todd shook his head. "That music is way too loud," he said as they got out of the car.

"The new neighbour is party central." Ben waggled his hand. "They dance at all hours, no physical distancing, and they're cheek to cheek, if you know what I mean. Cars stop all the time. He greets them on the street through their car windows. Drugs? Hopefully, he'll adapt."

"I doubt it." Todd said.

On the other side of a white picket fence, a robust, long-haired man wearing faded jeans torn at the knees and a black, blue and red King Gizzard and the Wizard Lizard jacket walked the grounds swigging from a beer bottle. Tailing the apparent hard-core rocker was a bikini-clad young woman who revealed more than a Sports Illustrated swimsuit model.

Ben and Todd turned away from the neighbour to see Heather Matheson and her daughter-in-law, Jenn Gabriel, leave the Matheson home.

"I'll give that creep a piece of my mind," Heather said.

Ben scrunched his nose. "A piece of your mind? You usually bake a double-chocolate cake for a new neighbour," he said to his wife.

"Not this one. He keeps slapping the young woman on the bum. I'm gonna give him heck, Hon Bun." True to her word, Heather crossed the street, Jenn beside her. Ben and Todd followed.

The barely dressed woman, both legs covered in goose bumps, bruises and cigarette burns, gasped at the sight of Heather and Jenn. The neighbour slapped the woman's behind as she raced toward the house.

Heather stopped, gaped at the bruised and burned young woman, shifted her weight and pointed at the neighbour. "I've asked you before to—"

The man ogled Jenn. "You've great boobs and a hell of a nice ass." He cupped his free hand. "Call me Big Dick. If you ever wanna see it, and..." He grabbed his crotch.

"Whoa." Ben stepped between Big Dick and Jenn before Todd could.

"Outta the way, Geezer." The neighbour pushed Ben.

"Jerk." Todd surged forward and pushed Big Dick.

The neighbour lunged and shoved Todd. "Eat shit."

"Asshole." Jenn slapped Big Dick.

"I know what Pocahontas wants." He flicked his tongue.

"Bastard." Jenn fisted her hands, ready to strike.

But Ben punched Big Dick first, hard in the chest, then pulled Jenn, kicking and screaming, away.

Todd again stepped forward.

Big Dick barged forward and punched Todd, drawing blood.

Jenn approached Todd, comforting him. She touched his nose.

"Oww, I think it's broken."

This time, Heather stepped forward, hands on her hips. "You beat girls, you brute."

Big Dick sneered.

Todd stepped between them.

Big Dick pushed him backwards into Heather, and she fell, her head bouncing off the ground.

Big Dick laughed.

Ben rushed to Heather. "Cupcake, are you all right?", he asked as Todd and Jenn joined him. Heather didn't move, her face looking as if the fall had drained her blood.

Neighbours rushed over. "I've called 9-1-1 for police and an ambulance," one said as seven others, five men and two women, advanced toward Big Dick. That made him back away from the short fence. "Keep away," he told the approaching posse.

A police patrol vehicle arrived, two uniformed officers exiting the white and blue Ford Explorer.

"Everyone calm down," one officer said. "Could someone please tell us what happened."

Ben, holding Heather's hand, nodded at Big Dick. "That creep assaulted my wife and broke my son's nose. And he insulted my daughter-in-law. I'd like to…"

The officer held his hands out, palms forward. "Whoa. Let's all remain civil."

Todd sneered. "Civil, around him? Get this: the creep calls himself…Big Dick." He pointed at the ogre. "You'll pay, big time."

"Your wife wants the Big Dick," the creep said, again grabbing his crotch. "Suck on this."

The officers calmed everyone and required Dirk Cannon, aka Big Dick, to visit police headquarters to respond to possible charges. Dirk entered his house, and the officers left as an ambulance arrived.

Two paramedics checked Heather's vitals and put her on a stretcher and into the ambulance. Todd told Ben he would follow the ambulance out to Queensway Carleton Hospital and have his nose checked out there. Ben and one paramedic stayed with Heather in the back of the ambulance while the other rushed to the driver's seat. The ambulance surged forward, siren wailing.

At the hospital, triage prioritized Heather for surgery. Hours later, Ben, Todd, now with his nose taped, and Jenn stood beside her bed.

The doctors had failed to save her.

"The police had better nail Creepo for murder," Ben said through his tears. "There were plenty of witnesses. And with cars stopping there all the time, he's a known drug dealer."

Todd shook his head. "They won't do much. They'll treat us all as one witness and just warn him. They've done zip about his drug dealing in the past. They didn't even take him to the station."

Ben growled. "Then charge him with reckless endangerment."

"Don't hold your breath." Todd shook his head.

"Then we'll send Dirty Harry."

The grief-stricken family left the hospital, and as they went through the main doors, Ben raised his right hand, thumb up and index finger aimed forward. "Feeling lucky today, Punk? Go ahead, make my day."

"Don't sound like Clyde." Todd said, frowning.

Three days later Ben left the house as a car stopped across the street. Big Dick strode to the curb, pulled a small package from a pocket, tossed it to the driver and then went back into his bungalow.

Feeling as useless as limp spaghetti, Ben snorted, "The bastard killed Cupcake." He strolled along the sidewalk, crossed the road and turned onto a path into the treed area. The leaves having fallen, he could see Big Dick's back porch.

He gasped.

A naked Big Dick and a nude woman came from the house onto the screened-in porch. They dropped to the floor and out of sight.

Ben turned to walk home. "That animal doesn't know how to love," he said to himself. He looked back. "I think they're done by now but can't be sure. Wish I had my scope." He imagined Heather saying, "Hon Bun wants to be a peeping Tom." He swore he felt her stroking his arm.

"Cupcake outshines that girl-child," Ben said. "Was she the same one as before? No, wrong shape and hair colour. What a pig."

Two Fridays later following a family-only funeral in a chapel, Ben, dark circles under his eyes, spread his arms to hug Todd and Jenn. He eased the urn from the stand, assured them he would be OK and said they should get on with their day. Leaving the chapel, he noticed a white-haired man outside.

"Sorry about Heather."

"Thank you, Clyde."

"If we'd shot them all like I said, the bugger couldn't have killed your Cupcake. So, you should nail him, from a distance. Up close, you'd see his eyes and choke."

"It wouldn't be right."

"I'll take the blame, Ben. I've cancer, got maybe six months."

"So don't waste what time you have."

"It's OK. I got plans. Just do it." Clyde walked away.

Feeling as if a doctor had injected Novocaine throughout his entire body, Ben went to his car and drove home. Noticing food baskets neighbours had left on the front porch, he entered the living room, sat on the sofa near the bedding he had put there, and placed the urn between two aromatic candles on an end table and under the east-facing dreamcatcher Jenn had given him.

Minutes later, as he collected the food baskets, music blared from across the street. Ben glared as Big Dick approached another car.

"Bastard."

On Sunday Ben learned that Todd's work would take him to Toronto the following Thursday. He arranged for Todd to give him some software that would scrub the gun club's computer hard drive of all deleted and overwritten files. Ben claimed there were rumours that someone had put pornography on the computer and then deleted it.

He picked up the software before driving to a big-box store to purchase a large plastic bottle of cola, masking tape, a dozen boxes of Jell-O, a dozen small plastic containers and two three-foot-long clear plastic containers. He brought them to the gun club.

In the kitchen, Ben emptied the cola bottle into the sink before preparing small containers of Jell-O and placing them in the refrigerator. While waiting for the jelly to set, he started the fireplace, then entered the office and, using the computer, prepared the club's books. Three hours later he put the scrubbing software into a desk drawer.

Once again in the kitchen, he dumped the almost-set jelly into the longer plastic containers sitting one behind the other on a bench to create a six-foot span.

That done, Ben opened the safes and removed another member's Beretta PX4 Storm, a pistol. It shot 40 Smith & Wesson ammunition. Ben's AR-15, chambered with a 5.56 mil-spec, could shoot different ammunitions, including 40 Smith & Wesson. Now he found the firing pin for the Beretta, inserted it, took four Smith & Wesson cartridges from his own ammunition and loaded them into the Beretta so they would discharge first. He knelt at one end of the containers on the bench and fired four times into the gelatin. The bullets passed through the first container before sinking to the bottom halfway to the far end of the second container.

Ben retrieved the bullets and examined them. Two survived undamaged and could be reused, the only markings being the striations from the handgun's barrel. He placed the two damaged bullets and the four casings into his pocket.

After putting the large containers near the fireplace to liquefy the jelly, Ben removed the firing pin from the Beretta, cleaned the pistol and, ensuring he removed his fingerprints, put it and the firing pin away.

Using the club's reloading press and reloading die, Ben, wearing cloth gloves, took two new casings and into each inserted primer for igniting gun powder, then some gun powder and two undamaged lead bullets. He then took his AR-15 and its firing pin from their safes. He wiped the new cartridges of any fingerprints and loaded the assault rifle so those cartridges would discharge first. Next, he shoved the empty cola bottle's neck over the front of the rifle barrel and secured the bottle with loads of masking tape, creating a silencer. Ben had learned this tactic from a Steven Seagal movie and had tested it years ago. He put the AR-15 into a black canvas bag.

Ben then dumped the liquefied jelly down the sink, mopped the floor and, using a knife, diced the containers. He locked the safes, extinguished the fire, reset the alarms and drove down Highway 417, the Queensway, that cuts through Ottawa, the bag in the trunk. Along the route, he pulled off and tossed possible evidence, after wiping it all clean, into public garbage bins, especially those at malls like Place d'Orleans, Carlingwood and Bayshore.

Late Thursday morning after Todd had called to confirm his arrival in Toronto, Ben drove to the far end of the neighbourhood's treed area. He took the bag from the trunk and walked over leaves, minimally covered by a dusting of snow, toward Big Dick's house, praying the cool air would deter others from using the paths on a workday. He planned to throw a stone at the porch to draw his target there.

Thirty metres from the house, Ben saw that Big Dick was already at the porch, facing away. Ben re-scanned the area and listened to ensure there were no witnesses, extracted the AR-15, the homemade silencer attached, and propped himself against a tree. His heart raced. His stomach churned. He pictured Heather. She shook her head. *Murder is wrong, Hon Bun.* Ben felt as if his heart was clogging his throat. "But Cupcake, he killed you." Hands quivering, Ben inched the rifle upward and peered through the scope. He could see that Big Dick was chatting on a laptop to a girl who looked 13. *What am I doing?*

Big Dick stood.

Ben gasped. The pig was naked from the waist down. The girl was staring.

Ben fingered the trigger but waited to squeeze. *Not yet. Why traumatize the girl?*

Rechecking the computer screen, Ben noticed that a man, likely the girl's father, had arrived and was waving his arms. The dad reached out, and the pig's screen went blank.

Big Dick closed his laptop. He turned, laughing, and stretched.

Ben's eyes blurred. He blinked. His heart raced. Eyes now clear, he aimed the AR-15.

Shoot.

Shoot.

Shoot! Ben squeezed the trigger. *Pfft...pfft.*

Big Dick grabbed his chest and backed into the laptop, knocking it off the table. He fell to the floor.

Feeling like a boxer had gut-punched him, Ben shook himself. *Move. It's done.* He scanned the area, put the AR-15 into the canvas bag, snatched the shell casings from the ground, went to the car, put the bag in the trunk and drove to the gun club.

There, Ben cleaned the gun and put it and its firing pin away. He cleaned the leaves and dirt from his sneakers, then diced the cola bottle silencer, the debris and silencer pieces to be placed as before in garbage bins, this time along with shell casings, around the city. Next he went to the computer and for two hours resaved the files he had updated on Sunday. Finally Ben opened the desk drawer, extracted the software and scrubbed the computer of deleted and overwritten files. Rather than leave the software at the club, he would give it to Jenn on his way home. Once there, despite believing that police no longer checked for gunshot residue, Ben planned to wash and dry the clothes he had worn and to take a shower.

That evening, after spying from the window for police activity and observing only regular motor vehicles stop across the street to wait briefly but fruitlessly for Big Dick, Ben sat on the couch, caressing the urn. "Don't be disappointed. The girl was maybe 13. What a dirt bag."

Ben heard vehicles stopping outside. He returned the urn to the table and looked out. Four police cars had arrived. Two officers twice knocked on Big Dick's door then crashed in.

Neighbours spilled from their homes, and police officers started interviewing them.

To avoid looking suspicious by staying inside, Ben donned his ski jacket, exited and asked three neighbours and a patrol officer, "Are they finally arresting Big Dick for dealing drugs?"

A neighbour shook his head. "I think the asshole is dead. The drug world is dangerous."

Police vans stopped. Officers in white bunny outfits exited one and entered the house. Four officers carrying flashlights went toward the woods. Two other officers placed yellow police tape around the outside of Big Dick's property.

Journalists arrived in cars and vans, the names of TV stations and newspapers on the side panels.

A man in a beige trench coat questioned other neighbours. They pointed at Ben, and the man strode over. "I'm Detective Sergeant Provost of the Ottawa Police Service. Your family confronted Mr. Cannon a few weeks ago. He hit your son into your wife, and I'm sad to say she fell and died. You and your son, both marksmen with rifles, threatened him. Where's your son, and can you account for your time late this morning and early this afternoon?"

Eyes agape as if surprised, Ben asked, "Does this mean a perpetrator shot Mr. Cannon this morning or afternoon with a rifle? They said it was a drug killing because he was dealing."

"We're investigating all angles. This isn't a typical drug killing."

"What's that mean?"

"Where were you this morning and this afternoon? Where's your son?"

"I was at my gun club on the Connaught range doing the books. I'm president. Todd is in Toronto on business."

Provost requested that Ben provide his and Todd's rifles and give police access to the clubhouse and its computer. "That'll save me getting a search warrant. We need to rule you two out as suspects."

Ben agreed to provide the rifles, mentioning that they were in the clubhouse. "We have the proper firearm licences, and the amnesty for owners of assault rifles remains in effect for several more months. And while you're there, you can check the computer; it and the rifles will prove my and Todd's innocence. But without a warrant, I cannot provide access to other members' rifles and handguns. Most members store them in our vaults."

"Do I need a key to enter your clubhouse?"

"We have a security code that I cannot divulge, so I'll go with you."

Dirk Cannon's body, covered by a white sheet, was wheeled from the house to a coroner's van soon after it had arrived at the crime scene. A man in a dark blue suit and fedora seemed to be in charge.

Provost said to Ben, "Excuse me for a minute." He went to talk to the man with the fedora, and Ben strained to hear the conversation. The only word he caught was "ballistics." *Getting the bullet won't do any good.* Still, a shiver ran through his body.

The detective returned to face Ben. "Let's go. I'll drive. My car is over there." Provost nodded toward an unmarked black car at the curb one house beside Big Dick's bungalow. "I'll have a forensics team meet us there."

Inside the clubhouse Ben opened the vaults and handed Provost his and Todd's AR-15s and their firing pins. "We'll want these back."

The detective held an AR-15 in each hand. "This is a nice setup. I notice the club has a reloading press and reloading die."

Two officers from the Ottawa Police Service entered and scanned the room. His hands occupied, Provost nodded at them before asking Ben, "Where's the computer? We'll want to take it with us to examine the hard drive and copy whatever is on it."

Ben pointed toward the office. "Please return it as soon as possible," he said to the two entering the office.

"Ballistics will tell us if either of these fired the fatal bullets," Provost said, lifting the rifles. "It's doubtful that they did since the perpetrator shot Mr. Cannon at close range."

Ben felt as if he stood naked in a freezer. No way the cops thought that Big Dick was shot at close range. The detective had lied to him. Provost did suspect him and was hoping for some kind of reaction. *My stunned look may have given me away.* "Really?" Ben shook his head. "How can a person shoot another person? That surprises me every time there's a murder. And up close? Good God. Maybe the girl he beat did it. She had bruises and cigarette burns on her legs." Ben felt his stomach muscles tighten. He had panicked and implicated that abused young woman. "Maybe she shot him in self defence; he beat her."

"Really? We'll check that out," Provost said. "But I doubt she did it."

On Sunday evening the newscasts for CBC, CTV and Global buzzed: a gunman had stormed into a house near the University of Ottawa the night before, wounding a dozen partiers and then holding them hostage. Videos showed him surrendering to the tactical unit and Detective Provost taking him into custody.

Ben froze. "Clyde?"

The news anchor reported that the shooter said, "They don't care about seniors. They party and party. Maybe they'll care when they learn that I shot Dirk Cannon."

Clyde was serious that he'd take the fall.

The doorbell rang, and Ben answered it. Detective Provost stood on the porch.

"Please come in, Detective." Ben's heart raced.

Provost entered. "We confirmed your son's alibi and forensics says his AR-15 didn't make the striations on the kill bullets. He's in the clear."

Ben smiled. "Todd is no killer. And the TV said you got your man."

"Your buddy Clyde didn't do it. Wrong firearm, which he recently illegally imported from the States along with a bump stock to create an automatic assault rifle of the AR-15. And if he killed Cannon, why only wound the partiers? A marksman, he could have killed them all."

"That's logical."

"Besides, we can prove his whereabouts at Cannon's time of death. He was partying in the ByWard Market, and patrol there remembers seeing him. And Cannon's girlfriends, he had two, also have alibis. The chief believes it was a drug killing."

"That makes sense." Ben's heartbeat slowed.

"Further, we checked your gun club's computer. You did save files that afternoon."

"I know. When do we get it back?" Ben's pulse slowed further.

"Soon. But you filed your info after the time of death. And the computer didn't contain any deleted files. Who can ever work so flawlessly? It was likely scrubbed. You see, Mr. Matheson, evidence consists of both what you discover and what you don't find. Little things often reveal the guilty."

"What?" Shivers raced along Ben's spine.

"I'm a stickler for detail, never believed the drug angle. Your AR-15 doesn't make striations exactly like those on the bullets that killed Cannon, but there are similarities. Forensics guesses the bullets were fired more than once by different guns. Your club has a reloading press and die. The false confession from a club member was his attempt to cover for you. You blamed Cannon for your wife's death. You had both motive and opportunity. Why not make it easy on everyone and confess?"

Ben felt as if his eyes had outgrown their sockets. "*You* believe I killed him?" His heart pounded. "Cannon was a bastard, but my wife never would've approved of my killing him."

"You should clear your conscience."

"If I did it, how would confessing clear my conscience?" Ben gulped.

"I know you did it."

"You can't prove I killed him if I didn't do it." Ben's heart pounded.

Provost shook his head. "I tried for a search warrant to examine all the guns at your club, but the judge denied the request as too broad. Then I applied to examine all the weapons at your club that take the slug used. We could fire them, reload the bullets and fire them again from another gun, try to match the striations. But the brass ordered the case closed as a drug hit. They won't waste time and money solving a drug dealer's death. So, the murder of Dirk Cannon is to become a cold case, *for now*." The detective turned as if to leave, then turned back. "You must surrender the guns in a few months." He smiled.

Ben growled. "Maybe if you had arrested the bastard back then, the drug lords wouldn't have gotten to him and he'd still be alive."

Provost shook his head. "We didn't arrest him because he was working with us to get the drug lords so he could stay out of jail."

Ben pointed at Provost. "So, the drug lords found out and killed him, not me. You likely gave him away."

"Maybe." Provost left.

Ben blew a stream of air. It felt like ants were crawling all over his body. He shuddered and sat on the sofa, the urn beside him, and with shaking hands lit the candles. Their scent filled the room, slowing his heart rate.

"Our wannabe Lieutenant Columbo knows but can't act, yet." Ben sighed. "You don't approve and what I did bothers me. I can't sleep but couldn't anyway because you're not here. Hon Bun misses Cupcake." He wiped a tear from his eye.

"How about I tell you a new joke? You'll love it."

"Did you hear about the drug dealer's ghost?

"No, you didn't.

"The police arrested him for...possession.

"You're trying not to smile, but here it comes. It's getting wider."

Ben laughed.

Joe Italiano learned storytelling by writing a Good News Bulletin during a recession while working as a government economist. He has placed "in the money" in three short story contests and has had short stories published in five anthologies. Having completed a draft of his science fiction novel, his current project is a novel featuring a Houston, Texas police officer.

THE KEY IS IN THE BUTTONS

12

ANNA DI MEGLIO

t all started last Friday when I arrived for my appointment at Doctor Bernard's office off St. Joseph Boulevard in Orleans, a suburb of Ottawa.

The waiting room was empty except for the receptionist and the life-size storm trooper watching over me by the row of chairs. To say that my chiropractor was a *Star Wars* fan would be an understatement. He even had *Star Wars* figurines in his treatment rooms.

As I sat waiting, I moved my neck from left to right hoping that the kink that had appeared the day before would go away. I'd worked all day at my computer trying to finish my manuscript and had to stop when the pain started to give me a headache.

I'm Terra Ramblings, author of the Yellow Peacock mystery series. Unfortunately, I've been forced to take a break but still hope to make my publisher's deadline with Doctor Bernard's help.

"No, no. I'm fine. Thank you," I heard a woman say in a shaky voice. I lifted my head and watched the woman standing at the receptionist's desk. She was digging into her purse. She brought out a tissue and dabbed at her eyes.

Lost in thought, I had not heard her arrive. As the woman paid for her treatment, the receptionist said, looking at me, "Go on to room number three, please."

Doctor Bernard's booming voice greeted me as soon as I walked into the treatment room.

"Is it your neck again, Terra?" he asked. He was of medium height, which is to say taller than me, with blond hair and friendly grey eyes that crinkled at the corners when he smiled.

"No tumbles down the stairs this time?" he asked, a smile on his face.

"Ha! No!" I laughed as I recalled the time that I had almost fallen down the stairs. I had started down deep in thought, as I had locked one of my characters in a cellar with a killer and had to figure out how to get her out alive. I stumbled over the cat sleeping on one of the steps and went flying. I plunged back into reality, grabbing the banister and hanging on for dear life, a feat which landed me with a pulled shoulder and at the chiropractic clinic once more.

"I've almost completed the manuscript. I'm so excited!" I smiled as I held back my shoulder-length brown hair from my neck so Doctor Bernard could examine it.

"It's a murder mystery, right?" he asked as he moved my neck from one side to the other.

"Yes," I said.

The next few minutes were spent in silence as he worked to realign my neck.

"OK, you're all set," he said.

I was already feeling better. "You're a miracle worker!" I told him.

He did not smile at my appreciative comment but instead looked at me thoughtfully.

"As a writer, you must be familiar with how to run a murder investigation? How a real one would be done, correct?"

"Well," I paused. "Yes. I've attended seminars and conferences where various professionals such as police detectives, pathologists and medical doctors have shared their expertise."

"Perhaps you could help a friend of mine?" Doctor Bernard

explained that the crying woman I'd seen earlier was his friend, and a friend of hers had been recently murdered.

"Just down the street from here. It's just terrible," he added. I had heard about it on the news but had not given it more thought.

"How do you expect me to help?" I asked. Did he think I had contacts on the police force?

"Maybe you could look into it?"

"What?" my eyes widened. "What can I do that the police aren't already doing?"

"Well, that's just it. The police don't seem to be doing anything. Please, just see what you can find out. Whatever you do will be better than nothing."

I thought about my plans to finish my manuscript. A couple more days surely wouldn't make any difference, would it?

I hesitated. Could I actually help? In a real murder case? It's one thing to write about it but altogether another to investigate a real killing.

"Help me, Terra. You're my only hope," Doctor Bernard joked, pointing at the Princess Leia figurine on the shelf. "Seriously," he added, "any light you can shed would be appreciated."

Maybe I'd just found another way to procrastinate and not work on my manuscript because I heard myself say, "OK, I'll do it!"

A quick phone call later and I was sitting with Mrs. Norton, the victim's mother, in her living room.

"Mrs. Norton, what can you tell me about your daughter?" I hoped this was a good first question.

Mrs. Norton sat across from me in an armchair, while I was on a matching chintzy sofa, a glass-topped coffee table between us. She was tall, and the furniture suited her height; only my toes reached the area rug. I felt like a six-year-old on a grown-up's sofa. Through the large window I could see, in the distance, a line of cars exiting the parking lot of the medical centre, which was situated across from the chiropractic clinic.

"Christy was a journalist. She had a column in the local newspaper but always had dreams of working for a big town newspaper. Dreams that were squashed when she was killed." She took a shaky breath, and tears spilled out of her eyes. She pulled a tissue from her pants pockets and quickly wiped her eyes. She had faded blue eyes, and her white-haired chin length bob showed remnants of ash blond highlights.

"She came back to live with me a few months ago after breaking up with her boyfriend. She was such a blessing in my life, taking over everything when my husband died. She paid all my bills, took me to my medical appointments and even went to the bank for me." Mrs. Norton stopped to wipe her eyes again.

"Do you mean she had power of attorney?" I asked.

"Yes, that's it."

"What had she been working on?" I inched myself to the sofa's edge, my feet firmly on the floor now, listening intently, hoping for something, anything that could provide a clue.

"Well, you see, she wanted to be an investigative journalist, but all her assignments were fluff pieces."

"Fluff?" I asked.

"An article that promotes an activity or a business. Like an advertisement, really, except written by a journalist."

"OK, got it." I smiled. I'd read many of those in the local newspaper.

"Do you know which business she was writing about?" I was grasping at straws, asking anything that came to mind. I wondered if this was how real detectives did it.

"Actually, I do. She would share what she was writing about with me at dinnertime. I so enjoyed those times." She smiled wistfully.

"Let me think." She rubbed her forehead then continued. "It was an article about the bowling alley out in the industrial park and a coffee shop and spa right here on St. Joseph Boulevard." I scribbled all this down in the notebook I kept in my purse. I kept it there to capture spur-of-the-moment ideas for whatever story I was working on, but today it was serving a different purpose.

"And I understand that you are the one who found her?" Doctor Bernard had told me this bit of information.

Mrs. Norton's eyes shone with tears, but she continued, her voice strained. "Yes, I found her in her car in the driveway. I had left to do some groceries, and when I came back... She had gone to meet her editor-in-chief earlier that morning."

As she spoke, a cat came into the room and started rubbing itself against my legs.

"Hello kitty, what's your name?" I asked.

"That's Pete, Christy's cat. Oh, how attached she was to the cat. Now, every time I see Pete, I'm reminded of her." She started to cry.

I didn't know what to do. I couldn't think of any words that could help assuage her pain, so I just waited and petted the cat. Its black fur was the colour of soot and was shiny soft. He slowly blinked his green eyes at me in appreciation. He wore a white collar from which hung a little green medal. I fingered the medal. The word Pete was engraved on one side. I flipped it over and saw engraved letters: LBTLSP.

Mrs. Norton had stopped crying. "Can I get you a glass of water?" I asked, thinking that this, at least, I could do.

"No, I'm OK. Thanks."

The cat sat and looked up at me. "Mrs. Norton, do you know what these letters mean: L B T L S P?" I read the letters out as I showed her the flip side of the medal.

"I don't know." She took a deep breath. "I remember she had the medal made a few weeks ago. She kept telling me that if anything happened to her, I should take care of her cat for her."

My eyes narrowed. Had Christy known she was in danger? That she could be killed? All I could think of was that her death was related to her work somehow. But why would someone be killed over a fluff piece?

I glanced at my watch. Half an hour had passed since I'd arrived. Maybe just a few more questions and then I would leave.

"Did she have an office in the house?" Maybe I could look at her notes.

"She worked out of her bedroom."

Mrs. Norton stood up and walked me to the small room. It had a bed, nightstand and desk and chair that barely fit. There was a laptop and some papers spread out on the desk.

"Did the police take a look at the laptop and notes?"

"Yes, but they said nothing came of it."

I read through the papers which contained notes about her interviews with three merchants.

The cat meowed. Pete jumped on the bed, then the nightstand and from there onto the small desk.

"You want to impress us with your jumping skills?" I smiled at Pete.

"Do you mind if I look in the nightstand drawer?" I asked Mrs. Norton. She nodded her permission.

I opened the drawer which contained the usual bedside paraphernalia: a book, some hand cream, lip balm—and a screwdriver? OK, a screwdriver was unusual.

I took the screwdriver and showed it to Mrs. Norton. It was a flat-head, long and narrow with a blue handle. Her eyebrows lifted. She was as surprised as I was.

I spun around the room taking in all the details. Where in this room could she have used a screwdriver?

The only items that would make use of the tool were the electrical outlet and light switch plates. My gaze fell on Pete who was sitting by the door. He yawned and looked up at the light switch. He then looked at me and back at the light switch.

My thoughts whirred and I recalled the letters on Pete's medal. LBTLSP. Look behind the light switch plate!

I'd read a book once where a key had been hidden behind a light switch plate. Could it be?

I quickly walked to the switch and unscrewed the plate. There was a piece of folded paper in the receptacle. I removed the paper, and it felt as if there was something in the folds of it, something hard.

I walked quickly to the desk, followed by Mrs. Norton. My heart beating quickly, I placed the piece of paper on the desk and unfolded it.

"A key!" exclaimed Mrs. Norton. It was brass-coloured and had square indentations.

There was also a note in Christy's handwriting, the same handwriting we found on the papers next to the laptop.

"And this paper says the key is for a security box at the bank down the road," I told Mrs. Norton.

"Oh!" Mrs. Norton said wide-eyed. She dropped on the bed, cupping her face. "It's my husband's security box."

I waited. Mrs. Norton rubbed her forehead absently as she made sense of her jumbled thoughts. "Well, it's my box now, but I've never used it as Christy did all my banking for me."

Mrs. Norton looked at me. "I hadn't thought about it until now," she said pensively.

"What do you mean?" I encouraged her to continue.

"The police found a similar key in Christy's purse. They'd asked me if Christy had a security box. I said no. I never thought about the one my husband used to have and that Christy now had access to."

"We should go check it out. Maybe it's a clue into her murder," I suggested.

"Yes, yes, you're right." She stood up, her eyes lost but lines of determination bracketing her mouth as she walked out of the room.

Pete rubbed against my legs then looked at me, eyes blinking.

"I did a good job, is that it?" I asked Pete. He meowed.

"Let's hope it's not a red herring," I told Pete. He ran out of the room ahead of me.

Mrs. Norton and I stared at the closed box in the bank's privacy booth where we were now both seated. I could see the trepidation in her eyes, as I was feeling it, too. What would we find? There was only one way to tell. I nodded to her and she slowly lifted the cover. We both peeked in. It contained only one item. A notebook.

"You read it," Mrs. Norton said. I took the notebook from the box. It was ordinary-looking, like one of the many sold at the dollar store.

I quickly scanned the pages, then went back to the beginning and read more slowly. Christy had used the notebook to document her investigation into the three same businesses that were the focus of her fluff piece.

"What does it say? Do you know who killed her now?" interrupted Mrs. Norton.

"I think so. I'll reread it more slowly just to be sure," I said, my mouth dry and my pulse pounding in my ears. As I read, I could see Mrs. Norton's anticipation rise, her fingers fidgeting with the strap of her purse.

Christy had come to suspect that the three businesses she'd been writing about were into some shady dealings. As part of her article, she had interviewed not only the owners but also some of their customers. To Christy's surprise one had confessed that she was being blackmailed by the spa owner.

"Oh, wow..." I couldn't help the words from escaping my mouth. Likely this is what led her to her death.

"What?" Mrs. Norton cut in, putting her hands on the table, staring at me with laser focus.

"She discovered a blackmailer," I answered.

"Oh, my..." she whispered as she slumped back in her chair, her eyes blinking rapidly taking in the information.

I continued reading. Her notes went on to explain how this client had mentioned to the spa owner that her husband liked to cross-dress. She'd not been worried, thinking that their conversation would remain private. She'd needed someone to confide in, someone outside her circle of family and friends. At her next spa appointment, she'd been shocked when the owner told her that if she did not pay

$10,000, the information about her husband would be made public. Her husband was a well-known lawyer in the community, and his reputation would be ruined if it came out. So, she had paid the money. Her notes recounted how she was able to find similar situations from clients of the other two businesses as well.

"More than one blackmailer," I updated Mrs. Norton.

"I can't believe it. She never said one word about any of this."

I turned the page and continued reading. Christy had also noted that the three business owners had the same tattoo on the interior of their right wrist: a circle with four dots inside of it like a button. She'd assumed there was a dot for each of the three business owners and she had been trying to find the fourth. She was sure she'd seen the tattoo before on someone else but couldn't recall where.

I stopped reading and pointed to the last page of notes. "It's dated the day she was killed. The writing is sloppy. I gather she was either in a hurry or panicked," I told Mrs. Norton.

"What does it say?" she prodded.

I read on. She'd gone to meet her editor-in-chief that morning to turn in her fluff piece and to discuss her next assignment. As she was talking with him, she noticed he also had the same button tattoo. She realized that's where she'd seen it before. She had tried to hide her shock at seeing it and hoped she'd been successful.

I stopped reading. Nothing else had been written. I sighed. Unfortunately, I knew that she had not been successful. All the pieces were falling into place. Her boss must have followed her home and killed her.

"What happened? Did she confront them? Did they kill her?" Mrs. Norton asked, her voice trembling.

"If I'm right, it's her editor-in-chief that murdered her. He was part of the gang of blackmailers," I said thoughtfully.

"Oh, my poor baby. She was doing her own investigative journalism. She was going after her dreams and put herself in danger's way," Mrs. Norton said. The woman was obviously saddened, her shoulders drooping, but then after a moment her face filled with determination. "We must finish this for her. We have to go to the police."

"Terra! You did it!" Doctor Bernard greeted me with a cheer as I walked into the treatment room a week later.

"Yes! I finished my story! I'm sending it to my publisher this afternoon." I laughed with joy.

"I meant you solved Christy's murder, although I'm sure finishing your story is wonderful as well," Doctor Bernard smiled. "Her friend was here earlier this morning. Christy's mother had told her the news."

"Yeah, it's great the murder was solved and even better that the editor-in-chief cracked like a nut under police questioning,"

"How did you figure it all out?" he asked, prodding my neck. I had spent another full day at the computer the day before, finishing up my manuscript. My neck was sore as well as my right hip. I'd have to set aside part of my royalties for a chiropractor fund.

Laying on the treatment table, I explained what I had done to solve the case. "Likely Christy was getting scared, or paranoid, and hid the second key behind the light switch plate," I said.

Doctor Bernard did a final adjustment. "Well done, Terra. You are one fine Jedi." He smiled as he gave me a hand sitting up. "You're all set."

"Thanks!" I exclaimed, my chest filled with pride. "I can now move on to write my next story!"

"May the creative Force be with you!" Doctor Bernard said. I laughed all the way to the receptionist's desk.

A lifelong lover of cozy tales, Montreal-born writer Anna Di Meglio believes life's too short not to be comfortable. When she's not crafting delightful whodunits filled with charming cats and quirky characters, you'll find her curled up in her favourite chair, wearing comfy clothes and sipping tea, embracing the comfort that inspires her stories.

BETTIN' MAN

13

JENNIFER JORGENSEN

Troy lifted the corners of his cards—three of hearts, five of diamonds—not great but he could hope for a straight. He made a point to breathe in quickly and heavier than usual.

"You a bettin' man, Troy?" Jake prodded.

Troy lifted his gaze. Strange question to ask at a no-limit poker game. Had he taken too long to make a move? His thoughts spun like a ball on a roulette wheel. *Could he go through with this?* His stomach tightened. The stakes that night were higher than the money he could not afford to lose.

He added a chip to the pot in response. It wasn't what the judge had meant when he'd ordered Troy to establish financial responsibility. But it could save his apartment and access to his kids.

Donny matched. Lucas decided to raise to $75.

Jake's fat thumb and index finger caressed two chips as he eyed the three other players.

"Why not?" he laughed. The chips flew in the air.

The man thought out loud, a trait Troy was counting on. Troy watched all three carefully. He had to find the cracks in their poker faces, the windows into their bluffs.

He viewed his cards, increased his breathing again and threw another chip in the pot.

Donny followed. "Call."

Why so curt, impatient? Does it mean he has a good hand? A bad hand? He'd have to keep track if that mannerism was a clue to what Donny was holding.

With all bets equal, Jake dealt the flop—three cards in the centre. All players added chips to the pot and Jake dealt the turn.

Troy checked. *He was not going to add to the pot with this hand.*

Donny followed.

Lucas, who had sat stone-still and not met any of their eyes the entire round, added another 75.

Jake tapped his feet and raised it an extra 75.

Troy folded.

Donny grunted and pushed his cards forward.

He must have had a good starting hand but it didn't last.

Troy watched and learned.

"Call." Lucas kept his head down. His Sens cap covered his eyes.

Jake dealt the fourth card. They both increased the pot. Jake's voice inflection stayed even.

Was Lucas even breathing? Could his pale skin blanch more?

The fifth card dealt. Both players stayed in.

"I have a straight," Lucas said as he flipped over a seven and an eight to go with the five, six and nine on the board. His muscles relaxed and he made eye contact with Jake.

"Impressive, my friend, but it doesn't beat a flush." Jake waved his cards in the air and whooped.

A good lesson on their body language.

Jake continued to deal and passed the next cards around.

Troy's cards weren't great, but they were good enough to justify staying in the game and to initiate the next step. His strategy wasn't foolproof, but at this stage, the risk was low.

Time to up the ante, so to speak.

"We need some tunes." Troy grabbed his cell and turned on CCR.

John Fogerty's raspy voice blared from the wall speakers...Call it Pretending.

Wagers were entered, more cards dealt. Troy's hand was still reasonable enough to not fold. *Yet.* The next card dealt didn't help his hand. *Perfect.* And as expected...

Three hard knocks shook the apartment's front door.

Donny and Lucas froze.

"What the hell..." Jake muttered.

Troy left the table, cards still in his hand, and disappeared around the corner to the foyer. He opened the door.

"Yes, Mr. Kovar?"

"Turn down that crap. There's a noise rule in this building, and I won't have it broken." He examined Troy's appearance. "And don't forget, you owe me rent."

The man left and headed to the stairwell.

Troy returned to the table and lowered the music. "Sorry 'bout that."

"You gambling your rent?" Jake said. "That's sad." He shuffled the deck with a loud snap. "I'll still take your money, but that's sad."

Donny turned to Troy. "Your cards left the table with you."

"Don't think it matters since I fold. I'll show you my cards at the end of the round to prove I'm not cheating." He laid his cards in front of Jake. "Search the foyer if you want."

Nobody spoke. He could feel their eyes on him as his skin heated. *Don't panic now.* Instead, he leaned his chair back and twisted to open the window an inch.

Donny broke the silence. "I fold too."

Lucas joined them.

"Hot dawg! I'm on a roll." Jake danced in his chair, his beer belly jiggling, and claimed the pot.

Troy wouldn't call two wins a roll, but he would call it a good start for setting the stage even as his stress level became more than a little elevated. Yes, he was betting his rent money, a month's worth, and he was hoping to increase it to three months' worth.

He knew these three guys from work—the massive Centre Block

restoration project on Parliament Hill—were his best shot. They were high rollers, not scared to bet the farm down at the Greely Casino—which was not an official casino, just an abandoned barn on a fellow player's actual farm in the rural south end of the city. Troy usually lost all his money there, betting big and losing big. But this time, gambling in his two-bedroom apartment in a run-down building that had seen better days, he counted on counting a lot of bills, if everything went to plan. And it had to, otherwise he'd be kicked out with nowhere to go.

"Cheese puff?" he offered to no one in particular while Jake dealt yet another round. *Keep it normal, just a night of poker with the guys.* He stretched out his legs and slowed his breathing.

Lucas and Donny took a handful but Jake refused. "I'm not marking up the cards for you to track them."

"Be a good boy then and use your napkin." Donny countered monotone, his pencil-thin mustache lifted in contempt.

"Chill Jake. Hard to track the cards if they are all orange." Lucas argued.

Jake lost his grin. "I play fair and square."

That was the main reason Troy invited him to the game. There could be no question of validity if—or rather, when—he won all their money. He wouldn't be surprised if Jake had contemplated inspecting the foyer.

Troy slowed his breathing, raised his expectations and lifted his two cards. The one thing he couldn't strategically plan for that night was the hand he was dealt. But, things were looking up, especially with the next three cards laid out. Before they finished that round, there was another hard knock at the door.

"Anyone want to come with me to the door and watch my cards? I'm not leaving them with you guys." *Oops, hope I didn't give my hand away.*

"Yes." Jake rose and followed him.

Troy opened the door to an already yelling Mr. Kovar, who paused briefly when a six-foot, muscular Jake came into view.

"Who the hell are you?" He didn't wait for an answer. "The one smoking the pot?" Mr. Kovar poked his head into the room and sniffed heavily. "I can smell it through the air vents." He lifted his chin. "I feel a breeze. You think an open window hides the scent? I should call the cops right now."

"Nobody is smoking anything. Come in, see for yourself." Troy lifted his arm as an invitation.

Mr. Kovar pushed past them and around the corner, taking exaggerated breaths as he stepped. His gaze stopped at the table.

"You boys have an illegal gambling den in here?"

Troy laughed. "Gambling with friends is not illegal."

Mr. Kovar glared. He continued to sniff around the room like a hungry dog. Not detecting anything to accuse them with, he stomped out without a word.

"What's his problem?" Jake shook his head.

They returned to the table.

"He's a small man whose biggest success is managing tenants. Lacking a healthy well-adjusted life, he has low confidence and so resorts to bullying to give himself some gratification."

Troy, Lucas and Jake turned to Donny stunned.

"When did you become Doctor Psychoanalyst?" Jake laughed.

"When I started playing poker. You have to know how people tick."

So much for uncovering Donny's weaknesses. Troy figured he hadn't prepared enough for that wild card.

"I'd guess he has no friends and is hoping we'll ask him to stay and have a beer."

That is not happening. But good segue. "Speaking of beer, anyone need another?" Troy got up.

"Sit, finish the hand." Jake barked.

Right, he couldn't mess up the next step. Timing was everything. His children were everything. He couldn't see them if he didn't have his apartment. His ex-wife would go back to court to say he was unfit to parent. The centre of the wall in front of him hosted pictures of his two sons. The Game of Thrones poster on the opposite wall hid the hole he had punched when his divorce had gone through. His TV, one of the few items his ex-wife hadn't claimed, hung in a corner. The place was small and old, but it was cheap, reasonably close to work and near his kids' Bells Corners Elementary School, and most importantly, it had a spare room for weekend visits. He had to keep it that way.

Troy cleared his mind and decided to raise to $100. He slowed his breathing. He hoped the others were watching for physical clues of his betting patterns. The guys matched. He had to appear calm.

But he couldn't keep his face blank as he overturned his cards. "Full house!"

Donny and Lucas folded, but Jake smiled brightly. "Four of a kind!" He laid out four eights and then pulled the pot towards him. "I'm rollin, rollin rollin."

Sheesh! How often does that hand happen? Don't worry. The night is young; there is still time. Troy would play all night if he had to.

Troy went to the fridge and grabbed four Buds. He didn't want to cloud his judgment with more beer, but it would seem weird if he was the only one not drinking. He held them all in one hand to close the fridge door, but they were wet with condensation, and he let them slip to the floor with a loud crash.

Lucas laughed. "Should we have a side bet on how long it takes your landlord to bang on your door?"

"That's one bet I won't take. You should open the door now for him," Donny added.

Troy replaced the beer with bottles not shaken and deposited them on the table. Jake dealt their next round. *Two of spades and a seven of diamonds.* Before he could preemptively fold, there were three loud knocks.

"I'm certainly getting my steps." He flashed the back of his cards at the guys. "I'm bringing these with me, anyone want to join?"

Nobody answered.

Good. They were comfortable.

He opened the door, apologized to Mr. Kovar and assured him that two beers each were their limit and he wouldn't need to call the cops when everyone drove home later.

He returned to the table and folded, as did Lucas, but Donny won the round with a pair of jacks.

They continued to play more rounds, the bets went up and up. Troy won a few but not enough to pay his rent.

His luck had to change. But he needed the right cards. And finally he got them.

His initial two cards were nothing special, but the community cards dealt after were very promising—a ten, queen and ace of diamonds were in the mix. If someone had the jack or king, they were sitting pretty. If they had both, they were laughing to the bank.

He observed the guys. Lucas's eyes were wandering, Donny's responses were patient and slow, and the inflections in Jake's voice told him his hand was crap.

Troy stared at his cards and breathed in hard and heavy. He hoped they were picking up his clues that he was about to bluff.

Donny spied a glance at him and raised the pot two-fold. Lucas raised it three-fold. It was getting late—the men had had a lot of beer and seemed to be itching to make things interesting. Troy continued to breathe heavily.

Jake eyed each one of them, keeping his head straight, then raised it more.

"Whooeee, someone could be rollin, rollin, rollin."

Perfect.

They were wagering in the thousands.

Troy grabbed his phone and put on CCR's *Rollin Down the River*. He increased the volume a bit then let his finger slip. The song screamed out the speakers.

"Shit!" He dropped the phone, scrambled to retrieve it and finally turned it down.

"Way to go. You're going to get kicked out with us." Jake grinned.

Troy didn't. He would get kicked out regardless if this didn't work.

All four cocked their ears toward the door. Troy breathed deeply in anticipation. Despite the underlying stress, he had to admit that he had enjoyed the night, hanging out, playing cards and drinking beer. The rental market was tight; he was surprised Mr. Kovar hadn't torn up his lease already. Raise the rent for the next tenant. But where would he go? He wouldn't even have one month's rent.

Despite the expectation, they all jumped when the knocks, five this time, shook the door.

This was it.

His face blank, cards clutched tight, Troy left the table, disappeared into the foyer and opened the door. The second he turned the knob, Mr. Kovar's voice rang loud and clear. He railed about the disturbance, the rights of the other tenants, threatened to call the police and city bylaw officers and barked that the only reason he hadn't terminated Troy's lease was that he was still hopeful he could recoup some of the rent money.

All through the shouting, Troy flipped through another deck of cards Mr. Kovar had brought. It was the same brand as the cards Troy had shown him when he'd knocked on the door the first time. Troy replaced the three and seven with the jack and king of diamonds. He gave the deck back to his landlord, winked and closed the door.

Final round! As long as the others didn't show the same cards, Troy would have enough money to pay rent, keep visitation rights and give Mr. Kovar his cut.

Jennifer Jorgensen resides in Ottawa with her husband, two children and two cats. She has won awards for Capital Crime Writers Audrey Jessop Short Story Contest, and her work has appeared in magazines On The Premises and Daily Science Fiction, the literary journal WayWords and in Year Six, A Black Hare Press Anthology.

THE CASE OF DESPERATION, DRUNKENNESS, DEBAUCHERY AND DESPAIR

14

BERNADETTE HENDRICKX

Curling her fingers around the ornamental bars of the Queen's Gate, Valerie called out to the officers hunched over the body until her caseworker, Celia, told her to calm down and stand back.

"I have changed, Celia," she protested.

"We have got to go, Valerie."

"This death has changed me."

"I imagine."

"I have acute and intimate knowledge," insisted Valerie.

"Let the police do their work," pleaded Celia, fighting back tears. "We will discuss later."

Valerie fell silent and did a personal check-in. Usually when Celia responded assertively to one of Valerie's important announcements, Valerie would cringe and retreat into a ball. Not literally, it was more like her chest would implode and begin eating itself up. Her small, neglected being had inherited sad DNA; her sensitive cells were susceptible to negative stimuli, to all those feelings. But now she felt nothing—*nothing*. The anguish was gone—she had ceased to catastrophize! A flower of cognition bloomed inside her; her power of insight could burn down a town!

It was all because of a murder, a slaying most vulgar and indecorous. A mere stone's throw from the pretty Victorian entrance to Parliament Hill lay the sordid crime scene, and she was a huge part of it.

"I have seen the patterns that will solve this murder case," she whispered, pointing at the body in the red-checkered lumberjack jacket.

Whispering made Valerie's pronouncements stand out with regular people but not with her caseworker; Celia looked pissed—and extremely anxious.

"You know it was *murder*?" Celia squealed in a tinny voice.

The young, wild-eyed community worker had a right to feel unnerved, thought Valerie. The cops she'd clashed with in Cuba had caused her and her family to seek political refuge in one of the coldest capitals in the world. Now surrounded by uniforms, she looked like she'd never escaped. Barriers were being erected to deflect traffic on Wellington Street, and camera crews had begun elbowing their way in, the stench of mid-summer sweat soaring as tourists and government workers, and houseless people like Valerie, congregated like bees in front of the gate to gawp at the body draped over the edge of the Centennial Flame monument.

Valerie smiled with clever comprehension. Friday late afternoon at the height of tourist season was the perfect choice for this murder. Even without visitors to Canada's national capital, Fridays were mayhem. Taxis and limos twisted through side streets, buses full of civil servants clogged the roads and hordes of suburbanites pushed in to snag seats at their favourite restaurants and buy goods at the ByWard Market. *Sensational* was the word that came to mind. The image of a famous person lying across a famous monument smack-bang in front of the renowned Peace Tower would be the talk of the nation—and Valerie's social circle—for years to come.

"He's not a homeless dude. He's a filthy politician!" she bellowed.

"Let's go," begged Celia. "Let's go."

"What were you doing there anyway?" grumbled Valerie, refusing to budge.

Celia stumbled backwards. "We'll be late," she nearly howled.

"Sorry, Celia. Reminds you of back home, eh? The goons, guns and political repression. Violence and detention."

Celia yelped in agreement.

"But listen, Celia. This murder, I am not just onto something. I *know*."

Celia stared at her so long Valerie laughed.

"I know what happened," Valerie declared to the woman looming over her, an undercover police officer who had shoved Celia and Valerie outside the gated area as soon as Valerie had pointed out the body and begun blabbing.

The plainclothes snoop ran her eyes over Valerie's heavily painted face, her scrawny Caucasian frame, her filthy Medusa-like hair, her bulging thrift store purse. She appraised Celia's black brawny body and her African queen tattoo, Cuban twist braids and deer-in-the-headlights glare—

"C'mon!" Celia began pulling Valerie away. "We have to go."

"You're right," sniffed Valerie, turning her back on the officer. "What does it matter? In the great scheme of things."

There was no way Valerie could explain any of it right now anyway. What she'd seen. What she knew. How the murder had gifted her a sense of relief. God knows it was the best thing to happen to her since the summer Dad took her—just her, all the other kids had to stay at home and help Mom—for a joyride and an ice cream cone at the Dairy Queen on Richmond Road. She hadn't felt this degree of specialness since that day; nor had she been able, until now, to access the wisdom inside her aging body. Without a doubt, the celebrity's murder had launched a sense of exultation and signifi-cance that enabled her to see clearly for the first time. Her vision was astounding, and it filled her with wonder.

The pair snaked their way between cops and cars across the jam-packed lanes.

"Listen, Val," confided Celia, once sure they were alone. "I am not involved. I was not there. Do you hear me?"

"I have changed, Celia." Valerie nodded distractedly. "I see myself clearly. I have found my life's purpose, like in that book you gave me."

"Right." Celia sidled along stealthily, urging Valerie to keep up.

"It's the prospect of having a home," puffed Valerie with passion. "You fought like the devil, and I will never stop thanking you for it. No more couch surfing or sleeping rough. No more compromising my health. I couldn't have achieved that on my own and I know it will make all the difference, and there is more that I want to do to make up for bad things I did."

"Please," said Celia. "I don't want to know about your bad decisions. I am two months away from securing *my* permanent home! Do you understand?"

"Si entiendo," said Valerie.

"And don't speak Spanish to me."

"Why not?"

"We're going to be late for your home transition meeting at the church. The committee folks won't be happy."

"Sorry," said Valerie, picking up the pace.

"Darryl is going to be there," Celia said encouragingly, breaking into a half-run.

"Darryl?"

"Yes. Big Darryl. The man who adores you."

"He does?"

"My goodness gracious, you're all he talks about, Val. Val this, Val that. He worships the ground you walk on."

Valerie stopped in her tracks. "He might've come down with a cold," she said slowly.

"Don't stop!" cried Celia. "Val, don't you see? The process demands you attend all the meetings. We can't be—"

Valerie broke into a run. She dashed into the church and tripped down the stairs into the meeting room and slid into a chair.

She wasn't late. And the city councillor was nice: "Must've been a chore getting here. Bit of a sensation on the Hill, eh?"

"Some murder," said Valerie.

"That so?" said the councillor. "Terrorists?"

"No."

"Protestors?"

"No."

"Who died? Do they know?"

Valerie shrugged then grinned at Celia who had just jogged in and sat down. "I'd rather not discuss it at this moment, thank you."

"Good afternoon," panted Celia, relieved to see Valerie. "We are so grateful you can accommodate our schedules."

Then Celia shot up from her chair. "Where's Darryl?"

Valerie hid in the washroom until everyone was gone. The meeting had been successful. She had made a good impression, and that was important because after everything she and the cohort had fought for, she could not lose her place. She had proven that she was a model citizen, that an unfair start could be overcome. Today's achievements and divine awakenings had assured her a redeemed life was possible. In her mind, she lined up the points of her individual goal plan and how easy it was going to be to adhere to them. She imagined little ways to make a stable home special without having to pay or steal. She would repair old furniture that came her way like she used to; she would find leftover paint and splash the walls in bright colours; she would save up for a crockpot and cook healthy meals and invite all her new friends over for dinner.

Or just Darryl.

Maybe just her best friend, Darryl.

But first she had to find the big lout.

Creeping up the backstairs, she entered the empty church and sat in the pew closest to the altar. There was so much good in her life now it made her cry. The flickering of the votive candles illuminated her heightened senses, her individual plan, her life's purpose. With repaired vision rose a new sensitivity, a reaching out towards her former, wounded self. She watched her sins dissolve into lessons, her lessons transform into ambition. God had finally entered her life, and she had an obligation to fulfill his first calling: she had to save Darryl.

Crouched down low, she stole along the south wall until she reached the back pew. Sliding onto the bench, she lay flat on her stomach and adjusted her vision. There it was! One plank in the outer aisle, the one extending beneath the bench seat in front of her, had scratch marks on one end and streaks of discolouration along the side closest to the kneeler.

Lowering herself onto the kneeler, she fished an old lockpick from her purse and, using it as a lever, raised the errant plank, sliding it away. Three items lay head to toe in the secret bed: an official will and testament, a wad of money and a small notebook.

She wasn't at all surprised to find Darryl's stash; he'd offered too many clues: lifting his head when he walked by, slowing down his step, staring longingly down at the floor where she now sat. It was just another "Darryl secret" he wanted to let her in on.

Valerie stifled a laugh. She had figured that lug out the day he joined the rehab program. His concussion from a workplace accident had been so severe he'd developed behaviours that, like Valerie, had kept him from holding down jobs and taking proper care of himself. Never mind that his actions didn't always meet his noble intentions, or that he was bad at masking his binge-drinking habit or that he dreamed up fantastical tales; she had taken to him like a moth to a lamp because, for once, she had felt seen and valued for who she was, warts and all. Like him, she was from a large family; like him, she'd been snatched from her home when the abuse hit the roof; like him, she'd expressed an occasional irreverence for the law.

"*All money and possessions to be divided equally among my children: Rory, Zak and Stephen,*" read Darryl's will. "*Invest wisely, you guys. Don't do as I did, lest you be done...*"

"He's got kids!" Valerie collapsed with the same sense of abandonment she felt when she was torn away from her parents. Here was a secret the charmer had never shared. Even with her. Sobbing beneath the bench, she drew towards her the last item in Darryl's cache: the notebook, which held one, single entry.

"*Saturday, July 14, 5:20 a.m. Desperation, Drunkenness, Debauchery and Despair: A Private Tale for Valerie. Thank you for believing in me. Love you forever, Darryl.*"

Sniffling and sighing, Valerie sat down to read. "No worries, you clod-pole, got you covered..."

We can skip the Drunkenness part, Val, since it goes without saying there was booze involved. It was a few hours before dawn, and I was totally ripped when I arrived at the abandoned cat colony behind Parliament Hill. It suddenly hit me how those cats got better treatment than any of us street folk. I miss those cats, my old buddies. Not as many live there as in the old days, just one or two sniffing around, probably looking for family.

Desperation you know about, too. I didn't want to stay at that rooming house, not after my stuff got stolen again. It's hard having nothing and then realizing that having nothing stolen from you means you at least had something. Everything of real consequence I have had to stash in a secret "coffer" that I bet my front teeth you have already found. I felt desperate to stay somewhere safe (and CCTV-free) where I could sleep it off without being disturbed (and so I wouldn't miss our important stakeholder or whatever meeting). I knew about a fine cluster of trees just north of the colony, so I threw down my old lumberjack jacket in the darkest, densest, most secluded spot there and settled in for a nap.

Well, it turns out the cat colony palace is still more of a sanctuary than we thought. I am lying there, close enough to catch figures prancing around the boarded-up shelter and I'm thinking, dang, why can't we colonize it? Add a few inches to the walls, raise the roof and you've got yourself a tiny home, Val—and just think of the view! You're on a wooded slope overlooking the magnificent Ottawa River where my ancestors used to log and trade.

So I'm high on the hootch, smelling the mist off the water and imagining you and me curled up under the stars and feeling like we're out of the city at a cottage or deep in the quiet forest, and that's when the Debauchery starts, Val, but not by me. The people down at the cat hut, they are going at it like feral cheetahs, and it's hurting my ears and my heart to hear them. I'm thinking they're going to kill each other!

That's when Despair walks in, Val. I inch down the hill so I can hear what they're saying. And guess what? They are slinging stuff at each other about politics—politics! It was sort of like a movie:

"Hey, baby, you'd better not kill that affordable housing initiative," moans the woman—she's got this funny foreign accent.

"But the debt, the deficit," squeals the man. "And the costs have gone up!"

"Like your private sector needs a break," chides the little lady, yanking at his boxers.

"There's been a policy shift," huffs the bro.

"I will bring you down if you break your funding commitment!" shrieks the woman, peeling off his shirt.

"Forget it, you loser, you've got nothing on me," snorts the guy. "Nothing!"

Then everything stops, and the dude who says "Nothing!" sees me standing there as drunk as ten lords trying to look the hero. The guy—he's completely starkers and looks terribly familiar, like his face is jumping off the front page of a newspaper—is wobbling and jabbing around with his fists, so I toss him aside, but before I can turn, the woman—also amazingly familiar—jumps forward and trots proud as a filly down the hill with all the guy's clothes and hops onto a speedboat towards the museum.

I swear they both looked like cheetahs, Val. Orange-blond bodies, spotted limbs—though the spots could've been from what the woman was wearing. Or my state of fear. (Or drunkenness.) And the man had orange, power-hungry eyes and sharp, greedy teeth.

Well, you can guess what happened, Val. I did a kung fu on the naked cheetah and bolted. If he's dead, I killed him. I'll be in hiding until I find out.

I love you, Valerie—for what it's worth.

Despairingly yours, Darryl.

(P.S. Tell Celia I caught Covid or whatever. And that I pray to God I still meet the criteria.)

"You came all the way to Canada for peace," said Valerie, patting Celia's hand, "and you get this."

Celia squinted tears into her coffee and scanned the café. "I don't want to have anything to do with this—this *assassination*," she hissed. "Just because I am against the politics of that cruel, narcissistic, anti-housing minister doesn't mean—but I—"

"You shouldn't have searched for me," said Valerie. "Now you are going to have to say you were with me, confess your involvement. It has to be done."

"Stop it, Valerie." She spoke under her breath. "I was only there to find you, to make sure you would make it on time to the meeting. If they interrogate you, you will say only that. OK?"

"But you know, don't you? *Don't you?*"

Celia began to cry. "The jacket! I realized at the meeting why Darryl wasn't there. Why the naked man lying over the Centennial Flame fountain was wearing a red jacket with the checkers. It was Darryl's. Darryl must have...he must have been helping him! He did nothing, but he knows he will be blamed. He won't meet the criteria and will lose his chance—oh, what did I do?"

"Is that all you know?" whispered Valerie, narrowing her eyes.

"They'll send me back!" Celia looked around in panic. "Oh, this is my fault, always letting my mouth get me into trouble. Now I've hurt the people I've tried to protect, misused my sacred heritage, disappointed my ancestors. My family will lose our protected persons status and be deported. I will go to jail. My dear kids, Val, my husband, will live in poverty. I love them like crazy. Do you know about love? Do you understand what you are doing?"

"Oh, I know about love," smiled Valerie, rising from her chair. "Believe me, I know. Now don't you worry about a thing. Follow me."

"You *are* different, Valerie," spluttered Celia as they exited the café. "Ever since you saw that orangutang politician zigzag to the fountain and stick his face in the water and—and *die,* you are not yourself. I see a holy light around your head, and it is freaking me out."

"*We* saw, Celia, *we* saw. You were there, too. You are just as much a part of this drama. You've got to be tough. It's part of your job."

Celia was fuming. "It's easier to be tough when we are safe from orangutang dictators."

"Orangutangs don't exist in Canada," mumbled Valerie.

"Sure. Just polite bigots destroying social housing."

"It is because of your tough compassion and advocacy that I have found my life's purpose," Valerie said to her kindly. "Thanks to you, I am a face of hope. Now keep moving. Enlightenment is near. Just don't mention a thing about Darryl. Or his jacket."

Celia screamed, "What do you mean by enlightenment? Where are we going? Why do I say nothing about your friend?"

Valerie pulled Celia into the doorway of the Community Police Centre. "OK, you're ready to know the truth! Well, for one thing, that undercover officer who dragged us away from the crime scene has been tailing us all morning and taking pictures of us chattering like criminals."

Celia gasped as Valerie waved the officer over. "Interview room, please!" she commanded.

"Yesterday afternoon I go to fetch Darryl for the meeting. The meeting was important; there was no way he could miss it. I figure he'll be hanging out where the cat sanctuary used to be. So I trudge down from the Library of Parliament—it's past two by now—and I come across evidence of vandalism—snapped branches, bent bushes, food scraps, trash—but Darryl's not there. Not that I think Darryl had anything to do with it. He's got respect for property, and anyway, he can't risk losing his spot for the supportive housing unit. As soon as I call out for him, I hear this eerie groan, like from a wounded, other-worldly beast. I think it's Darryl waking up from an uncomfortable night, so I scramble up towards the sound and find not Darryl but a stark-naked man in a red lumberjack jacket writhing back and forth on the ground. He's jerking about, his limbs keep stiffening up, and he's sweating like he's about to have a heart attack—oh, and he's got a large bruise on the side of his face, no doubt from a fall. 'Poppy,' he gasps. I say, 'My name's not Poppy, it's Valerie. Can I help you, sir?' But all he can say is, 'Poppy! Poppy!' Then he says, 'Drink! Drink!' So I'm thinking the poor guy needs a drink of pop or something stronger, and I remember the fancy can of pina colada lying on the porch of the shelter. So I go get it, smell it, and seeing as the can's empty, I bag it like in the cop shows and put it in my purse. Then as I'm about to leave, I notice all kinds of other proof of foul play, like a condom wrapper, lots of blond hair and a furry piece of cloth with spots on it."

Valerie placed the items, each in a clear, sealed bag, on the table. "Bagged those, too."

Celia, the undercover officer and her colleague, a homicide investigator, stared with disbelief at the mound of evidence.

"You always carry crime scene bags around in your purse?" interrupted the investigator.

"I am houseless," said Valerie simply. "I survive."

Celia glanced from Valerie to the poker-faced investigator and began to wring her hands.

The investigator examined Valerie's hair. "There are objects in your hair: twigs, string—are those golden fibres someone else's hair? We may need to do some analyses to confirm your story."

"Guess I picked up a few things on my adventure. And just look at my nails."

"And your friend—?"

"Darryl."

"Darryl. Did you find him?"

"Shepherds of Good Hope." Valerie smiled at Celia. "Slept there, right Celia?"

"Transitional program." Celia nodded weakly.

"Are you familiar with the deceased?" asked the homicide investigator.

"Not personally. I only recognized the murder victim when I met up with Celia at the monument. It was too dark in the woods to see who he was."

Several seconds elapsed before the investigator continued. "This is a serious crime."

"Oh, yes!" exclaimed Valerie. "Of national importance!"

"Obstruction of justice in a major crime investigation is a criminal offence. Are you aware of that?"

"Oh, yes!"

The homicide investigator pressed his face close to Valerie's. "Perhaps you can explain to us then, Valerie, how you're so sure the death was not by natural causes."

"Like a heart attack?"

"Yes."

Celia whimpered.

"Well, if you'll just let me finish!" grunted Valerie impatiently. "As I was saying, I bagged all the evidence, and by the time I return to the man, he's disappeared. So I go back up the hill calling out as I go and, lo and behold, he's made it to the top and is cooling off in the fountain, or so it seems, and that's when I hear Celia sob and say, 'He's dead'. I check out the scene, and it's true; he's not looking very alive with his body spread eagle covering the shield of Ontario—I don't think that was on purpose, sir. I doubt that as a highly respected politician he was protesting or trying to send some kind of a message. So I do my civic duty and examine the situation and tell Celia not to worry, and that's when you arrive and encourage us to leave."

After a brief silence, Valerie said, "Celia can corroborate it."

"Thank you. Celia?" The investigator studied the dark circles under the young woman's eyes, her chewed-down nails and the steady stream of tears.

"Calm down, Celia," Valerie advised her. "It's better to tell the truth."

"This is not the movies!" exploded Celia. "You are not Hercule Poirot or Miss Marple!"

"She's right, though. It is better to tell the truth," piped in the undercover cop.

"Everything will be fine," smiled Valerie. "God has a plan."

Celia sobbed with resignation. "I am thinking he is houseless," she blubbered. "I want to help. I see he is desperate for water, trying to drink from the fountain, and is breathing heavily. I am shouting for help and dialing 9-1-1 when he turns and looks me in the eye, and it is then that I know who it is. He's the bully who wants to destroy all our work on permanent housing. Not just for the houseless—"

"Like me," interjected Valerie.

"Yes, like Valerie and Darryl and so many more," cried Celia, "like refugees, low-income earners. He wants—wanted—to eliminate not just the programs but all the sources of funding. He hates us. He's against anybody not like him. He wants us to go back to where we came from. He's a—a greedy, ignorant, racist, bigot orangutang!" She was shaking. "I can't—I—"

"Trust the process, Celia," begged Valerie.

"He—the ape—I think he is drunk," erupted Celia. "He is lying there making ugly looks at me, and I am standing over him making pissed-off looks at him. Suddenly his arm jerks around, and he points and shouts 'fo-reign in-ter-fer-ence!' straight into my angry face. I am so upset, I cannot tell you. And even though I see he is without charms or protections, I lose my mindfulness. My heart calls up the devil and my intention grows dark. That's when I transmit to his orange eyes *el mal de ojo*—the evil eye—and I yell a curse in his ear, a very bad curse, the worst and most powerful curse you can imagine, and right away he dies. He chokes right in front of me. His eyes go blank like a dead rabbit."

Both officers looked away.

Then they covered their faces.

"I can assure you," said the investigator gently, "that your evil spell may have only shortened his life by a few nanoseconds."

Valerie grinned; Celia stopped crying. Clutching onto Valerie, she whooped with relief. "Are you sure? Are you sure?"

Valerie nodded, as did the officers.

"But then, why did you keep saying it was murder?" Celia asked, turning to Valerie. "I thought you were talking about me! You said you knew—"

"Poppy!" Valerie fluttered her eyelashes. "I happen to know about poppies—discoloured skin, trouble breathing, small pupils, confusion: all signs of poppy seed poisoning. Such a distinguished, sensible man would never have overdosed. He must've known he'd been poisoned. And robbed. And disrobed. But he was stuck on the hill for so long that he ran out of time to get help, so he died."

"Well done!" confirmed the investigator with unconcealed admiration. "Thebaine is an opiate alkaloid. Taken in high doses, it's a highly toxic stimulant, potentially—and certainly in this case—deadly."

Celia still seemed confused.

"The man kept saying 'poppy,'" explained Valerie. "Thebaine comes from poppy seeds." She pointed with pride at the empty can in the bag. "I've been an alcoholic all my life, and this did not smell like Malibu Pina Colada to me!"

Darryl wept at the crimson vibrations of the Ottawa River and the fungal smell of fall. "Celia and I got you a little something," he said. "To thank you."

Valerie beamed at the beautifully wrapped gift on the picnic table. "Thank me for what?"

"You know darned well, pussy cat."

"Knock it off, we're a team!" Valerie smiled serenely. "Just glad we were able to keep you out of the wicked mess."

"You saved my pretty *derrière*," said Darryl, raising his can of ginger ale. "Cheers."

Valerie laughed. "Mine, too." Unwrapping her gift, she marvelled for the thousandth time at how life could suddenly pluck up an entire history and toss it to benevolent gods. "A crockpot!" she exclaimed. "And there's a...a *key*—?"

"That's your key." Celia bore a wide grin. "To your apartment!"

Valerie sprang up to hug her. "You did it, Celia!"

"No, no, *we* did it, dear Valerie. Darryl included."

"Gosh, guys." Valerie was stroking her present. "Can't wait to have you over! Try some of Mom's old recipes."

Celia giggled with glee as she handed Darryl his key. Turning it around in his giant hands, Darryl shook his head back and forth with great emotion. "*Gracias, ángel.*"

Shyly, tearfully, he added, "Hey, Val, got you something else."

"No way!" Valerie planted a fat kiss on his cheek.

"Some extra resealable baggies for your purse. You never know when we'll need them next."

Bernadette Hendrickx is a teacher and an award-winning theatre professional who has written and co-authored dozens of plays, skits and poems, and helped winners of the Broken English Writing Competitions (with CBC Radio One and Television) dramatize their works. Her poem Tulips at Costco appeared in Off Topic Publishing and her short story Nice is forthcoming in the anthology One of Us is a Robot by Chicken House Press.

PRESSURE POINT

15

MADONA SKAFF

I t was official. I had no life.

Was I out partying with friends on a Saturday night? No. I was sitting in my car outside a client's upper-class home.

I had made it a rule never to socialize with my patients. But after two years in the city, I hadn't made any close friends. Though occasionally I joined my co-workers for drinks, they didn't share my interests. I had to turn my life around before I became a little old lady living alone with my 100 cats. I already had a good start with three rescued strays.

I wouldn't say I was lonely—well, maybe I was.

Which is why I'd easily become friends with my client Gail. Five months ago she came in for physiotherapy after the cast on her ankle had been removed. Jasmine, her daughter, had helped her hobble into the treatment room. At 59 Gail had taken up skateboarding with her husband who successfully executed an ollie. Gail managed to pop her skateboard into the air. At a critical moment, the board abandoned her and landed safely on the ground. She did not.

I always looked forward to my sessions with Gail, whose positive attitude had been refreshing. Her unparalleled discipline in doing her daily exercises at home had resulted in a quick recovery. After only three weeks of intensive therapy, her limp had disappeared.

Although I was happy that Gail had recovered quickly, I hated to see mother and daughter go, especially Jasmine who was my age.

As it turned out, I was to see Jasmine again. She returned a week after our tearful goodbyes. At 35, she was in much poorer shape than her mother and prone to frequent muscle injuries and strains, probably because she was a typical weekend warrior who mostly sat at a desk working temporary secretarial jobs Monday to Friday. She came in every couple of weeks. The one hour always flew by as we chatted about an assortment of topics.

Last month she'd brought me a gift, a small box wrapped in gold paper. Knowing that she had a love for jewellery, I was worried that it was something inappropriately expensive.

"I appreciate the gesture," I had said. "But a gift isn't necessary."

"If you don't want it, I'll take it back. I promise." She'd spoken so earnestly that I felt I had no choice.

I unwrapped it, opened the box and stared at the contents. Confused, I looked up. "Uh, thank you."

"Don't you remember? Last week you said that when you moved to the city, one box was lost. The only thing you regretted losing was the blue yo-yo you'd had since you were a kid."

I couldn't believe that she'd remembered the passing comment.

When she called earlier this week begging to be slipped into my already full schedule, I agreed to stay late. I figured it would be a nice ending to a strenuous eight hours of non-stop, strange injuries: a jogger with a twisted wrist, a golfer with a sprained ankle, a driving instructor with whiplash. OK, that last one wasn't so strange.

Hearing the receptionist greet her, I turned expecting to see a bubbly Jasmine. Instead, I watched her limp into the treatment room, her face tight with pain.

Three weeks ago she'd seriously injured her lower back. It had taken several sessions for her to become relatively pain free.

"You were doing so well. What happened?" I helped her onto the treatment table.

"Pulled a muscle." Her voice was flat. I could see her pallor beneath the impeccable makeup. She took a deep breath to keep her voice level. "I took your advice and started an exercise class. And I cut out chocolates and snacks. Look." She pulled at the waistband of her shorts. "I'm down to a size 12."

"Eating healthy is great." I examined her back, finding several tight, angry muscles. "There's no point exercising hard if you wind up in traction."

"I know, I'm sorry. My back kept trying to tell me that those weights were too heavy, but I didn't listen." Jasmine laughed, then winced. She brushed back a lock of blond hair from her eyes. She executed that signature move a little stiffly, but it subtly revealed the opal earrings which matched her engagement ring. I remember her telling me that her fiancé had left town the day after she'd announced their engagement. I couldn't imagine wearing a constant reminder for six months.

"Oh, you've bruised your hands," I said, "and you have some nasty scrapes, too."

"I've been working in the garden," she said, giving me a proud smile. "Getting fresh air, just like you suggested."

I sighed. Some of the cuts were old, but several were recent. Maybe even from today. She seemed to try too hard in just about everything she did. I wanted to shake her and tell her to use common sense. If she could just be herself, instead of hiding her insecurities beneath a façade, I knew her confidence would grow.

"Lie down on your stomach and let's see if we can get you straightened out. And before you go, I'm going to give you a list of *safe* exercises. Maybe skip your exercise class, this week. OK?" There was a weak nod of agreement.

"How's the pain now?" I asked 45 minutes later.

"You're a miracle worker." She sat up slowly and tenderly stretched her back. "Still hurts, but not so bad. By the way, before I forget to tell you, it's my mother's birthday on Saturday. She'll be turning 60 and she'd love for you to come."

I suppose I'd always thought of Gail as a substitute for my own distant mother. And Jasmine was like the sister I wish I'd had instead of the bullying one who made my teen years even more vulnerable.

"I'd love to."

I sat in my car now, admiring the two-storey house that sat nestled part way down a wooded hill overlooking the Ottawa River. This was no cookie-cutter neighbourhood. Her house was among the varied mid-century homes, and there were also many modern ones, all uniquely designed. The houses were dotted among mature trees and winding roads. When I got out of my car, I noticed how steep the land sloped behind the house. The trees waited patiently for the weather to warm up and the leaves to arrive.

Gift in hand, I walked up the cobblestone path and rang the bell. Jasmine opened the door and, when she saw me, gave me a wide smile.

"Elizabeth, I'm so glad you came!" She pulled me inside and gave me a big hug.

I felt a bit awkward and tried to politely pull myself away. My family never showed any sort of emotion—not the positive type anyway.

Finally released, I stepped back searching for something to say. "I love your dress. Pastels really suit you." Well, that was a pathetic opening line. But her blue dress *was* extremely flattering.

"Thank you. Come in." She ushered me into a high-ceiling lobby with an elegant chandelier and impressive spiral staircase.

She hung up my jacket in the front closet, asking, "Can I get you a drink?"

"Red wine please." I followed her past the living room with its oak floors to the kitchen.

Suddenly the peace was shattered by squeals of laughter and the clatter of tiny feet running along the hardwood floor of the dining room to the ceramic floor of the kitchen. I laughed as twin young boys zipped by. Close behind was a harried looking woman. Though a brunette, and younger and slimmer, she could have passed for Jasmine's twin.

She skidded to a halt a short distance from me. "Sorry. I guess 15 minutes is the hiding limit for four-year-olds."

"I didn't realize this was a surprise party. I parked in front of the house." I looked at Jasmine. "Should I move my car?"

"No, don't worry." The woman indicated herself and the boys. "We're the surprise. Oops, gotta go." And with that she chased them down the hall and up the staircase.

"I didn't know you had a sister... "

"That's my cousin, Nora," Jasmine whispered, her face tight. "They just showed up an hour ago. Unannounced."

"Guess they came for the party?" Talk about stating the obvious.

"They already visited from Newfoundland at Christmas for two weeks. And now her husband is travelling again, and she hates to stay alone. All that extra work for my mother, especially with those— kids."

"Looks like it's been hard on you, too." Despite the forced calm expression, I noticed a certain tightness in her eyes, almost as though she was fighting not to frown.

"You have no idea," Jasmine sighed loudly. Lowering her voice, she added, "I guess I'm just reliving my childhood. When my cousin's parents died, my parents adopted her. Even though she was five years younger, she appointed herself the know-it-all 'big sister'." She made quotes with her fingers. "Always criticizing me. Ordering me around."

I could understand her feelings.

I heard the front door open.

"Hello, we're back," a man called out from the foyer.

"Daddy's home," Jasmine said, her face brightening. "Come on, I'll introduce you."

"Glad to finally meet you Elizabeth," he said, giving my hand a warm squeeze. "My wife can't stop singing your praises."

"I've heard a lot about you, too, Mr. Colt." Jasmine had mentioned that he'd been a bodybuilder in his younger days. It still showed. "How's the skateboarding coming along?"

"Call me Mark, please. Last week I did a full 360 aerial!" he said with a huge grin. To Jasmine, he added, "A little tough with your mother *screaming* at the top of her lungs for me to be careful. And in front of all those teenagers. It was *so* embarrassing." In a stage whisper he added, "I said she's my mother."

"Daddy, cut it out! " Jasmine gave a tiny giggle, then asked, "Where's Mother?"

"Parking." To me he explained, "It's a tight squeeze in the garage with Nora's car, so I got out first. It's her car and she won't let me drive after one *tiny* four-wheel skid, she barely lets me *sit* in the car."

The front door opened and Gail came in.

"Elizabeth!" She bear-hugged me just as the boys exploded down the stairs with a chorus of "Grandma, grandma, grandma!" Nora followed close behind.

Gail knelt down to reach the boys, and the four of them coalesced into a huddle as tears streamed down Gail's cheeks.

"Surprise, Mom!" Nora said when the hug finally dissolved.

"This is the best birthday present ever!"

"When I spoke with Jasmine..."—Nora hesitated ever so slightly—"I know your big day isn't until Thursday, but we couldn't miss the party tonight! So we jumped on the first flight we could get."

"Oh if only you lived closer," Gail said as she gave the boys another hug before standing up.

Watching the family reunion warmed me until I glanced at Jasmine. Her brow was creased, the corners of her mouth curved down. I was about to speak to her when Gail unexpectedly pulled me into a group hug.

Happy chatter continued as we took our seats at the dining room table. Dinner consisted of Gail's favourites: Caesar salad, lasagne and garlic bread, all prepared by Jasmine. Throughout the meal Jasmine had wordlessly bustled back and forth from the kitchen bringing more garlic bread, more vegetable sticks and more wine to the table.

"How's your husband doing?" Gail asked Nora. "Isn't this the second mission this year? And it's only April."

"At least Eric was home for two days before they shipped him overseas. He's going to be gone longer this time."

"The military shouldn't be deploying young men with families." Gail shook her head.

Military deployment? Jasmine's off-the-cuff comment about his travelling, I'd thought he was a businessman or something mundane.

"Why don't you take time off from work and stay here?" Gail continued. "I hate the idea of you and the boys all alone in that big house."

"I wish I could," Nora said. "I have a new case, and we go to trial in two weeks. But after that..." She let the sentence hang, and I thought I saw a shadow of a sly smile.

Jasmine stood abruptly, muttering that she had to get something from the kitchen. Nora offered to help.

"Help those kids of yours eat properly. I just vacuumed," Jasmine snapped.

I thought, for four-year-olds, they were very neat. I discreetly brushed crumbs from beside my own plate. I couldn't understand why she was being so uncharacteristically rude. I looked around, and the other adults seemed just as surprised by the outburst as I was. They each gave me embarrassed smiles.

Jasmine came back to clear the last of the dinner dishes, again declining, though more politely this time, any offers of help from the rest of us.

She returned with an exquisite two-tier birthday cake decorated with white and purple icing. A large 60 candle glowed brightly on top. She started us on a chorus of Happy Birthday, but her smile disintegrated when the boys joined in with their own loud, off-key version. The rest of us grinned affectionately.

After the cake we went into the living room. But rather than join us, Jasmine headed for the kitchen with tight, brisk steps. I followed with an offer to help. All this running around wasn't good for her back.

"The coffee isn't quite ready," she said, as she yanked off a sheet of paper towel, leaving half of it behind, then dabbed sweat from her upper lip and brow. "I'll tidy up while I wait for it. You can take the cream and sugar if you like. I won't be long." She smiled, but I could hear the struggle to keep her voice pleasant.

I debated staying, but looking at how she crushed the paper towel in her fist, I thought better of it.

"All right." I picked up the crystal cream and sugar bowls.

As I left the kitchen, I overheard her mutter, "I just wanted to celebrate *one* birthday without *her*."

I could relate to her mood change. Whenever we had those rare family gatherings, I always turned into a glowering, silent mannequin. Self-preservation for my mind.

In the living room I placed the cream and sugar on the coffee table, then sat next to Mark on the sofa.

Nora said, "I had the boys' tricycles and my dirt bike sent here. The crate should arrive Monday. I also shipped my cross-country skis."

"Your skis?" I asked, "Are you expecting snow in April?"

"It's happened before. Besides, I checked and the Gatineau Hills still have some snow-covered trails," Nora answered, giving me an almost-wink.

Mark turned to his wife. "Do you remember, Dear, when we bought the girls cross-country skis? The second day, Nora was careening through the woods behind our property."

"I aged 10 years every time you skied past that cliff," she said to Nora.

"Sweetheart," Mark said, "it's hardly a cliff, just a sharp drop. Barely 15 feet high."

She huffed and said to Nora, "My heart wouldn't start beating again until you were safely back in our yard. And you," she shook a finger at her husband, "always encouraging her. And now with that dirt bike again. I can just see her zooming down the trail..."

"But Mom, it's no fun without speed," Nora said with a laugh.

"For pity's sake Nora! You're a mother now!" Gail said. "You can't keep acting like you did as a teenager."

"Mom, I'm careful." Nora patted her mother's arm, adding, "I just want to test out my mountain bike after its tune-up."

"I would have thought you have enough places in Newfoundland for that," I said.

"Sure, but nothing like the hill behind our house here."

"Gail's right. It looked steep," I added, the ever-concerned physiotherapist in me coming out.

"No, there's a nice switchback trail that a lot of us neighbourhood kids wore down while we were growing up. Easy and safe."

"I hope we have enough time to test it properly. You didn't say how long you can stay," Mark said.

"Well," Nora paused for a moment, that same sly smile on her face. Then the words rushed out. "Eric got the news three weeks ago, and I called right away to tell you. Jasmine answered the phone, but she insisted I wait to tell you so you don't get your hopes up if the orders don't come through. But after three weeks of torture keeping quiet, I can't wait. After this mission, Eric's going to be posted here in Ottawa! And—I got a job at a local law office—as a junior partner. We'll be back before the fall!"

I joined in the ensuing hoopla. As the echoes of our celebrating faded away, Jasmine silently came into the room, carrying a tray with a silver coffee pot and five delicate china cups. She filled all the cups, passing one to me, to each of her parents and then took one for herself, leaving Nora's on the tray. She sat in a corner armchair apart from everyone. They tried to include her in the conversation but with only one-word answers, they eventually gave up. I moved to sit in the armchair next to her.

I leaned close to whisper, "I understand how you feel. Try to make the best of it. For your mother's sake."

Cold silence.

"Your dad's great."

"Well, yeah."

"I'd love to see your garden," I said cheerfully, hoping she'd be proud to show it off.

"Haven't done much lately." The new scratches on her hands said otherwise.

"It's just that you've been working hard on it and..."

The twins' game of tag crashed into the coffee table, knocking over the last cup. Everyone jumped to their feet to check if the boys were scalded. Jasmine inspected the mahogany table for spills. The tray had retained most of the coffee with only a few escaped drops. The boys were fine. Jasmine picked up the tray with the pot, then stomped to the kitchen. I followed.

"I don't understand why my parents let those monsters run free. I know *she* won't discipline them." She washed and dried the tray, her hands trembling.

"You need to relax. If you're tense, your muscles won't loosen and your back won't heal as fast as it should."

"You're right," Jasmine said as a smile replaced the frown, a little too quickly I thought. She purposefully folded the dishtowel and laid it on the counter. "Shall we?"

I dropped the topic. As Jasmine returned the tray to the coffee table, Nora noticed her hands.

"Those scratches look bad. Why didn't you wear the work gloves I bought you at Christmas?"

"I prefer the feel of the soil on my hands."

"Honey," Gail said, "you won't have any skin left on your hands to feel anything when the first flower comes up."

Jasmine returned to the kitchen with a huff. I prudently stayed behind this time.

"I'm just trying to help," Nora said.

"I know, Sweetie," Gail said. "She's been a little stressed lately, especially after running into Raymond and his new girlfriend last month." A tense silence followed.

"I do believe," Mark said, "that it's time for you to open some presents." His attempt to lighten the mood worked. We all laughed as the boys grabbed their brightly wrapped boxes from the corner and dropped them at Gail's feet with a thud. I just hoped there wasn't anything breakable inside.

Monday morning another emergency call came in from Jasmine. I decided to skip lunch and slip her in. I was worried that all my therapy had been undone, but when I saw her, she looked fine. I guessed she was probably sore from all the running around on the weekend. She had barely settled down on the treatment table with a heating pad when the receptionist handed me a message. I stared at it, feeling my face grow cold.

"Jasmine." I removed the heating pad.

"Has it been five minutes already?" She looked up. "Are you OK? You look pale."

"Jasmine," I hesitated, then said as delicately as I could, "there's been an accident and you need to go home."

"An accident?" She gingerly sat up. "What happened?"

"They didn't say," I replied deadpan, not liking the idea of lying to her but not sure how she'd react. "Just that it's serious. I'll call you a cab."

"No, I can drive."

"Maybe it's best if I go with you."

"That would be nice." She gave me a tiny smile.

As she changed, I pawned my afternoon patients off on my co-workers, promising to make it up to them. I walked with Jasmine to the underground parking lot to a red Porsche.

She seemed calm. But I was afraid that once her mind started imagining the possibilities, her concentration would go. After some arguing she agreed to let me drive. I was glad she didn't ask me for any details.

On the way she played with the radio, changing stations every few seconds. I noticed fresh cuts on her hands. Also, her ring had lost its opal. She really should have worn those gardening gloves, I thought, no matter who'd given them to her.

When we got there, the police and ambulance were still in the driveway.

"She can't be hurt that bad if they haven't whisked her away," Jasmine said conversationally as I parked the car on the road. She got out before I could ask who she was talking about. I shut off the engine, struggled to pull the key out and hurried to follow her.

Red-eyed, her mother ran out of the front door and down the few steps to throw her arms around Jasmine's neck as she cried, "I told him not to go. But he wouldn't listen. That man would never act his age." She broke off with a loud sob.

"What?" Jasmine stepped away from her mother.

"Nora's crate arrived this morning while she was out. Thank God the boys weren't here. Your father opened it up and took her dirt bike out—just to test it he said."

"Daddy?" Jasmine's voice quivered.

Her mother loosened her grip, then with hands on her daughter's shoulder, she said, "He was happy biking along the road, but when he got to the top of the hill, he cut through the woods. I called for him to stop, but he couldn't hear me. He went off the trail and down that dreadful cliff!" She wrapped her arms around Jasmine's neck again as she sobbed silently. Jasmine stood silent, her eyes unfocused.

"Jasmine!" Nora ran out of the house towards them.

Jasmine's eyes narrowed with anger. "How..."

"Jasmine!" Nora reached them and embraced them both. "Oh Jasmine. Dad..."

Jasmine shoved both away and ran towards the ambulance attendants as they brought a stretcher out from behind the house.

"Daddy, no!" she screamed as she tore at the body bag. The attendants restrained her until we were able to drag her into the house.

A half hour later Gail came into the living room to join Nora and me.

"The paramedics gave her a sedative," Gail said, collapsing into the sofa with a heartbreaking sigh. Nora poured her a cup of coffee, added a touch of cream and a spoonful of honey and put it in her hands.

"Gail, I'm so sorry about your husband," I said. She nodded. Not knowing what else to say, I took a sip from my cup. The odd coffee and honey combination was pleasantly soothing. I turned to Nora. "And I'm sorry about your uncle."

"My—who?" Nora straightened from her slumped position, wiping at her raw nose and eyes with a tissue.

"Mark, your uh, uncle." Even as I spoke I knew that I'd put my foot in my mouth.

"He's my father. *Was* my father. Why would you think he was my uncle?"

"Jasmine said that you two were cousins..." Why did I keep talking? I knew from her reaction that I'd made a terrible mistake.

"Damn," Gail whispered, then turned to Nora. "We've had so many arguments over the years. She thinks that we love you more because you've given us grandchildren. And that we're prouder of you because you're a lawyer and she's a secretary at a temp agency." She turned to me. "Jasmine refuses to believe that we could love both our daughters equally." She gulped her coffee as though fighting to gather strength.

Gail rubbed her temples and added, "I'm sorry, I thought she was over all her childhood jealousy. Nora, she seemed OK for the last while. Oh, this is just too much now. Please excuse me." She put down her cup and left, looking suddenly old and frail.

"I'm so sorry," I offered lamely.

Nora sipped her coffee, then said, "I've always known how she feels about me. It's not like she ever tried to hide it. I mean with Mom's birthday this week, the boys and I had planned on coming here tomorrow and then spending the week. If I hadn't called and talked to dad... he thought I knew about the change of plans. I knew she wasn't happy when I told her three weeks ago that we were moving back home, but I never thought she'd try to keep us from the party." She slumped into her chair and stared at her cup.

After another useless apology, I left the troubled, silent household.

Two police officers stood near their cruiser in the driveway, the male officer talking on his cell. As I came down the steps, I overheard snippets of the conversation. I moved closer.

"Looks like some kids were building a fort or something in the area." He paused. "Yeah, they'd built up a wall of rocks, about 30 centimetres high, but the way it crossed the actual path made it seem like the path veered off. Guess the guy was coming down too fast on his bike and didn't have time to react. He rode right off the edge." Another pause. "Okay, we'll see you back at the station." He hung up and said to his partner, "Such a senseless accident."

"I know," she said. "It's lucky no one else went over the edge." They stopped talking when they noticed I had stepped closer.

My head spun. Nausea fought to close my throat. Jasmine's repeated back injuries started three weeks ago, the same time that she'd found out Nora was moving back home. Three weeks of scratches and bruises on impeccably manicured hands.

On some level, I still liked her. But how could I reconcile the happy, generous person I'd come to know with the bitter, angry one I'd seen at the party? And today...

She really should have worn the work gloves her sister had given her to protect her hands. And her jewellery.

Through the nausea, I managed to say to the officers, "If you take a closer look at the area, you might find an opal stone among those rocks."

Madona Skaff is the author of several mystery and science fiction short stories. She also writes the Naya Investigates series about a young woman recently disabled by multiple sclerosis, who turns sleuth to solve crimes. Her recent novel Shifting Trust is a near-future SF Thriller.

CRAZY ABOUT HIM

16

RUBY URLOCKER

got into the Royal when I was doing better. I had lost a few pounds. My skin looked healthy, probably from all the hot water and tea I was drinking. I knew something about myself, back then. I knew how to look good. I knew how to shower every day and wear fresh clothes that made me feel like my own character starring in some romantic movie. Sure, I didn't know myself as well as I had years before. But I was recovering.

I was lucky to get into the Schizophrenia Recovery Program. It wasn't a regular inpatient unit like they had in the main building. This was a little offshoot building right next to the regular Royal. Now, let me explain, for those who don't know. The Royal is a mental hospital in Ottawa, supposedly the best in Canada. The Royal, to me, would become an oasis where everything was polished and clean, I could paint and exercise and people in their twenties were all on disability, expecting to move into little apartments with rent subsidies and sometimes hoping to get part-time jobs. We generally didn't *talk* about schizophrenia, or at least the worst of it. We were in a recovery unit and focused on rebuilding our lives. There were two long hallways with a nurses' station in the middle. I'd pass the nurses' station when I got my steps in walking the hallways, back and forth again and again. Whenever I passed the station, I felt like the nurses could read my mind.

The unit was rather quaint with nurses answering your questions and actually sharing things about themselves like normal people. They treated us like we were normal, made jokes and asked us questions. There was nothing too hospital-like about the place. It was just a slightly medicalized large house where we were served free meals and got to come and go as we pleased. The lack of formality counted for a lot.

I had a lot of mental health issues, though they were mostly in remission. My medication didn't cause too many side effects. The keto diet was helping to reduce my anxiety and delusions. I didn't feel emotion deeply because the medication worked its magic to zap the happy chemicals, but I wasn't a zombie. I was going for jogs every morning and generally feeling OK.

The morning of my admission, they welcomed me into my own room. It had big windows, yellow walls and a bed without any sheets on it yet. A nurse came and asked me a bunch of questions—whether I'd ever been suicidal. I had. Whether I was hallucinating. I wasn't. Whether I had anxiety. I did. The whole process was like an in-depth interview that took 45 minutes. After the nurse was finished, I just sat, then lay down, on my cold, blue rubber mattress and reflected on life. I thought about how far I'd come from the days of being a paranoid schizophrenic losing jobs, breaking relationships and setting things on fire. I didn't feel like I'd won in a huge way, but I was past acting inappropriately to friends and colleagues due to my judgment being off or due to occasional paranoia about the world being run by evil people plotting to kill me.

I went into the kitchen. There were about seven black wooden tables with two to four plastic chairs at each one, big windows looking onto a walkway and an ill-used, dying vegetable garden. There were two watering cans lying around as if someone had attempted to get the garden together but then stopped. There was one man sitting at the furthest table away, his leg moving up and down nervously while he just sat there and stared into space.

The people on this unit were supposed to be largely stable, focusing on wellness elements of their lives after schizophrenia. There were groups, like art and therapy groups and stuff like that. After the first few days settling in, I was allowed to go for my morning runs, but I had to sign in and out. Curfew was every night at nine. So we had to be back on the unit by that time, or else just notify the staff we were going to be late.

I got to know the names of some of the other people staying there. I interacted with a few of them. Then there was Josh. One day when my dad was dropping me off at the hospital after a visit to his place, he asked if I knew the young man standing, smoking outside. "He looks like a surfer," he said.

I smiled at the description. Josh often lingered in the background of the kitchen-living room, keeping to himself, not talking when it was crowded. He did look athletic and was dressed in clothes that looked like what a rich person could afford. During the first interaction I had with him, he commented on the varsity jacket I'd gotten at Bayshore Mall after a long bus ride. I was still nervous about the bus turning around in the depot on its way there, but I'd gone because I wanted new clothes to help me feel like myself.

There was this one morning group called *I'm Recovering,* the only one that was mandatory. We talked about coping skills and planned for emergencies when symptoms were on the rise. The recreational therapist who ran it wore snappy yoga clothes and had a hard smile. Josh got switched to being in my *I'm Recovering* group due to new admissions coming. He was fun in the answers he gave. Even goofy. He said his favourite book was *1948.* He meant *1984* but was being silly. He said in one answer to a question, "I like expressing."

"Expressing? Expressing what?" asked the group leader.

"Myself."

He was spontaneous and kind of strange.

I hadn't thought about any young men in quite some time. René, my ex-boyfriend from high school, and everything that had happened there both terrified and excited me. I've had occasional entanglements with young men since, but they never led to anything. René had been my one and only.

I looked quickly around the kitchen, where everyone was eating lunch one day, to see who was there. Josh had his hood up and was sitting as though he were protective of his food. He seemed fragile and dangerous at the same time. His blue eyes looked complex. If René was anyone in this unit, he would be Josh, I told myself. There was a bit of resemblance.

Josh generally didn't come to many of the groups and stayed in his room most of the time. But I thought I saw him watching me when he was around, and I started to feel...a small spark.

It was late evening when I was in the kitchen again. I tried to tell myself I wasn't looking for Josh, but there he was all the same. I had bought some dried coconut pieces that came in a bag from the Shoppers at Westgate where everyone went to splurge on candy. Westgate was a small mall of sorts; half the stores were dead. There was a crappy Thai place and a restaurant that was the life of the party and a magnet for everyone living nearby, a fifties-style diner called Rockin' Johnny's. I'd bought the coconut pieces on impulse and afterwards couldn't figure out why, especially because they weren't keto. They were dry and I wasn't loving them.

Josh's eyes perked up, finally, when he saw me, and he looked curious.

"Whatcha eating?"

"Coconut pieces," I said. "You can have some. They're not very good."

He came over to me. It felt right to give him food. He took a piece. "Damn," he said. "I think this is delicious."

I gave him another piece.

Right then, I wondered if the nurses were watching me from their station and if I was doing anything taboo. Maybe we weren't supposed to share food. The station had such a presence about it, it was hard not to think the nurses were all scanning my mind.

For the first time, I looked Josh over completely. He was in a thin red shirt without sleeves, had on what looked like very expensive dressy pants with a belt and was thin enough to even be *too* thin. He had bleached blond hair just starting to grow past his chin. He was good looking. And he had a kind of wanting darkness in his eyes that I had not seen in a young man since René. He looked like he was starving.

I gave him the whole bag, holding it out on a whim.

"You mean it's all for me?" he asked.

"Yeah," I said. "It's all for you."

He grabbed the pack and shoved several coconut pieces into his mouth. "Thank you," he said.

I thought he really was starving, judging by his behaviour. A few days later I walked back to the Shoppers and bought some unhealthy snacks for him. A few chocolate bars. Some chips. I was glad everything with my debit card still worked. An older man at another hospital had told me there were some sketchy things going on with that particular bank.

Whenever I ate in the kitchen then, that day, and the days after, Josh's eyes would follow me. Our interactions were short, and polite, but they made me feel warm on the inside. I recall telling him one evening in the kitchen that I liked his voice.

His voice was a memorable deep voice with sort of...ripples? You could recognize his voice from far away. It was a signature thing about him.

"Thanks," he said. "I always feel like it's too raw."

We stood there for a little while. "Lucy, how are you?" he asked, eyes suddenly open to me.

"I'm good," I said. "How are you?"

"Could be doing better." Then, abruptly, he left. It seemed like he was running away from something, or that could've just been my imagination.

A few more days passed. I met with the doctor and told her everything was fine, thank you. Not sure if I wanted to get into anything personal. I couldn't tell her about Josh. I knew they didn't like us dating each other in a recovery environment. Not that we were dating or anything close to that, but my heart was starting to stir for him. I looked at him eating his pierogies in the cafeteria one day. *He's René,* something in my awareness said.

"What?" I said aloud.

My vision snapped. For a moment everything was blurry, out of focus. Like the world wasn't the same.

I looked at Josh closely. He *was* the same height as René, more or less. Skinnier, but René could've lost weight. And his hair, he'd told me it was dirty blond in its natural form. Just like René's.

Visions of René overtook me that night, especially those when everything was solid and good between us that one spring. It could be that René wants to do things over with me, I thought. That he knew I'd be at the Royal. That Josh is going to just turn into René and show up like that all of a sudden. A surprise.

Josh's face looked different. By all standards, he wasn't René. But something in me made me think that he was. Maybe it was the way his eyes met mine, with a kind of softness or silent regard for me.

I was sitting on the living room couch watching TV when Josh came in. His eyes looked slightly bloodshot, and he lingered in a tired way. "I went over to Bowman's," he said, referring to the restaurant across the street. "I am super drunk right now. Don't tell Doctor Wood."

I smiled at him. "OK."

He sat down at the other end of the couch and just started opening up. "Things have been kind of crap between my parents. They're fighting more and more. And the depression always hits worse in the summer for some reason, even though it should be in the winter. Then there's me not wanting to get a job. I just...don't want to. And that makes me worry about my future and all."

"Well, one thing at a time. We're all here to focus on our health, right?" I said.

"Yeah..." he said, slowly. Then he nodded. "That's a good point. You're always reassuring to talk to. You know that?"

He looked at me, and in his eyes, I felt love blooming. All at once I wanted to be near him to focus on whatever he said, to focus on his face. He had almost this light around him. Like an aura.

"There's this small party happening. Me and a few of my buddies are going to this abandoned house. Is there any chance you'd take me up on that?" His eyes bore into me, deep and solemn and perceptive. It struck me that Josh was a very intelligent person.

I thought about it. "Will there be, like, drinking and stuff?"

"Yeah, probably."

I was about to say no when I looked at the side profile of his face and saw his slightly pale skin. I could tell his cut, triangular nose was just like René's, now that I was looking at it up close. He was acting as a whole other person, complete with mannerisms and behaviour and everything, but I felt more sure of the fact he was René in complete disguise. He was almost asking me out. He was asking me out in a roundabout way. I had to say yes. Maybe it could be an adventure. Maybe once we were at the party...we could have some real alone time. Maybe he was looking at me so much because he liked me *that way.*

"Ok," I said.

"Really? You'll come?" His face lit up with hope. It was so easy to make him happy. "I didn't think you'd wanna say yes to that. What we're going to do is... just tell your doctor that you're staying over at your parents'. And I'll tell Doctor Wood that I'm staying at a friend's. That way they won't have to know we're at the abandoned house together."

A queasy, wrong feeling overtook me. I wasn't usually someone who lied.

"It means a lot to me that you'll come," he said. "Thanks a ton. It's kind of awkward these days with some of my friends, and...I'd feel better if you were there, to be honest."

I felt really flattered. I felt *close* to Josh/René. We sat for a little while longer in silence, and I felt myself imagine that we could communicate with our minds. I kept whispering, telepathically, *I love you. I love you, Josh.* He looked at me again—as if he could hear my thoughts. He gave a whistle. "You're quite the looker," he said. "D'ya know that?"

I went to bed that night feeling excited. Maybe too excited. René was falling in love with me all over again. This was going to be our second chance. His eyes, the more I looked at them, were exactly like René's. René's had been light brown. But he could easily be wearing contacts. I felt my intuition grow stronger as I lay awake that night. I longed to touch him, to hold him. I'd been wanting to since we broke up nine years ago when I'd first gotten sick, slapped him in my desperation and then broke down in a way he couldn't carry. My thoughts went back to that dark place and all the negativity I'd swamped him with, all the times I asked for more and more love and didn't give enough back. I'd broken him. But I had always dreamed of some new, happy moment when he would come back.

I tried to get some sleep but couldn't. I kept replaying all my moments with Josh, all our short but sweet interactions. He was someone who liked to be helped. He'd asked me for money several times, and I'd always given in. He was so thankful, telling me I'd saved him. He'd looked me right in the eye to thank me. He was a proper gentleman.

I finally fell asleep at 2 a.m. I slept in and missed morning huddle and the first group in the morning. There was a knock at my door. "Hey," said Josh's deep voice. "Can I come in?"

I sat up and opened the door. "Hi Lucy," he said. "The party's gonna start at six. It's a long walk there, but we can make it on foot."

His face looked tired, but it brightened again. "We're gonna have so much fun. I'll introduce you to all my friends, OK?"

"OK," I said. And my heart lifted.

We started walking at 5:15. The days were long, and I only needed a light jacket. I wore my varsity jacket. The sun felt warm, and the trees fluttered their leaves in the breeze. I felt happier than I'd been in a long time.

"You don't talk much," Josh said.

"Oh," I said.

He laughed. "Guess that means I have permission to talk about myself."

"I like it when you talk about yourself."

"I like it when I talk about myself, too," he said cheekily. "Well, what else can I tell you? I have two sisters." *Oh my God,* I thought. *Just like René.* "I got schizophrenia first when I was 17. I tried to kill myself. That was a hard year. Now I just do minor things like...cut myself or burn myself with a cigarette. I have one mark here." He showed me the back of his hand. I reached out and touched the spot tenderly. He didn't protest, and holding his hand was an amazing little shock to my system.

"I did really well in school," he continued. "Got excellent grades. If I could be anything, I'd be a scientist. I want to try to find the cure for cancer."

I listened. The walk didn't feel long with him there, and his skin kind of shone in the light. I felt privileged that he was telling all these things to me. He had a directness to him, an honesty, even though he told lies to others. I kept glancing at his face, and then his eyes would meet mine. There was an intimacy there.

But slowly, I had this uncomfortable feeling of nervousness in my stomach. Something wasn't right. Something in reality felt altered, as if the movie was supposed to play out one way, but someone was messing with it. I felt a pressure in my side, like a warning. When we reached the house, I gasped. It was truly an abandoned house, a white one with boarded-up windows and a door slathered with uneven red paint. I felt tense as we went to the side of the house and slipped in through the side door. There was loud electronic music playing. The song *Latch,* by Disclosure. An oldie. The inside of the house was even less inviting with a massive hole in the wooden floor-boards and bricks lying around. Josh's several friends were in the white kitchen with their shoes on, and there was dirt all over the uneven flooring. There was an unplugged fridge. I opened it up and saw cans of paint in it. There were spray-painted smiley faces in dark green randomly around. One was inside the fridge, on the back, another on the left wall of the kitchen. Then there was one on the staircase leading into the basement. I wondered if they were gang symbols for something. *We really shouldn't be here.*

Maybe this was all a setup. It was a fake house. Josh's friends were hired actors. Maybe this house was covering up something really, really bad, and Josh needed my help with facing the dangers. For a moment, I was even afraid of Josh. Maybe he was a criminal. Maybe this was a makeshift house for the darkest of deeds.

But Josh was standing close to me, closer than he ever had. I'd been so alone since getting my first psychotic episode. Now here, René was returned to me, the past back in a different form.

Josh's other friends were drinking and passing around a joint. I didn't want to think about the implications there. Josh introduced me to them all, and I quickly forgot their names. One had glasses that made his eyes look big and a hoodie. One of them was so young, he still had braces. There was something weird with age going on.

"How old are you, Josh?" I asked.

"I'm 21," he said.

I was 26. It made me feel gigantic. I felt almost maternal towards him, but then I figured he could lie about his age and make himself look younger if he was really René. Maybe people in this society did that all the time. Plus, him being younger was kind of cute. A slow song, *Perfect* by Ed Sheeran, started to play. Josh very lightly took my hand. I wanted to ask him what he was doing. But I knew. We started slow-dancing in the middle of the badly half-renovated kitchen. I felt his smooth arms along my waist and along my back, and I couldn't have asked for a sweeter moment. Maybe this was the summer I'd come alive.

One of Josh's friends returned from exploring the basement. "Guys!" he said. He seemed really excited. "You'll never guess what! There's like $800 down there in fives and twenties stuffed into the pillows of some old bed. And there's a jagged knife and some...well, you'll see for yourself." He held out square, thin, happy cartoon-pineapple bags in his hands. They were drugs of some kind, that I knew.

The music stopped, as if it, too, were surprised. "Josh," the friend said quickly. "You're the only one with a backpack. Lemme put that stuff in."

"No way. They're gonna inspect my bag when I get back to the Royal."

"Well, what are we supposed to do?"

"We could take the stuff now, then store the money in our pockets," said Josh. I was taken aback by his easiness with substances, not for the first time. "As for the knife, I think we should leave it here."

"OK," said the friend whose name came to me—Clifford. He was tanned with long black hair.

The door opened. Two middle-aged men walked in. "You!" The shorter of the two shouted with a threatening look. The second, taller man assessed the supplies of theirs we had found. "It's ours," he said. His voice was stern and emotionless. He had one tattoo of a mermaid on his chest, partially visible from under his grey, too-small sweater. He wore tattered jeans and a big belt, was overweight and had unwashed, scraggly hair. The shorter man was bald and less over-weight. When he checked me out, his eyes made me fill rigid with fear like a little kid in trouble.

There was a zip, like lightning, through my mind. My fears turned to a severe feeling of a drop in my stomach. "We're sorry," I said. "We didn't mean to. We'll give it right back."

"Princess, we don't care if you'll give it right back. You still took our stuff. This is our place. You kids should mind your own business."

The way these two men looked at me, it was like they knew about me and Josh—like they were hired from some mega organization that had built files on me for years, knowing where I was, who I loved. This was not the first time I'd thought like this. Maybe this was the truth, and it had been censored by my medication.

The bald man came forward in big, heavy boots that had no shoe-strings and were open, revealing hairy ankles.

Scrambling, Josh picked up the knife we had found, but in an instant, before the bald man could do anything, I grabbed the knife. They were here to kidnap him, maybe take him to a prison to do experiments...

The knife slid from Josh's hand easily, like butter. I tried to hold it tightly, but my hands were shaking. "Stay away from him!" I cried out as I pointed the knife at the bald man.

Though short, the bald man seemed to loom in front of René—my René—with the edge of true menace. The look in his eye spoke of bad haunting nights and of pure evil that will control an individual, making them into something they're not.

Then the man reached out an arm and roughly grabbed Josh's shoulder. I swung the knife at the man and stabbed him. Right in the chest.

He groaned and his eyes looked manic and filled with pain.

I stabbed him in the shoulder, then in the chest again.

"Lucy! What are you doing!" Josh cried.

But I was caught in a hypnotic moment where I had to expend all of my strength. My senses went into overdrive. I'd wronged René. I'd emotionally harmed him in a way that no words could repair, and I had to go back in time and save him now.

The taller man reached for a phone in his pocket and tapped something before he ran away from the scene. The wound in the bald man's chest was flowing with blood, soaking his shirt. I stabbed again, this time in the stomach, and the cut went so deep, I swear the knife touched bone.

Then he fell to the ground, his eyes looking sleepy and dull, all their life fading away.

Josh swore. "Lucy, what did you do?" I saw anger in his eyes, which were once so beautiful. "Lucy, holy...why did you literally kill the guy?"

I felt shock. I felt numb, like passing out. "He was going to hurt you," I said.

"Jeez," he said.

Josh's friends looked guiltily at one another. "What should we do?" asked Clifford.

"Let's just get outta here," said Josh. "Cliff, can we stay at your place?"

"At my place? No! My folks are gonna be there."

"We can't go back to the Royal until tomorrow morning. We're gonna have to sleep here," said Josh.

I looked at the bald man's body. "I'll call my dad," I said lamely. "I'll tell him what happened."

"Are you an idiot?" Josh said to me.

"I'd rather just tell him."

"You're not going to frickin' tell anyone. You'll drag me and all of us into it, too. We'll all suffer legal consequences. No, we're spending the night here. Then we leave at two different times tomorrow. And we tell no one. No one."

The innocence I had seen in Josh was now nowhere to be found. I felt tears form and tried to hide them. *Where are you now, René?* I felt like I was lost in a dark tunnel. He had been the light, but he was fading away. I wanted to call him back.

Josh's friends were around the dead body looking at it, then stepping back, their mouths open. The young kid with braces looked at me with real horror in his eyes.

There were sirens outside.

Oh no.

The taller man must've called the cops in an attempt to save his friend.

Josh came really close to me and spat in my face. "Killer," he said.

He fled with his friends out the back door. The front door opened and police came in; I put my hands up to my face and felt like screaming. Josh had left me here. With my guilt. I tried to save him from something invisible, a predator that stalks around my mind going in circles, toying with my imagination. I faced the police as tears streamed down my face, and I confessed everything while they shone a flashlight on me. I needed someone to forgive me. I needed

Josh to take me in his arms and let me cry on his shoulder, but as they put the handcuffs on my wrists, all I felt was cold hard metal around me.

Looking back, I know it was my desire for romantic love that was the most dangerous, toxic thing to me. My very essence, what is natural to me in my mind and personality, is dangerous.

My dad and my lawyer convinced me to plead insanity. I know I was, literally, insane. I can never live in conditions as healthy as the Royal again because of where the freedom of my own mind took me. I'm now in an institution, on heavier meds, probably permanently. I've gained a lot of weight.

Sometimes I still wake up happy and light, feeling that kernel of intuition that René loved me. Maybe he still does. I know it's irrational, probably just a coping mechanism. Yet, I still think I will live to see the day René comes back. It feels so real. Why would I ever let go of that?

Ruby Urlocker has been a creative spirit since she was a young child: drawing, writing, singing and more. In adulthood she has great struggles with mental health issues but is still creative to this day.

IMOGEN ST. PIERRE IS DEAD

17

KATHY MACLELLAN

mogen St. Pierre is dead. I can't stop thinking about that terrible night. But Imogen is dead.

I first met Imogen at Ogilvy's, the elegant department store, the tallest building on Rideau Street. I was on my way up to the third-floor dressmaking room with a pattern and fabric I'd just purchased on the ground floor. When the immaculately dressed, white-gloved elevator operator opened the grilled door on the second floor, I stepped out, thinking we'd arrived at the third, and collided with Imogen.

"Oh, excuse me," she said. "I'm so sorry."

"Not at all," I said. "I should have looked before I leapt. Too busy gawking at this new pattern."

"A poodle skirt! So divine," she said. "We have a number of them in ready-to-wear, with simply fab appliqués—funny sayings, cars, cartoon characters, martini glasses, so cute!"

"No pink poodles on a silver leash?"

"Pink poodles," she laughed, "very big in 1954, but that was last year. Would you like to see what's ahead for 1956?"

In her circle skirt, perfectly accessorized with a button-down blouse, wide belt, saddle shoes and a chiffon scarf around her neck, she was the epitome of class and style. Everything I wished I could be. I looked at the gold lamé bag tucked under her arm and then at my watch: 10:00 a.m. "Aren't you about to take your morning break?"

Her tinkling laugh struck just the right balance of elegance and friendliness. "Customer service is paramount at Ogilvy's. Come on in and have a look."

She never did take that morning break. By lunchtime, my armload of tartan boxes decorated with the famous Ogilvy hunting tartan contained, among other things, a poodle skirt, two coordinating polka-dot tops, ballet flats and an adorable pair of white socks with poodle appliqués.

"All ready for a sock hop," Imogen had joked when she rang up my purchases. Then she had offered me her employee discount.

I'm Cornelia Ahearn. I live in a four-storey mansion overlooking the Ottawa River a few miles east of the city. My father drinks and rages, but he's never yet cut off my clothing allowance even though I can well afford to pay full price.

I appreciated Imogen's offer of a discount and her service so much that I treated her to lunch at the Chateau Laurier Hotel. In the weeks and months that followed, Imogen and I went to a sock hop, a movie, dinners, parties and concerts. She worked part time at Ogilvy's to pay her way through nursing school. She had been raised by her Aunt Moira, who had recently died. Imogen cared for her aunt for years, and the nurses who helped her at the end inspired her to become a nurse. We were both 21 and ready to take on the world, but opportunities for young women were few and far between. My father's wealth gave me an expectation of a comfortable life, but Imogen had to make her own way in the world. So, it was nursing school for her and society events for me. Sometimes I wondered which of us had the more tedious existence. In any case, with her sense of style and my money, we never lacked the right shade of lipstick to pair with the latest fashion craze or the latest "it" place to go.

My brother, Vincent, sometimes accompanied us in the evenings. Vincent was tall and athletic, with expensive suits expertly tailored to show off his broad shoulders and slim waist. Imogen had an eye for

Vincent, but he was more inclined to play the field. One night the three of us borrowed Father's Chevrolet Bel Air and set out for the bar in the basement of the Standish Hall Hotel in Hull. It was an icy Tuesday night. The weather was terrible. The streets were empty except for a huge bus with a Duke Ellington sign over the windshield parked in front of the hotel. We entered the Standish, went downstairs, and sure enough, it was the Duke Ellington band. They were on tour and played the Standish as part of a long-standing agreement with the owner. There were maybe 20 of us there, but the band played song after song.

Vincent and Imogen made a lovely couple on the dance floor, but as I sipped my rum and Coke, my eyes were drawn to another gentleman, tall and blond in a stylish, grey, three-piece suit, who approached and asked me to dance. I floated in his arms as he whirled me gracefully around that beautiful art deco hall. We stopped and chatted with band members between songs. He could talk to anyone and make them feel respected, valued and interesting.

He was Clifford Ogilvy, heir to the Ogilvy fortune, a grandnephew of Charles Ogilvy, who had founded the great department store in a tiny Rideau Street shop in 1887. We liked Clifford from the beginning, and soon we went everywhere together—Clifford, Imogen, Vincent and I. We laughed and danced under clear, starry skies, blind to the rumbling storm clouds on the horizon.

My father approved of Clifford, which didn't surprise me. He was well spoken, well dressed and well connected. He ran Ogilvy's with such fairness and generosity that most of the employees, including Imogen, practically hero-worshipped him, and I found myself falling for him too. My heart was over the moon when, on Christmas Eve of 1955, Clifford proposed, and I accepted. He presented me with a blue sapphire ring encircled with tiny diamonds that glowed and sparkled in the candlelight.

Father was thrilled. He'd recently quarrelled with Vincent for having refused to marry a certain society debutante. Father rewrote his will, making Clifford and me his sole heirs.

We booked a secret weekend away at Montebello to celebrate.

Clifford and I had both grown up enjoying family dinners and ski weekends at Chateau Montebello. The exclusive, luxurious resort, operated by the Seigniory Club, was private and for members only—the perfect place to mark our engagement.

We'd never have been able to sneak away without help from Vincent and Imogen. They were to be the best man and maid of honour at the wedding, and I couldn't have been happier. Vincent didn't know the terms of the new will, and I saw no need to mention it.

A month later certain telltale symptoms encouraged me to think that I had some exciting but unnerving news for Clifford. We'd planned a night out with Vincent and Imogen, although Vincent had become mysteriously absent of late and had cancelled on us at the last minute. I doubted he'd found out about the will. I suspected a new romance and I hoped Imogen wouldn't be too disappointed. We were to meet at my place for a drink before going to a musical at the Capitol Theatre.

I had taken special care to look my best that night. I'd had my hair done, bought a new dress and accessorized it with my mother's long rope of pearls. The doorbell rang as I carefully applied my new lipstick. Clifford and Imogen arrived together. I could hear them hanging their coats in the cloakroom under the stairs as I came down. I expected to meet them in the parlour, but they weren't there. I circled the ground floor and didn't find them in my father's study, the dining room, the kitchen or the living room. I checked the empty parlour again. A suspicious giggle prompted me to open the cloak-room doors, and there they were. Cheeks flushed, hair mussed, in each other's arms. I closed the door and tossed the ring over my shoulder as I went back upstairs. I ignored all entreaties and swore I'd never speak to either of them again.

The engagement was off, and my goose was cooked. My momentous news would begin to show in a few months. I'd be unmarried, caught out, unable to hide my shame. I couldn't face my father, who wasn't above violent rages when things didn't go his way. I couldn't even confide in Vincent. I couldn't bear to hear his disapproval, his taunts, his male superiority. What could I do?

I approached a convent a few miles downriver from my house: the Roman Catholic, francophone Villa St-Louis in Orleans. Unfortunately, they weren't sure I was a suitable candidate. Did I speak French? No. Was I a Catholic? No. Was I in fact, the raised eyebrows implied, nothing but a spoiled rich girl who'd never done an honest day's work in her life, totally unprepared for the rigours of convent life? I hadn't even mentioned my compromising situation.

I threw myself on their mercy. I would work hard, I promised, to atone for my sins, without mentioning any specific sin. I would learn French. I would renounce Presbyterianism and take whatever steps were necessary to become a Roman Catholic. They weren't convinced. I had to come up with something dramatic and convincing, at least for the short term.

"I will endow you with all my worldly goods," I said, fingers crossed behind my back. "My father has made me the sole beneficiary of his will and his considerable fortune. I will humbly leave everything to you, if you accept me into your community."

The good sisters seemed to perk up at that. Skeptical frowns turned upside down. They decided we could see how things worked out for a few months, a kind of probation. That suited me.

I moved in that very day. No need to go home and pack. I would be given novitiate clothing and minimal toiletries but was not encouraged to think of owning anything else. Poverty, chastity and obedience were the order of the day. I didn't even have to face my father. I asked for pen and paper and wrote him a letter.

My father, of course, hit the roof. He phoned the convent. They let him speak to me, but I hung up on his outraged tirades and refused to come to the phone again. He showed up at the convent gates, drunk and raging. He was going to destroy the will that he made in my favour and leave everything to Vincent.

I didn't care. I just wanted to hide from the world and all the people that betrayed me. I didn't stay in bed, though. I got up every morning, went to Mass, prayed and sang with the nuns, performed my chores and learned my catechism. I paid lip service to it all. But all I ever thought about was revenge. I found poison ivy in the garden, itching powder recipes in the library and, near the river, the best stones to throw through a window. In the kitchen I learned how to sharpen knives.

The convent trained young women in many areas, including housekeeping, gardening, nursing and hospitality. We practiced hospitality when people made retreats at the convent, living with us for days and weeks at a time.

In the second week of May 1956, a group of student nurses was getting ready for a two-week retreat at the villa. I was on my hands and knees scrubbing the kitchen floor and didn't bother to look up when they came in on a tour of the building. They seemed very young, fresh out of high school, but one slightly older woman who seemed to be in charge laughed at something, and my blood ran cold. Imogen St. Pierre.

I managed to avoid her the rest of the day and most of the next one, but that evening she caught up with me as we left the dining room.

"Cornelia, can we talk?" she asked.

"I have nothing to say to you, Imogen."

"I just wanted to say that I'm sorry."

I marched on. "Spare me."

She caught up and stepped into my path, beaming. "Clifford said I took his breath away."

I stopped. "He said that to me," I said, shaking out the voluminous robe that hid my shame. I brushed her aside and kept walking. "I don't need to hear it again."

"Please, Cornelia. Be happy for us." She put her hand on my arm. I shook it off, but not before I noticed the ring on the third finger of her left hand. A blue sapphire, encircled with tiny diamonds.

"You're married?"

"I didn't plan to work after the wedding, of course, but I got my nursing certificate, and they desperately needed another supervisor on this retreat, so I agreed to come along."

"You're married?"

"We didn't want to embarrass you with a big society wedding, so we eloped. I'm Mrs. Clifford Ogilvy now." She chuckled. "The other girls in ready-to-wear couldn't believe it."

She laughed again; the irritating, tinkly sound sent hackles up my spine.

"Go away, Imogen, and never speak to me again. I don't want to see you, hear you or think about you. Father, Vincent, Clifford, you. None of you exist, so leave me alone."

But she did exist. I couldn't miss her going up and down the stairs and in and out of rooms with her gaggle of girls making plans, gossiping and giggling. I did my best to erase her from my mind. In the end, the only way I could do that, the only way to ease the pain, was to think dark thoughts.

On Tuesday, May 15, I went to bed early, right after compline, the last required prayers of the day. As usual, I tossed and turned, exhausted from the bitter scenarios that kept me up night after night. Also as usual, I listened to the roar of airplanes overhead. We were in a cold war against Russia and, as my brother Vincent had often liked to point out, the nearby Rockcliffe air force station housed some of the most sophisticated flying machines in the Royal Canadian Air Force arsenal, including CF-100 "Canuck" Mark V interceptor jet fighters. The planes were fully armed with rockets and machine guns, he loved to say.

That night, a deafening boom threw me from my bed. I'll never forget the terror, the panic or the blistering heat. Splinters of glass and fiery embers rained in through my shattered window, igniting hot, crackling fires all around me. I grabbed my robe and opened the door, only to be pushed back by thick black smoke that stung my eyes and seared my throat.

I held the edge of my robe over my nose and mouth and plunged into the hallway, following a group of elderly nuns who led the way to the third-storey fire escape. On the lower floor, fire blocked our exit, so we had to jump.

The three-storey brick building had 70 rooms, but only 35 of us were in residence at the time. Imogen's group of 16 student nurses had stayed downtown to see a play. Imogen hadn't accompanied them. She had a sniffle, poor baby, and had stayed with us.

Neighbours ran across farmers' fields to help. We knew them. Many were regular attendees at Mass in our chapel. Ray Rainville lived less than a mile from the villa. I watched him catch an old nun who leapt from the third floor just ahead of me. He said that Father Richard Ward, our chaplain, was blown 150-feet away by the blast. The priest died in the arms of Joseph Potvin, another neighbour.

A group of decrepit sisters with burns, blisters and broken bones huddled together in their nightclothes on the lawn outside the burning building. I joined them, and between what they said, neighbours' reports and what I later read, I eventually pieced together what had happened.

Two CF-100 fighters had been dispatched from the Uplands air base to investigate an intruder in Canadian airspace. It turned out to be an RCAF North Star cargo plane, travelling from Resolute Bay in the Arctic to St. Hubert near Montreal.

One CF-100 returned to base. At 10:17 p.m. the other one suddenly vanished from the radar screen. In less than a minute, it fell 33,000 feet at 700 miles per hour and plunged into our chapel. The deafening explosion sent debris and flames hundreds of feet into the air.

According to the news reports I read, it was the worst air disaster in Canadian military aviation history, and no one knew what caused it. There had been no sign of trouble, no distress signal, no use of ejector seats. Radio silence. One possibility was that a malfunction in the oxygen system caused the two men to lose consciousness.

The blast could be heard 15 miles away. It threw residents of nearby Hiawatha Park from their beds. It shattered 24 windows in St. Joseph School, a mile and a half away.

Within five minutes our roof had collapsed. I heard that two hours later the 40-foot chimney and a few steel girders, melted and warped by the blaze's heat, were all that was left. Stoked by aviation fuel and coal stored in the convent's basement, the explosion and fire destroyed our home, the Villa St-Louis.

Huddled on the ground, I gazed at the ambulances and neighbours who were gathering up the injured to take them to the Ottawa General Hospital where they would be cared for by Imogen's student nurses. But I wasn't injured. I refused to go to the hospital. I insisted on being taken home. Father gruffly accepted me, despite my now obvious condition. But I swore I would never again let anyone get the better of me.

Among the 35 residents of Villa St-Louis, 13 died—11 Grey Nuns, a lay-woman cook and Father Ward. The two young flying officers also died. And Imogen St. Pierre.

I was the last to get out alive, but Imogen was right behind me. She was in shock, so shaken that she barely felt me slip the sapphire ring off her finger as I helped her out onto the fire escape. We stood for a moment, arms wrapped around each other, gazing into the hell fire below. Then I pushed her into it.

"God has sent us this cross from the sky," said one nun, in a clipping I saved from the Ottawa Citizen. "It fell on our chapel. May His will be done."

Kathy MacLellan is a writer, actor and puppeteer who has criss-crossed Canada and the U.S. as a performer and co-director of Rag & Bone Puppet Theatre for many years. Writing credits include an ACTRA award, plays, puppet shows, dozens of CBC-TV episodes for shows such as Under the Umbrella Tree, Mr. Dressup and Theodore Tugboat, and her Miss Maple Mysteries podcast series.

NOT ALL POLAR BEARS ARE CREATED EQUAL

18

ELIZABETH HOSANG

"Happy Birthday!" Donna said, wrapping Andrea in a hug.

"Thanks," Andrea replied, releasing Donna and taking her coat. "Everyone's in the living room. The bar is on the kitchen counter, so help yourself."

"And where do presents go?" Donna asked, holding up a brightly wrapped box with a big yellow ribbon.

"You can put that in the kitchen for now, thanks," Andrea replied.

A chorus of greetings met Donna as she made her way through the Bells Corners townhouse, along with one growl. Alarmed, Andrea dashed into the kitchen where Bolt, her police dog, was standing guard in front of Donna.

"Bolt, heel," Andrea commanded. Instead, the dog sat, his eyes locked on Donna. Andrea grabbed the dog by his collar and yanked. "Bolt, heel!" she said again. The dog followed her away from the startled guest and out into the back yard.

"Sorry about that," Andrea said, returning to her guests. "I should have put Bolt in his kennel earlier."

"Not a problem," Donna said. "Is Bolt going to sniff us on the way out instead of having us blow into a breathalyser?"

"Of course not."

Three hours later most of the guests had waved goodbye. Donna and a few of Andrea's fellow officers with the Ottawa Police Service remained, lounging in the living room where they exchanged stories about stupid criminals.

"So, do we get to spend more time with your new partner, or is he banished to the doghouse for the rest of the night?" asked Jerry Swan.

"I suppose I can bring him back in," Andrea said.

"Sizing up your replacement?" Donna asked.

"No," Jerry replied amid chuckles. "I totally get why she wanted to transfer to the K9 unit."

"Yeah, she can put a muzzle on her partner when he gets annoying," Donna said.

"You know police dogs aren't trained to be cuddly, right?" Andrea said as she brought the German Shepherd, who was walking in lockstep with her, back inside.

"Hey there, Officer Bolt," Jerry said.

Bolt trotted straight over to the discarded boxes and wrapping paper, which had been piled haphazardly on the living room floor. He carried a box in his mouth and dropped it at Andrea's feet. He sat and looked up at her expectantly.

"Is he indicating?" Jerry asked.

"I think he is," Andrea said. She picked up the box and tossed it over to her former patrol partner. "Bury it in the papers again." Andrea bent down and held Bolt's face in her hand, keeping his focus on her. Once the box was buried, she stood up.

"Bolt, seek." The dog whipped around and dug through the papers, coming up with the same box. He walked over to Andrea, again dropping it at her feet.

Andrea picked up the box and looked at it. "Anyone know where this came from?"

Donna leaned over. "I think it's the one I used to wrap the vase I got you." She looked around at the cops staring at her. "I don't have drugs at my place! I'm a Crown attorney for crying out loud!"

"Where did you get the box?" Andrea asked.

"It came in the mail," Donna said. "See, this is where I ripped the label off." She pointed to the torn cardboard. "I ordered something off the Sell My Crafts website, then reused the box for your present. Maybe the shipper had something illicit in it before using it for my order."

"What had you bought?" Andrea asked. She opened a desk drawer and pulled out a laptop.

"It was this ugly polar bear thing," Donna replied.

Andrea set the laptop on the coffee table and logged in. After a few keystrokes, she spun the computer around. The Sell My Crafts home page was displayed. "Show me."

Donna frowned, then started typing. "Give me a minute. I'm trying to remember how I found it." She looked around at the police officers who had set aside their drinks and were staring at her intently. "Does everyone have to watch?"

"Why? What did you buy?" Jerry asked. "Was it a sex toy?"

"I wish," Donna said, her cheeks turning red. Finally, she sat back, grabbing a cushion from the couch and clutching it in front of her chest. "There."

A stunned silence followed her pronouncement. "What the hell is that?" Andrea asked. A lumpy white blob with a few black marks was pictured on the screen.

"It says it's a polar bear," said Leo, Jerry's new patrol partner.

"It looks like a wad of wet toilet paper," Jerry said.

"Does that say $300?" Andrea's voice rose an octave as she said the price.

"It was late, I'd had too much wine, it's done. Let's move on," Donna said.

"How did you even find this?" Jerry asked.

"I was looking for a gift for my niece. She's very keen on environmental causes, and I wanted a locally made igloo or a polar bear statue. See? The company is based in Ottawa."

"It was $300!" Andrea repeated.

"Andrea, focus! Your attack dog is eyeing me like I'm bacon," Donna said.

"Right," Andrea responded. "Well Bolt definitely doesn't like this box. I think we need to take a look at that figurine. Hopefully you didn't throw it out, even though the garbage is exactly where it should be."

Donna sheepishly admitted that she still had it. She couldn't throw it out after spending that kind of money on it, but she didn't want to saddle her niece with it either.

"Sorry to break up the party," Andrea said, standing, "but lawbreakers never sleep." Most of the remaining guests said their goodbyes, leaving Andrea, Donna and Jerry to go over to Donna's place. "We need someone to keep an eye on the suspect during the search," Jerry quipped.

Andrea took her coat from the hall closet and grabbed Bolt's leash. Twenty minutes later they were in Donna's apartment, and Bolt headed straight for the bookshelf where the so-called polar bear sat next to a figurine of a moose dressed as a Mountie, hoof raised to its Stetson in a salute.

"There's no question, Bolt doesn't like your polar bear," Andrea said, zipping open a satchel and pulling out a pair of latex gloves. She held the figurine up to the light. "It's been glazed, but the bottom is rough." She tapped it with a knuckle. "It's hollow, too."

Moving into the kitchen, she laid an evidence bag on the table before placing the figurine on its side. Reaching into her satchel, Andrea pulled out a scalpel sealed in plastic and scraped the bottom of the so-called bear. As she pressed the blade against the figure, the bottom crumbled inward.

"Wow." Jerry picked up a white clump and crushed it between his gloved fingers. "Andrea, either you've been pumping iron, or that's plaster of Paris."

Andrea grunted in reply and cleared away the rest of the plaster, leaving the entire bottom of the polar bear open.

"You could easily fit several grams of something inside this, then seal and ship it," she said. She put the figurine in an evidence bag while Jerry swept the remains of the crumpled bottom into another bag. "I'll take it to the lab for complete analysis."

Andrea pulled off her gloves and turned apologetically to

Donna. "Sorry about this, but I can't play favourites." She picked up Bolt's leash. "Do I have permission to search the rest of your apartment?"

Donna sighed. "This is about that time I wouldn't let you copy from me in fifth grade math, isn't it?"

Andrea smiled.

"Go ahead. Might as well get it over with."

"I'll wait here in the kitchen with the suspect while you search the premises," Jerry chuckled. "She might have more questionable artwork. Maybe an Inuit carving she uses as a weapon. Wouldn't want her trying anything funny." Donna responded with an expressive hand gesture.

Andrea rolled her eyes as she and Bolt moved down the hallway to the bedroom. "Bolt, seek." She followed Bolt as he sniffed his way around the room, lingering briefly over the pile of dirty laundry in the corner and shoes in the closet. She could hear Jerry in the living room giving Donna a formal-sounding caution about the dangers of shopping while under the influence.

Andrea and Bolt then worked their way through the bathroom, linen closet and kitchen before returning to the living room, where Bolt once again indicated the figurine.

"Find anything?" Donna asked, rubbing her hands nervously. "It sounded like he indicated something in the kitchen."

"He didn't indicate," Andrea said. "He was just very interested in the green bin."

"Leftover Greek takeout," Donna said.

"That explains it," Andrea said. "He did indicate some crumpled flyers in your paper recycling in the second bedroom."

Donna blinked anxiously, then brightened up. "The polar bear came wrapped in flyers."

Andrea nodded. "Makes sense. We'll bag those too. I'll put in a call to the sergeant to see if she is good with me bringing things in myself."

"You think she's going to send a full investigative unit?" Donna asked. "Because if so, I'd like to tidy up my bedroom a bit first."

"I don't know," Andrea said. "It might look suspicious if you actually did laundry." She grinned at her friend.

The next day Andrea and Donna sat at a conference table at police headquarters. Bolt sat next to the wall behind Andrea, turning his head to sniff at people filing into the room.

Constable Bob Warkentin was last to arrive. "So, counsellor, I hear you like to make late night purchases on sketchy websites."

"It's a perfectly respectable site," Donna fired back. "It's not like they were statues of girls from Japanese animation with beach-ball boobs." There were a few snickers around the room. Bob worked in the cybercrime department and had more than a few questionable figurines on his desk.

"If I could have everyone's attention," Sergeant Toni Andretti said loudly enough to be heard over the snickering. The room immediately went silent. "For those who were not invited to Constable Andrea Romero's birthday party, her new partner, Bolt, was on the job even if no one else was. Crown attorney Donna Park brought a gift wrapped in a box that she had received in the mail containing an online purchase. Bolt indicated that the box was positive for narcotics."

The sergeant pressed a button on a remote, and the smart board in front of the room lit up, showing the lump of ceramic from Donna's apartment. "We have verified that this product is indeed sold on the Sell My Crafts website by a company called Northern Treasures, and that Ms. Park purchased it. What we have not confirmed is her blood alcohol level at the time." There were snickers, and Donna blushed. "For those who do their shopping sober, Sell My Crafts is a website for small businesses. Sellers may be individual hobbyists working from their kitchen or small companies who don't want to pay the overhead of running their own site. The website charges a fee to the sellers but has no other affiliation with them."

Toni clicked the remote again, and the screen showed the web page for the Northern Treasures store. "The company offers a number of items. The item purchased by Ms. Park is listed as a polar bear sculpture." She clicked the remote again and brought up the page showing the figurine Donna had bought. There were murmurs, snickers and exclamations over the price. "The site offers other items of similar quality, including an alleged igloo, snowman, iceberg, penguin and Christmas tree."

"Are those prices for real?" someone asked. "It looks like someone slapped papier mâché on a toilet paper roll."

"Who would pay $300 for that crap?"

"A lot of people," Toni replied. "Fortunately for us, the website also likes to sell their usage data. We have confirmed that the company's figurines sell quite well, much better than those in the same price range from other vendors. In fact, more frequently than one would reasonably expect based on quality." There was another round of snickers in the room. "We therefore have applied for warrants to examine the company's financial records. In the meantime, we have been doing some routine background checks on the company. Bob?"

"I've done some standard database searches on this company," Constable Warkentin said. "There's nothing on Northern Treasures in our files. No complaints or investigations opened into them. They aren't even an incorporated entity. The Northern Treasures store does have a good seller's rating and customer reviews, although almost all of the reviews were written in the first week after the seller set up, suggesting the seller created them. Anybody can create dummy accounts and use them to make fake reviews."

"So just to be clear," said Steve Mazur, a senior analyst, "we are investigating this company and applying for warrants because they are selling ugly figurines?"

"Ugly's an understatement," Jerry said.

"Crude," Toni said. "Let's use crude in the reports."

"They are selling crude, expensive figurines," Steve continued.

"A lot of them," Jerry said.

"Which our Crown attorney purchased, even after seeing what they looked like," Toni said.

"Have you had your eyes checked recently?" Jerry asked, turning to Donna.

"Or cleaned your monitor?" Bob suggested.

"It was late, and I'd had a little too much Merlot," Donna said. "Can we move on?"

"I understand how people become junkies, but buying that?" Bob said.

"However it happened," Toni said, her voice a little louder than usual, "the lab found trace amounts of meth on the inside of the box. We now have to answer the question: was this just a recreational user letting their stash get too close to materials from their other hobby, or do we have a distributor?"

A chorus of voices responded, "Distributor."

"Why else would anyone buy those things?"

"If it is a distributor, the question is, why weren't there any drugs in Donna's polar bear?" Andrea posed.

"There was a personalize option," Donna responded. "For $50 they would write a name or dedication on it. Maybe that's how buyers flag that they want something special."

"That fits," Bob said. "I was able to get the order history for the seller. There's a personalize option on almost all of the products that have the word snow in the text. Snowball, snow cone, snowstorm, that sort of thing."

"Okay, so next step, we need to order a few items," Toni said. She looked around the room. "Who wants to get started on their Christmas shopping?"

Two weeks later the same group was back in the conference room. Spread out on the table before them was the ugliest collection of pottery Andrea had ever seen. "Let me get this straight," she said. "Every one of these cost $300?"

"$350," Toni corrected her. "We added the extra charge for personalization."

"At least they don't charge shipping," Andrea muttered.

The sergeant continued, "We bought three kinds of figurines, and for each we ordered one without personalization, one personalized with just a first name and one with a short phrase containing the word snow. In each case where we asked for a phrase with snow in it, the figurine held four grams of meth crystals."

Toni then nodded at Steve Mazur, the analyst, who cleared his throat. "The RCMP laboratory checked out the meth composition, which sent up flags all through their narcotics division before they finally got back to us. The drugs match a new dealer the RCMP has been tracking for the last eight months. Overdoses throughout Canada have been traced back to this particular product. Needless to say, the Mounties are eager to work with us."

Bob spoke up. "The company's profile on the Sell My Crafts website doesn't list a publicly visible email or physical address, but to set up their account, Northern Treasures had to provide that information. The street address is an OC Transpo parking lot for out-of-service buses in Orleans, but the phone number is real and has a 613 area code."

"The cancellation marks on the packages show they were mailed from different Kanata post offices." Toni said. "Between the phone number and the fact we could prove the packages were mailed within the National Capital Region, we were able to get a warrant for the company's online transactions.

"It looks like they distribute right across the country. A lot of their orders are for multiple figurines, meaning possible dealers. We also got warrants for the company's email and listed phone number. We've identified the woman running the organization as Simone Richard."

A rap sheet with mug shots appeared on the smart board. "She's got several priors for distribution but no violent felonies," Toni continued. "It seems she's running a meth lab network west of Ottawa, mostly on remote farms that are no longer operating. The labs bring their product to Richard's farm just on the edge of Stittsville. That's where she makes the, um, figurines. The bodies are ceramic, but the bottom is just plaster, so it chips apart easily."

Steve spoke up again. "More importantly, it looks like they are planning to expand. They have visitors coming from Florida in five days to study their setup."

Toni clicked the remote, and several arrest photos appeared on the screen. Steve resumed narrating.

"These three individuals are believed to have ties to a Mexican cartel," he said. "But so far law enforcement has been unable to prove that. They will be here for one night, staying at the Richard property."

Toni spoke up again, tapping the table for emphasis. "It is very important that we arrest them with Simone. It's unclear how they will be arriving in the country, and simply following them from the property won't be as convincing as taking them at her home. The plan is to descend on the farm and all of the known labs at the same time. The RCMP will handle the labs, but since the farm is technically inside the city limits, we will be leading the raid on Ms. Richard. The briefing with the RCMP teams will be this afternoon at their headquarters."

Donna had been slouched in her seat, eyes closed, one hand partially covering her face. Now she sat up and opened her eyes, sighing resignedly. "You didn't happen to tell the RCMP how this got started, did you?"

"I'm sorry, counsellor," Toni said with a barely concealed smirk. "I'm afraid we agreed to share all information with our federal colleagues."

"So now everyone knows I make bad shopping decisions while drunk?" Donna asked.

"Look at the bright side," Andrea said, patting her friend's shoulder. "Maybe you can expense the Merlot."

Andrea sat in a briefing room at the RCMP headquarters, studying the satellite view of a farm, as Claude Robidoux, head of the RCMP SWAT unit, indicated features with a laser pointer. "There are three buildings on the Richard farm: the house, barn and double garage. We've driven by a few times to get street-level views, but it's on a country road, so there aren't any good places for prolonged observation. Across the road is an open field, and 40 metres on either side is a thin line of trees marking the property boundaries. The images taken from the drive-by surveillance show two vehicles on the property in the mornings and evenings with plates indicating they belong to Simone Richard and her adult son, Gilles. Both drivers' licences list the farm as the residence." Two licence photos appeared on the screen. "There are no signs of anyone else living there and no mention of anyone else in their emails. We have traced deliveries of pottery supplies to the residence: clay, glaze and plaster. Seems they have a kiln in the barn. We have also documented a large number of small pickup trucks driving to the farm with plastic containers in the beds and then leaving with empty beds. Two days from now their visitors from Mexico are due to arrive."

Three new mug shots appeared on the screen and the Ottawa sergeant took over. "We want all of them," she said. "The visitors will be staying at the farm, and we'll have undercovers watching for them. We'll go in at 5 a.m., early so there won't be much, if any, traffic." Toni Andretti looked around the room to make sure everyone was staying focused. The next part was crucial.

"If anyone is awake," she said, "we launch tear gas. Patrol cars will block the road on both sides of the house. K9 units, you will back up teams on the perimeter. If we get any runners, we need you to bring them down. According to the Guns and Gangs Unit, there are no signs that Simone or her son have connections to any of the motorcycle gangs or other gangs, so we don't know if they're armed. However, most outlying farms have a rifle or two in case of coyotes, and the visitors have histories of using firearms. Since they are arriving from out of town the night before, we don't know if they'll have time to pick anything up or if they'll risk bringing firearms across the border. To be on the safe side, we are assuming they will be armed."

Toni took the remote and went back to the overhead of the farm. "We will drive to the tree line here, and here, then get out and go in on foot. There should be a full moon, which will provide good visibility. We haven't had much snow so far this year, so travelling across the ground on foot shouldn't be a problem."

She then brought up a map with locations marked. "The Mounties will have deployed to their targets earlier. For the Ottawa police team, we will rally in the parking lot of the grocery store, here. It's off the main highway, so away from traffic at that hour. Do not stop at the Tim Hortons around the corner for coffee. We don't need anyone tweeting about the large number of police vehicles in the area."

Then, looking straight at Donna's direction, she added, "And no late night online shopping either. We don't want to alarm them with unusual website traffic."

Everyone turned to smirk at Donna, who, in turn, glared at Andrea. "Next time I come over, Bolt better be in the yard."

At the sound of his name, the dog let out a gentle "Woof," prompting further laughter.

Three days later, in the wee hours of the morning, Andrea was behind the wheel of her custom K9 squad car, which had a special compartment for her partner. She turned down a small side road, looking for the parking lot which was the rally point for the raid. It was just past 4:30, but there had already been a few cars at the Tim Hortons when she had passed by. Hopefully the people waiting to get their double-doubles were focused on the results of last night's hockey games and not on the unusual number of police vehicles that had driven by.

At last she pulled into the parking lot. Whimpering and growling since she had loaded him into the car, Bolt broke into an excited bark when she stopped. "Quiet," Andrea said, but she could hardly blame him. She was wound tightly herself. She opened the rear door and Bolt hopped out, tail wagging furiously. Andrea gripped his leash tightly. "Bolt, heel."

"Morning," she said to Jerry and Leo, who had just arrived as well.

"Everybody ready for this?" Jerry asked.

Bolt lunged forward, and Andrea restrained him. "The sooner, the better," she replied. The four made their way towards the large truck in the middle of the lot. They climbed into the personnel transport, and Andrea took her place on the bench near the back.

The mood inside the truck was tense. Officers checked their weapons, performed quiet comms checks or rubbed their good luck charms. Bolt whimpered in anticipation, and Andrea stroked the German Shepherd between his ears to keep him quiet.

A crackle in Andrea's earpiece preceded the message they'd been waiting for. "This is command. Thermal imaging shows five inside the house, four upstairs and one in a room on the west side of the main floor. No animals in the house. The raid is a go. Repeat, the raid is a go."

After a short ride bumping along the country road, the truck stopped and everyone stood. "K9 unit and Team 3, go." Andrea and Bolt climbed down from the truck, followed by the team that would approach the house from the east. She kept her hand on Bolt's head to prevent him from barking. She could make out the house in the silvery moonlight. The armoured vehicle drove down the road, then halted to let the other teams out. Voices crackled in her ear as the officers checked in.

Team 3 crouched low and made their way around the house to cover the back exit, but Andrea hung back. From her vantage she could see front and back and could back up teams positioned at either end of the house. She watched as Teams 1 and 2 converged on the front. An officer crept up to the enclosed porch and peered through the pane. A voice crackled in Andrea's earpiece. "No one visible."

"Take the front door."

There was a faint tinkle of glass, and the officers disappeared into the house. A light went on in a second-storey window, followed by shouting and shots fired. At the sound of gunfire, Bolt barked excitedly. Andrea tightly held onto his leash. Bolt kept barking while Andrea peered through the dark. A motion to her right made her turn her head. Someone had opened a window on the first floor and tumbled out. "Halt! Police!" Andrea clicked the talk button on her mic. "We've got a suspect coming out of the ground floor window, east side." Bolt was barking frantically now.

"Bolt! Seek!" She unclipped the leash, and the German Shepherd lunged forward, powerful legs eating up the distance between him and his target. The dark figure was almost to the barn when the dog leapt, landing on the suspect's back. The weight of the dog bore the perpetrator to the ground. Bolt jumped clear and whirled around, grabbing the prostrate suspect's arm.

"Call him off! Call him off!" a deep male voice bellowed as Andrea reached him, her sidearm drawn.

"Bolt! Release!" Andrea called. "Hands above your head."

"The damn dog bit me!"

"And if you don't behave, he's gonna bite you again," Andrea said. "Now hands over your head!"

The man complied. "Bolt, watch," Andrea said. The dog growled as she stepped forward and grabbed one hand, pulling it behind the man's back and attaching a handcuff. As she reached for his other arm, the man shoved himself up and kicked at her. The next moment Bolt's jaws were locked on the man's forearm. He cried out in pain as Jerry came running up, his gun drawn.

"I told you he'd bite you again," Andrea said. "Bolt, release." As the dog's powerful jaws let go, Andrea pulled her suspect's arm down and attached the handcuffs.

Several officers ran up and hauled the man to his feet, then dragged him towards the front of the house. Four other people in pyjamas and handcuffs were being stuffed into patrol cars, and crime scene techs started to swarm the house. Andrea's runner struggled as he was dragged to a car, but a fierce growl from Bolt quieted him right down.

"Good boy," Jerry said. "Hey, Andrea. Maybe you should lend him to Donna to monitor her late night shopping!"

Elizabeth Hosang is an author of short stories in the genres of mystery, science fiction and fantasy, one of which was a finalist for the 2017 Crime Writers of Canada Award of Excellence. Her work has appeared in over 20 anthologies, and in 2024 she compiled some of her early works in a self-published collection.

UNDER THE CIRCUMSTANCES

19

LIS ANGUS

know something's wrong as soon as I enter our Barrhaven townhouse, closing the front door behind me. There's a disturbance in the air or maybe something I smell—a faint odour that jogs a dark memory. I pause, my senses alert. Instead of dropping my keys and purse on the hall table, I hold on to them.

At a glance, everything in the living room looks the way we left it this morning. Ella's Grade 4 science project is still spread over the coffee table, and my accounting textbook is beside the couch where I was studying.

But Oscar, our aging tabby, has retreated to his safe spot under the couch. That's where he hides when strangers appear. Only his glowing eyes are visible.

I hear a noise deeper in the house—a shifting sound, like a foot moving on the floor. The skin on the nape of my neck tingles. I back up, my rear hitting the closed door behind me.

A shadow moves in the next room, and a lanky figure steps into the archway. "Hello, Sarah." His voice is deceptively soft. "Don't hover there. Come on in."

A cold shiver runs up my spine. "What are you doing here?" I ask. But I'm not really wondering; I always knew this was possible.

"I've come for Ella. You can't keep her away from me. I'm her father." This time, the menace in his tone is obvious.

I've been dreading this for three years, ever since we escaped and left him behind. Using a new last name and staying under the radar, we've built fresh lives in Ottawa. Ella has made friends at school, and I'm to finish my accounting qualification next year.

No. This can't be happening. My mind reels. *We're having fish and chips for supper and we're going camping this weekend.*

I can't let my abusive husband wreck this now.

Michael and I met at university in Saskatchewan. I was drawn to his quiet manner, and we laughed at the same jokes. We married right after I graduated. With my freshly minted but impractical arts degree, I got a job working in a hardware store while he finished his final year in veterinary studies. We had a little apartment, and life was good.

After Ella was born, though, he insisted we move to the rural community where his parents lived. His family had very conservative views on the roles of men and women. His father, manager of the local feed mill, was the unquestioned head of the family. His mother took pride in being a traditional housewife: cooking, cleaning, sewing, gardening, doing up preserves. She had nothing but scorn for women who worked "outside the home."

Michael got work at the local vet clinic, and I looked after Ella and the house we rented. He started pressuring me to model myself after his mother. I tried, learning to bake pies and can vegetables. But as time went on, he increasingly treated me like his subordinate and an inferior one at that. Our marriage, which had started so happily, no longer felt like a partnership.

And he began changing in other ways. His quietness turned into brooding. He became suspicious of outsiders and discouraged any friendships I started. He started claiming a variety of strange and shifting allergies: foods he suddenly couldn't eat and things that he said made him itchy like fur, feathers and some kinds of detergent.

When I questioned any of these, he became enraged, viewing any disagreement as disloyalty. The first time he hit me, he begged my forgiveness and promised not to do it again. I believed him that time. This was the guy I'd married, after all.

But it did happen again. And again. He stopped being contrite—now he blamed me for causing him to do it. He started lying to explain my injuries and made me tell the emergency department that I'd broken my arm by falling off the porch.

Why I went along with it, why I stayed as long as I did, is a mystery. I know it's an old story shared by many abused wives. We tell ourselves that staying is better than leaving.

Ella was my saving grace; watching her grow was a pleasure. Michael loved her too, and I told myself that his attachment to her was a redeeming quality. He disapproved of any hint that I was teaching her feminist views, though. I received a couple of black eyes over that.

The final straw was the day he hit Ella. She'd started school that year. Over supper one day, she declared she'd like to be a teacher when she grew up. That was acceptable—Michael's mother had been a teacher before marriage—but then she said, "Or maybe I'll be a doctor or an airplane pilot."

He frowned. "Those would get in the way of looking after your kids."

She looked at him and raised an eyebrow—a trick she'd been practicing in the mirror. "Maybe I won't have any kids. Women can choose, you know."

He stared at her and suddenly swelled up with rage. When he flung his arm out, it wasn't a slap: he backhanded her so hard she flew off her chair and hit the wall.

We left a week later. I grieved for the marriage I thought we'd had.

He moves forward into the living room now. "Ella's coming home with me," he says.

My throat tightens. *No. I can't allow that.*

I'm still backed up against the front door. If I can open it, I can run to the neighbour's and get help. I reach behind me to turn the knob.

But he's already in my face. He grabs my arm, drags me away from the door. "You're not leaving," he says. I can see the steel in his expression, the tension in his jaw. He flings me toward the couch, and I land heavily, my cheek scraping on the rough upholstery.

Menace is radiating off him, and with a sinking heart I recognize this stage. He has already worked his way up to fury. From there, it was never much distance to full violence.

My purse is on the couch beneath me, under my right hip, close to my hand. Sitting up to mask my movements, I reach in and feel for my phone. Without looking, I adjust it in my hand, my fingertips gripping the side buttons. I try to remember what to press to activate the emergency SOS feature.

But something in my face or body alerts him. He leaps across the room toward me, yanking my arm up and sliding his other hand down to grab my phone. His face looms over mine, and I smell the acrid scent of his breath.

He smiles a cruel smile, the one I'd come to know so well. "No way," he says. "I'll just take that." He drops me back against the sofa cushions and moves across the room, slipping the phone into his shirt pocket. He gazes out the front window. "Ella'll be home from school soon, right?"

Yes, her school bus will be coming down Fallowfield Road in about 15 minutes. If he knows that, knows our daily routines, he must have been watching us. Maybe for days.

"How did you find us?" The words spill out of my mouth.

He smiles again, this time the false-charming one he uses. "Your mother told me you were here," he says.

My heart sinks. Yes, my mother never accepted how dangerous

he'd become. I'd tried to get her to promise to keep our secret, but I should have known he'd get around her.

I have to get away. Have to try something else. "I need to go to the bathroom," I say. Maybe I can slip out the window there—I think it's big enough, and it wouldn't be a long fall to the ground.

He smiles crookedly. "All right."

Maybe this will work. But as I head down the hall to the bathroom, he follows close behind. He stops me from closing the door. "We'll just keep the door open, won't we?" he says.

He leans against the wall across from the bathroom. A black feeling comes over me. With him watching, I can't even try the window.

I go ahead and pee. He glances away, a small concession to my privacy. Taking advantage of his short lapse in attention, I palm a nail file that was lying on the counter. I leave the bathroom, edging my way past him.

"Wait a minute. What do you have in your hand?" His arm is blocking my way.

"Nothing," I say.

But he forces my fingers back and takes the nail file from me, giving a short humourless snort. "That wouldn't do you much good, Sarah."

He's right. It wouldn't have been much of a weapon. I turn away and walk into the kitchen. "I'll make tea." I feel his eyes burning into my back, but he doesn't stop me.

I fill the kettle with water and plug it in. He's still in the hallway, watching me, but his main attention is on the front window. He's waiting for Ella.

My anxiety rises: she'll be here soon. Her school bus drops her at the corner, and she walks the block to our house with Alice, the next-door neighbour's daughter. Alice goes to the same school but is in Grade 5.

My mind spins. I have to get out of here and get Ella away. I glance at him: he's not watching me at the moment. I head for the back door, trying to look casual, but I trip over the open cardboard box that we've been filling with camping supplies for the coming weekend.

My stumble makes a noise. My eyes shoot toward him. He sees me.

I'm out of time. I'm still grappling with the back door lock when he slams into me. "No you don't," he shouts, throwing me against the wall.

My shoulder explodes in pain and I fall to the ground. I know right away the shoulder is dislocated—I've had this before. The pain is as excruciating as I remember.

I see the rage building in him and I recognize the ramping up process. His eyes are wild. He's working himself up for unbridled violence. The fury in his face is something to behold.

I have to do something, even with my shoulder in agony.

Beside me is the box of camping supplies. I reach blindly into the box with my good hand and grab an aerosol container—it's either the bug spray or the bear spray; I have no time to check the label.

As Michael lunges toward me, I reach out and spray it in his eyes. He collapses, shrieking, his hands clutched over his face.

I check. It was only the bug spray. It's stinging him now, but it won't hold him long.

Reaching with my good hand to unlock the back door, I gather my feet under me.

But as I go to stand, his arm shoots out and he grabs my ankle. His fingers close in an iron grip. I gasp in terror. My shoulder explodes in pain again, and I realize I've fallen against the cardboard box of supplies. I reach in and grab a jar at random. Using every ounce of strength I can muster, I throw it at him.

The jar hits him square on the temple. He falls to the floor, the jar landing next to his face.

I stare at him. The jar has a crack down the side, and something has leaked out of it. Peanut butter. A streak of it slides down his cheek, along with blood, and his hand has smeared it further.

We never had peanut butter in our house back then. It was one of the things he said he was allergic to, so we just didn't buy it. Now I wonder if it was true, not just something he made up.

As I watch, his eyes bulge and he clutches his throat, gasping for breath.

Holding my shoulder carefully, I lean forward and extract my phone from his pocket. I will call 9-1-1.

But not too quickly.

First, I'll get Ella to go next door with Alice. Under the circumstances.

In her early career, Lis worked with children and families in crisis; she later transitioned into a career as a business writer and editor. She's had short stories published in the anthology Covid Chronicles and in Black Cat Mystery Magazine. Her first novel, Not Your Child, placed second in the RWA Unpublished Mystery/Suspense Daphne du Maurier Award in 2021 and was published by The Wild Rose Press in 2022. She lives south of Ottawa with her husband.

THE GREELY WIDOW'S SECRET

20

JOANNE WHITE

The call came in at 3:14 a.m. Kat Collins sat in her cruiser on the corner of Hawthorne and Hunt Club nursing her hour-old coffee while updating files and call logs. Night shifts left her half-wired and half-dead at the same time. Caffeine, fresh or not, usually helped get to the finish line. The dispatcher's voice crackling over the radio made her sit up at attention.

"Possible break and enter. 4067 Miller's Lane, Greely. Caller, elderly female, heard an intruder around her home. No forced entry observed."

"10-4. ETA in less than 15 minutes," Kat replied. She cracked her window, allowing the biting March air to seep in while muffling the deafening siren. Kat chose a wail—a slow, automatic rise and fall of frequencies, the kind you'd hear when a cop car was gaining on you from behind. *Nothing ever happens in Greely,* she thought, flicking on the lights. *Might as well make an entrance.*

Greely was really part of the City of Ottawa, but it felt like a quiet village, and Kat called it home. It was mostly farms and sprawling rural properties where neighbours could go days without seeing each other. Kat had training academy friends who recommended it for its out-of-city lifestyle. Single, she chose a manageable townhome. With her secondment to the Ottawa Police Service from the RCMP, buying her own place made sense.

Kat pulled into the long craggy driveway. Another cruiser was already there. Constable Ryan Bishop stood by the front porch, speaking with the homeowner, a petite silver-haired woman wrapped in a thick woolly robe. *Backup.* Kat was still getting used to that luxury. All those years working in Newfoundland, that was never guaranteed. Most times, she was on her own, answering calls and playing Russian roulette with the human condition—some nights a drunk fisherman swinging fists in a snowstorm; other times, a teenager high as a kite, ready to jump off a wharf just to see if they could fly. Kat had already collected many battle scars, each with a story of a close call or narrow escape. Ottawa was different. Here, there were resources. It felt safe. Predictable.

"Mrs. Pritchard, may we come in?" Ryan asked as Kat climbed the steps.

The elderly woman stood in the doorway, her posture straight and expression attentive despite her advanced age. "Come in out of the cold," she said. "I swear I heard someone at my back door. I'm sure they were trying to get in."

"Do you live alone, ma'am?" Kat asked.

"Yes, since my husband passed away a number of years ago."

Kat caught the shift in the widow's gaze toward the wall, where a collage of photos told a story. Formal shots, candid ones, the same man appearing beside her again and again. Even without knowing the woman, it was clear who she'd lost.

"Can you show me exactly where you heard the noise? My colleague will check outside."

Mrs. Pritchard led Kat through the hallway to the rear of the house. The place was old but well kept—clean, paint a little faded but not peeling. *So obvious she took pride in it.*

"It was right here," she whispered. "I heard the noise. Then a faint rattling, like someone was trying the handle."

Kat swept the area with her flashlight, noting the hardy lock and absence of damage. "Did you see anyone outside?"

"No," Mrs. Pritchard replied, her voice wavering. "By the time I gathered the courage to look, there was no one there."

Kat offered a reassuring smile. "We'll make sure everything is secure. In the meantime, please stay inside."

Mrs. Pritchard nodded while Kat radioed her colleague.

"Bishop, do you need any help with the perimeter?"

"Negative. You finish inside. Be back shortly."

Kat took her notebook from inside her soft body-armour pocket and flipped it open to write.

"Tell me everything from the beginning, Mrs. Pritchard."

"Like I told the operator, I heard something at the back. My room's upstairs, but I'm telling you the back door rattled. Somebody was trying to get in," she added firmly. "I called 9-1-1 just after three o'clock."

Kat tucked her pen away and unlocked the back entrance, glancing out over the worn steps. The porch light flickered, casting long shadows across the frost-rimmed yard. She spotted her partner's flashlight cutting through the darkness several feet away.

"Is this light always on, Mrs. Pritchard?"

"It's on one of those timers for the nighttime. Had it installed a few years ago."

Both constables meticulously continued their searches, mostly for Mrs. Pritchard's peace of mind.

"There's a shed and barn at the edge of the treeline," Bishop reported. "Nothing remarkable. All locked up."

"10-4," Kat replied.

"Nothing suspicious. I'll brief telecoms."

Kat offered a reassuring smile and rested a hand on Mrs. Pritchard's shoulder. "We'll stick around for a bit, ma'am. Could've been an animal or even the wind. Sound carries differently at night."

The widow didn't look convinced. "A lot of things don't work like they used to," she said quietly, "but my ears are just fine." Her gaze flickered to the dark beyond the porch light. "Maybe I'm losing my marbles?"

Kat shook her head. "You're not." She knew better than to dismiss a gut feeling. You listen when someone says something's off, even if you can't see it yet. However, after an extensive search turned up no sign of forced entry, no footprints in the hard ground and no evidence of anything but the usual creaks and rattles of an old farmhouse, there wasn't much more they could do.

"Is there anyone I can call to stay with you? Friends? Family?"

"It's only me. I have friends from the seniors club and the Anglican church, but I'm not bothering anyone this hour of the night."

"We'll be close by if you need us," Kat said as she jotted down the non-emergency police number for Mrs. Pritchard, then left her to the quiet of the farmhouse.

Three days later, just as Kat began the day shift, Mrs. Pritchard called 9-1-1 again. This time, it wasn't a suspected intruder.

This time, there was a body.

Kat sped down the gravel road, her radio buzzing as more units responded. Dispatch advised of a possible 10-7, meaning temporarily out of service or cop code for dead body. *That meant backup. Lots of it.*

By the time Kat reached the property, the place was swarming. Two cruisers, an ambulance and a fire truck crowded the driveway. Another unmarked vehicle containing a two-person ident team rolled in behind her. Officers moved quickly, voices overlapping as they secured the scene.

They found Mark Sutter, a well-known Greely handyman, slumped against the side of the barn, his flannel jacket saturated with blood from a single gunshot wound to the chest.

"Still has a wallet and phone," Bishop observed, crouching beside the body. "Looks like whoever did this wasn't after money."

Her breath visible in the cold morning air, Kat turned toward the farmhouse where Mrs. Pritchard stood just inside the doorframe, her hand pressed against her mouth, eyes wide and glistening with something caught between fear and disbelief.

"Perimeter's being secured," Bishop said. "Don't know what we have yet. Need to rule out an active shooter."

"I'll head to the house," Kat said. "I'll get Mrs. Pritchard out of the open."

Bishop gave Kat a nod, and she headed to the residence.

"Mrs. Pritchard, let's go sit down in the kitchen. I know this is difficult, but I have a few questions."

"I...I don't know what to say, constable," she muttered.

"Let's start with this," Kat replied. "What happened today?"

"I...I got up. Had my tea and went to the sink, and I saw him... lying there."

"What did you see?"

"M..m..Mark...I knew it was him because of his jacket."

"Did you hear anything?"

"No."

"When was the last time you saw Mr. Sutter?"

Mrs. Pritchard sat back, arms crossed tightly over her cardigan, her face pale in the morning light.

"Yesterday afternoon," she said, her voice tight and brittle. "He was doing some work for me and told me he was going to the Home Hardware in Manotick."

"What time was that?"

"I don't know. It was after the twelve o'clock news." She blinked rapidly while twisting her handful of tissues.

"You're doing well, Mrs. Pritchard. What did he need at Home Hardware?"

"You'll have to ask them," she said, shaking her head. "I have an account there."

"When did Mr. Sutter start working here?"

"He put some pot-lights in the dining room and ripped out the cupboards in the laundry room. Mark's done lots of odd jobs for me... and everyone around here." She paused to sniffle. "Who would do this?" she whispered, more to herself than anyone else.

"That's what we're going to find out."

Kat stood to obtain a visual of the officers outside. A few other colleagues had arrived. Most of the activity remained near the barn. She stepped out to give the widow a break and get an update from Bishop.

"Barn doors are shut. Padlock still in place," he explained. "We'll let ident do their thing. Get what you can from the widow. There are a few squads following up with neighbours who showed up at the checkpoint."

The first break in the case came within the hour.

Ident's search of Sutter's truck turned up an old picture tucked in the glove compartment. The colours had all but faded, leaving behind a washed-out, sepia-toned image, enough to make Kat pause. The photograph depicted a young man and woman standing in front of the Pritchard barn. Kat donned her rubber gloves to grab a closer look, studying the faces frozen in time.

"That's her," Kat mouthed to her colleagues.

"Who?" said Bishop. "The old lady?"

Kat wet her lips, swallowing before she could get the next word out. "Yes."

"Are you sure?" Bishop asked, peering over her shoulder. "This photo's pretty dated."

"I'm very sure. There're pictures of her all over the house. Look Bishop, a mole just above her lip."

"How the hell would I recognize some old lady's mole, Collins? I was outside in the cold the other night while you were studying your new friend's pigmented lesions."

Kat glared but said nothing. *Not worth it.* She knew his comments were a stress reaction.

One of the ident colleagues chimed in. "Is that the homeowner's husband?"

"Good question. I ...I don't know," she answered. "The man here looks quite a bit younger than her."

They motioned Kat forward. "Well go find out."

Kat's rapport with the elderly widow—and the fact she was a female officer—made her the clear choice to go back in for a follow-up interview. *Send in the woman for the woman. Doesn't matter if she's a victim or a suspect.*

Inside, the widow drifted from the dining room, moving slowly, like someone waking from a dream they didn't want to leave.

"Mrs. Pritchard, we found this in Mr. Sutter's belongings," Kat said, showing her the print. "Could you tell me about the male beside you?"

A heavy silence filled the space.

"That is you, isn't it?"

The widow went rigid. "Where did you get that?"

"Mark Sutter had it in his truck."

Her hands trembled ever so slightly as she reached for the edge of the table, gripping it to steady herself.

"That's...that's my brother, Samuel."

"And where is he now?"

There was a long pause. "Haven't seen him since 1984. He was tangled up with some no-good yahoos and never came back."

Kat listened attentively, asked several probing questions about Mrs. Pritchard's brother. Kat noted the widow's reluctance to answer.

"Mrs. Pritchard, anything you recall, no matter how small, could be important. Why would Sutter have a picture of you and your brother?"

"How would I know? He was in my house enough times. Maybe he stole it. I need a glass of water. I feel dizzy."

Kat knew a sidestep when she heard one. Bishop reappeared at the doorway, and Kat quickly briefed him on the scant details.

"Can you query Samuel Hillier, date of birth April 1, 1967. Lots not adding up here."

Bishop soon had hits trickling in. Samuel Hillier was a drifter, in and out of trouble, mostly for summary conviction offences. In 1984, he disappeared without a trace; a friend reported him missing. The police chalked it up to his transient lifestyle and assumed he'd just left town.

"Last known address?" Kat inquired.

After a brief pause, Bishop found the information. "Bingo. We're at it now."

A puzzled look passed between them.

"What are you thinking Kat?"

Kat's gut churned. Something told her that Samuel hadn't left on his own. *Then there was Mark Sutter. Why did he have that photo? They had to be connected. What had he uncovered that cost him his life?*

"I have to get her talking. Just give me more time. Keep the brass outside."

"That's not easy to do. Sarge is here now. I'd say you have three minutes, tops!"

"Stall him."

"You owe me," he whispered.

Kat returned to Mrs. Pritchard. Her tone more direct now, she leaned toward the woman. "What makes you think Mark Sutter would've taken the picture from your house?" Kat asked.

At that, the widow started fanning herself, her breathing growing shallow.

"I need my pressure pills," she muttered, clearly struggling.

"Try to breathe," Kat said gently. "I'll have one of the firefighters take your pressure. We need to keep going with this." She reassured the widow that she'd be all right, then stepped back, allowing a fire medic to take over for a moment.

"Don't let her out of your sight," Kat instructed sharply. "I'll post a uniform on the door and be right back."

"Whatcha do Collins...interrogate her into a heart attack?"

"I think she's playing us, Bishop. A few minutes with the medic might calm her down."

"Take a walk with me to the barn," Bishop prodded. "Ident is finishing the perimeter. Time to move inside now."

Upon entry, the musty odour of rot and sourness crawled up Kat's nose while dust swirled in the glow of their beams. They exchanged a quiet moment, and then all eyes gaped toward the floor. The floorboards were unmistakably disturbed, half of them pried up, evidence of something being found and hurriedly put back.

Bishop looked at Kat. "Help me with this," he said as he knelt by a loose floorboard.

They pried the floorboard up. Beneath it, packed in the frozen earth, lay a human skull, soil clinging to pieces of weathered bone.

"Sweet Jezus. How many goddamned bodies are on this property?" Kat exclaimed.

"This wasn't buried yesterday," Bishop said. "I'll radio Sarge. Go back in. Detain her."

Kat hurried across the yard, meeting the firefighter who gave Kat the greenlight. Within moments, the widow regained her composure, pushing herself to stand.

"I need to be up," she said, as if standing would clear the tension building between them.

"Sit down."

"No...," she insisted.

"I said sit down," Kat snapped. "You're going to want to be comfortable for this."

The woman lowered herself into a chair.

"Whose body is in that barn? You're the only one alive here on this property so you better start talking." Kat's tone shifted, the patience she once had wearing thin. "Before you respond, I'll advise you're being detained for questioning, and anything you do say may be used as evidence. This is serious, ma'am!"

The widow looked away, her demeanour remarkably colder than it had been earlier. She blinked once. Then nothing. No nod, no shake of the head. Just that blank, impenetrable stillness.

"I've had enough," Kat barked. "You're not getting out of this by going quiet. Start talking now!"

"My brother," Mrs. Pritchard admitted in a shaking voice. "Samuel was either drunk or high as a kite or both." She looked down. "He threatened me, beat me up over the years."

271

"Now we're getting somewhere. Continue."

"Samuel stole from us. I don't even have a wedding band." She showed Kat her left hand. "He took everything we had for those rotten drugs. My brother was not a nice man."

If death was a reasonable punishment, there'd be lots of bones under barns, Kat lamented while taking crucial seconds to formulate the next series of questions.

"How did your brother end up buried in your barn, Mrs. Pritchard?" Kat demanded. "I want answers and I want them now."

The widow barely crumbled. If anything, she hardened. Her eyes narrowed to pinpricks. Whatever she was about to say, it wasn't coming easy. Kat didn't push. She waited.

"It was my husband," she replied in a quiet, exculpatory whisper. "George shot him to protect me. We didn't know what to do. So, we...we hid him."

That explains one body. Kat's eyes widened. *Samuel Hillier was murdered. Who else knew the truth? Maybe George wasn't the only one who had a hand in that night? Where did Sutter fit in all this mess?*

"So, work with me here. My next obvious question...who killed Mark Sutter?" Kat asked, though in her gut she already knew the answer.

The widow's lips pressed together. Her eyes darkened, insolence settling in. "I want a lawyer."

Kat stepped forward positioning herself over the widow with quiet authority.

"Mrs. Pritchard, you have the right to retain counsel." She continued reciting the formal declaration. "If you don't have your own lawyer, the court can appoint one for you. I can make a call right now. Your choice. However, keep in mind that there're two dead people on this property. The next officers coming in aren't going to be as accommodating as I am. I can tell you my sergeant will not care how old you are. Innes Road lockup is no church picnic."

The widow remained defiant. The silence that followed felt deliberate. Kat worried that whatever crack she'd opened was about to seal up.

"Look lady, my partner is outside drafting a warrant. George is all around us," she said as she extended her arms to the various visual reminders. "What would he want? Show me where the gun is— because either way, we're going to tear this property apart, including this house. Make it easy for yourself."

The widow's eyes filled. She stood, peering toward the photo on the mantel. "I told you this would come back," she whispered. "I told you, George."

Kat turned her around and placed the handcuffs on the slim, wrinkled wrists, wondering how those frail fingers managed 12 pounds of trigger pull.

"Mrs. Pritchard, for now you're under arrest for improper disposal of human remains. I expect that to change as the day goes on. Let's go!"

The widow's voice came, quiet and resigned. "Look in the silver-ware box in the china cabinet. Don't wreck my house."

"You hear that, Bishop?" Kat called out as her partner came inside. The crease in his brow said that he'd heard enough.

On the shelf below the blue and white china pieces, the .38 six-shot Smith & Wesson revolver sat in a red-velvet lined wooden chest. Bishop emptied the four remaining shots rendering it safe.

"When we send this for fingerprints, are we going to find yours?" Kat asked while she escorted the widow to the nearest marked vehicle.

"That greedy bastard," the widow exclaimed. "How dare he try to blackmail an old lady!"

"So, Sutter was onto you? That's it?" Kat inquired.

The widow turned her head stoically, saying nothing.

"No one deserves to die like that," Kat said, her voice angry. "What I don't understand is who showed up on your porch the other night?"

"I'm not saying another word."

Kat tucked the widow into the backseat of the cruiser and, spotting a younger uniform, instructed him to keep an eye on their new malefactor.

Kat went back toward the house and relayed the latest to Sarge and Bishop.

"Nice work, Collins," Sarge added while patting her back. "Neighbours said Sutter was snooping around lately and asking questions about the Pritchard family tree. They tried to warn Mrs. Pritchard, but she shrugged them off."

"Why?" Kat asked. "Sutter had no record. What pushed him to try to shake her down?"

"Gambling. He racked up a serious tab at Rideau Carleton Casino. He asked for money up front from other neighbours."

"If he found something in that barn, the fella should've come straight to the police," added Bishop. "Instead, he went to the old lady trying to squeeze a few bucks. Greed always has a way of flipping the table."

"There's still something I can't figure out," Kat said, scratching her head. "Why did she call us the other night?"

"Maybe her conscience, Collins," replied Sarge. "Or Sutter could've been there giving her a scare."

Kat wasn't convinced.

"Don't go too deep, Collins," Bishop added. "Like you said, maybe it was just the wind."

Joanne White hails from the coal mining town of New Waterford, nestled on picturesque Cape Breton Island, Nova Scotia. She began her career with the RCMP in 1989, serving in various roles across Newfoundland and Labrador, Saskatchewan and Ottawa. Since retiring from the RCMP in 2017, Joanne has continued to contribute internationally, working as a Senior Police Advisor in Tunisia, Liberia, Mali and Kosovo.

In 2022, she published her debut novel, Bay Island Girl. Joanne resides in Ottawa with her husband, two daughters and beloved pets. When she's not writing, she enjoys quilting and working on improving her golf swing.

MASKED HYSTERIA

21

MAYA VALENZUELA

The TV blared from the next room: an Ottawa neighbourhood under siege, residents feeling unsafe in their homes. It was much the same story on repeat for the last week.

"They think they have new information, Mom." Anthony bounced into the kitchen where his mother sat idly leafing through cookbooks at the kitchen table. Lina needed something to keep her mind busy. If she had to watch one more news story about the neighbourhood bandit, she was going to explode.

"Hun, it may not be a great idea to watch that before bed," she mumbled, but he was already gone. The television volume suddenly got louder, and his little voice echoed off the walls to be heard over the din.

"Listen to this, Mom. They may have found him this time."

A woman's voice clear and sonorous could be heard despite what sounded like idling vehicles in the background.

"Vanessa Rodriguez coming to you from Riverside South, the idyllic suburban neighbourhood that prides itself on being one of the safest in our nation's capital. Where neighbours know each other, everyone leaves their doors unlocked and people let their children play outside until dusk. But for

the past week, this normally peaceful scene has been thrown into an uproar and become a neighbourhood under siege with a ramping up of crime, destruction of property and several break-ins. But why here of all places? Why now?" Ominous music interjected.

"I'm here with Patrick Neko, a resident of Riverside South for 25 years. What can you tell us about what's been happening lately? Could you maybe speak to the most recent development when your house was broken into two days ago?"

"Yes." An old man's voice broke in. "You know the side door going to the kitchen? Well, he let himself in while I was asleep, bold as brass. Scared my wife half to death."

"Was the door unlocked or anything taken?" The reporter questioned him.

"I could have sworn I locked it before I went to bed—that was what scared me the most. I woke up because I heard noises in the kitchen, rustling on the counter, bags and that kind of thing. I ran into the kitchen as he was running out. He must've heard me." He coughed before continuing. "The place was a pigsty. Looked like he helped himself to whatever was lying around, but the strangest thing of all was the cutlery."

"The cutlery?" the reporter asked.

"Yes, the drawer." The man's voice was incredulous. "It was wide open and basically everything had been taken. I was completely stumped. What would someone want with our forks and knives?"

"And were you able to get a look at him as he was leaving? Seems that no one has been able to properly identify him so far."

"I didn't have my glasses," the man apologized, "but I'd say smaller than I thought he would be..." He paused as if trying his best to remember. "Yeah, short, might even say he had greyish hair though it was hard to tell in the dark. And a mask. He was running out the door. Must've heard me, and I scared him, but on my life I swear I saw a black mask. That's what I told the cops."

Vanessa pressed on. "Right. Have the police been any help? Up until now you're the only one who has any idea what he might look like."

"The cops took my information down and said they'd look into it. It's not been enough though, no. My wife is terrified. Doesn't want to be in the *house alone when it starts to get dark. I'm hoping the information I provided will take us one step closer to locking this guy down for good. It's not right what's happening here."*

"Thank you very much for your time, sir." Vanessa again turned to the camera.

"You heard it here first," she said. *"People in this community are afraid to be alone as a night stalker targets their homes. This is the first time the bandit has actually taken something though. Could robbery be the next big thing on his spree of crime? And why cutlery of all things? The same questions remain: who is he and why is he doing this? Police are asking anyone with information to please reach out to the telephone number on the screen below. And in the meantime, take the necessary precautions and lock your doors. This is Vanessa Rodriguez..."*

The sound tapered off as Anthony ran back into the kitchen.

"It's not just about destroying garbage cans and sheds anymore, Mom. He's breaking into people's houses. He's taking things! You heard what that guy said about a mask? Says he got a pretty good look at him!"

"I heard, hun." Lina closed the books in front of her and pulled out the adjoining chair. "Sit for a minute, OK?"

Anthony sat down with a thud. His small face was animated.

"You need to listen to me, OK? This is a very real situation right now, something we need to let the police handle."

The little boy puffed his cheeks out in exasperation. "You heard what the lady said, Mom. They're barely doing anything!"

"I'm not joking, Anthony. This guy could be dangerous. We have no idea where he came from or why he's doing what he's doing."

The front doorknob turned suddenly, and the door opened with a creak. Lina jumped as Emmet came in from outside. Anthony whirled around, his chair scraping the tile and shouted, "Dad!" He jumped on the grown man like a flash. The static mood in the kitchen all but dissipated.

Emmet smiled. "Oof buddy, you knocked the air out of me. Why are you still awake?" It was almost 11:00 p.m., and he tousled the boy's hair playfully as he glanced at Lina who shrugged sheepishly.

"I was watching TV about the bandit, Dad. You know he's started taking stuff now, and a guy actually saw him. The cops know what he looks like and they've still done nothing to catch him!"

Emmet exhaled slowly. "Before bed. Buddy it's not the best idea."

"That's what I told him." Lina grinned. "Why don't you go climb into bed, and I'll be there in a second, all right? I want to talk to your dad for a few minutes."

"But Dad just got home," Anthony muttered quietly, though a look from Lina stopped him in his tracks. "Yeah, fine." He shuffled off down the hall, his bare feet making small smacking noises against the wood. Lina listened.

"All the way into bed, buddy, and close the door. I'll be there soon."

The boy's small voice responded sheepishly from where he had planned to eavesdrop through the open bedroom door. "OK, OK." Faintly, the door clicked shut.

"So?" She turned inquiringly to Emmet who sat heavily into the little boy's abandoned chair and rubbed his tired face with both hands. Having kicked off his boots, they now lay in a dirty heap beneath the table. For once, Lina was too distracted to care.

Emmet had just returned from his shift with a community watch program hastily organized by Lina and Emmet's next door neighbours, Sheila and Rob Jenkins. The catalyst had been the attack on the Jenkins's shed. The couple had been woken by what they described as earth-shattering bangs and then they had found their shed windows smashed. Some of the metal shovels were taken, too, only to be discarded on the lawn. Worst of all, the outside of the shed was covered in what could only be described as animal waste.

"If the police aren't going to do anything to keep this neighbourhood safe, then we need to step up," Sheila Jenkins had all but shrieked, her voice trembling in a manic sort of way, into the phone to Lina. "It's a matter of keeping our children safe, our neighbourhood safe. We're not even close to downtown, Lina, where this type of thing actually happens!" She had paused dramatically. "What kind of miscreant does...well..."—she paused again —"THAT to somebody's property?" Sheila was a well-intentioned, neighbourhood busybody, and an attack on her property meant that she would not rest until the culprit was ascertained and punished within an inch of his life.

The call to arms initiated, Emmet's eternal can-do attitude made him a natural, although not necessarily willing, participant. Lina knew, however, that it was no longer enough to simply lock doors and windows and standby while the police dealt with the issue. She and her husband now found themselves caught between putting on a brave face for the little boy in the next room, by not letting on that the issue of the bandit in the neighbourhood was getting worrisome, and going out on shifts in the middle of the night, wondering what they might see or encounter. For all Anthony knew, Emmet had just come in from working late and had definitely not been out prowling the neighbourhood armed with a baseball bat and a mug of coffee.

"It was Rob and I tonight." Emmet said. "Honestly, I knew we wouldn't see much."

"I'm not sure how you stand that guy." Lina sighed; she knew her comment wasn't helpful. "And what exactly are you supposed to do if you do see something? I don't like the idea of you out there with a baseball bat. I'm afraid someone is going to think you're our perpetrator instead of a neighbourhood superhero."

Emmet laughed, "I doubt it, and would this guy even touch us if we bumped into him? Isn't it funny how absolutely nothing we've heard has indicated that the bandit is violent?" He had been feeling this way from the start, a sort of gut feeling of disbelief. "He hasn't even stolen anything of value for goodness' sake Lina. Some forks and a couple of shovels? It's being built up into mass hysteria over property vandalism and some breaking and entering."

"How can we even be sure he's breaking in?" she interjected. "Have you heard anything at all to prove that this guy breaks into homes? I have a feeling he lets himself in through doors that are already open." She exhaled slowly. "That's what Anthony was watching tonight on TV. They had a guy talking about how he had actually seen the bandit, but he himself wasn't even convinced that the door to his house had been locked. Said the guy shuffled around the kitchen going through bags and things they had left on the counter. Maybe he was hungry? Would that explain the need for cutlery?"

Emmet shrugged, "That's exactly it," he agreed. "There's got to be more to this than…"

A thundering crash interrupted Emmet mid-sentence.

Lina stood up quickly, her eyes wide. Noise travelled fast in the small, two-bedroom bungalow.

With Emmet hot on her heels, she rushed into the hallway towards Anthony's bedroom and barged through the door.

"Anthony! Are you OK?" Her voice didn't sound like hers; rather it sounded panicky and high-pitched.

She scanned the room. Anthony wasn't in bed. The sheets and comforter were in disarray. His desk was pushed across the room and under the window—the *open* window with its curtains rippling in the cool night air.

Her heart pounded against her rib cage. Bile crept up the back of her throat.

"Emmet!" she cried, grabbing his arm. "He's gone!" Her voice cracked.

Before Emmet spoke, a shadow outside the window made them freeze. A beam of light streamed into the room from outside, momentarily blinding them before a small, freckled face appeared.

"Mom, Dad!" he hissed. "Look out here!" Anthony's normally animated face was serious. "You need to come outside, right now!"

Relief flooded through Lina, but just as suddenly, she was livid. "Anthony, are you kidding me right now? You almost gave me a heart attack." She rushed forward to grab him. The boy dodged her hand easily and shrugged his shoulders.

"I'm sorry. I didn't mean to, Mom. I heard a noise and didn't want to bother you and Dad."

"So you took it upon yourself to investigate?" Emmet's deep voice bounced jarringly off the walls in the quiet of the small room. "By climbing out your bedroom window? Do you have any idea how dangerous that was?" He rubbed the bridge of his nose. "Could you turn off the darn flashlight?"

"Oh yeah," Anthony stammered and clicked it off. "Sorry! Look, you can punish me after OK? You need to get out here right now and see this."

The head disappeared as quickly as it had appeared, but the small voice floated back in to them as it moved away from the window. "Mom's really going to freak out." And then he was gone.

Lina had forgotten to turn on the front porch light as she and Emmet raced outside, and it took Lina agonizing seconds before her eyes adjusted to the darkness. She reached behind and grabbed Emmet's arm, and together they went further into the dark.

"Great, this is just great," she muttered. "I still can't believe this; it's almost midnight, and we're out here hunting down a nine-year-old vigilante." Emmet didn't reply, and Lina continued on passionately. "When I catch him, I am going to ground him and the very earth he walks on."

Emmet remained silent. She turned to look at his face and saw that his eyes were wide and his face gaunt. She followed his gaze slowly. Her jaw dropped. She had been so consumed thinking about Anthony that she hadn't taken a moment to really look around her. Their yard was completely destroyed.

Two metal trash cans lay on their sides, contents completely overturned and strewn about the grass haphazardly. Broken fragments of potted plants dotted the porch steps and dirt was everywhere.

"The lawn's been dug up!" she stammered. Deep trenches had been freshly dug across almost the entire front lawn. "Did you notice this when you came home tonight?" Her voice shook.

Emmet was running his hand through his short hair, clearly at a loss for words. "There's no way this was here when I got home tonight," he said.

Lina's mouth was a thin, set line. "Emmet, how does someone do this much damage in an hour? If this wasn't here when you got home earlier, then they must have arrived shortly after. If there was someone out here, how did we not hear anything?"

"We did though, didn't we?" Emmet's usually even voice wavered slightly, giving away his anxiety. "The crash we heard that sent us running to Anthony's bedroom—it must have been when the garbage cans were overturned. That's the only thing that makes sense."

"I'm calling the police." Lina turned to him assertively. "We moved to this neighbourhood to keep Anthony safe, and this isn't funny anymore. We need to get someone over here now."

"Wait!" Anthony's voice rang out. The boy appeared seemingly out of nowhere, decked out in his pyjamas, darting towards them from the side of the house. He tucked his flashlight away into the fanny pack around his waist and waved a small hand at them. "You need to follow me."

Unable to hide her fear, Lina whispered urgently, "Anthony, this isn't a game. If someone is here, we need to get back inside now," but she was interrupted mid-sentence.

"*SHH*, Mom," Anthony whispered. "You need to be really, really quiet, OK? Please! Follow me right now and I'll explain everything." He was already backing away towards the side of the house.

Emmet's deep voice pushed her forward, "Follow him, Lina. I'm right behind you."

They picked their way slowly over the gravel path leading to the side of the house. Their compost bin had been opened and thrown down aggressively. Bits of eggshell and food scraps now littered the beautiful new stones Lina had put down last month. She had a vivid image of the food rotting when the sun came up. The smell made her want to gag.

"Just a bit further. Follow me to the shed," Anthony whispered loud enough for them to hear as he quickly picked his way over the rocks. "And be really, really quiet." He was just light enough that his footsteps made little to no sound as he moved towards his target, a lightness his parents tried to emulate.

Anthony came to a quick stop, reached into his fanny pack to extract the flashlight and held a finger to his lips. The small tool shed was now in view and he moved towards it and turned on the light, aiming it at the ground in a sweeping motion.

"Spoons," Lina heard Emmet whisper quietly from behind her. "What in the world?"

Spoons and forks, small spades, tin cans, tinfoil balls, metal scraps and even a hubcap glinted in the light. Anthony watched his parents eagerly. Then once he was satisfied they had seen everything there was to see, he moved the flashlight beam slowly up the side of the shed until it rested steadily on the roof.

Lina and Emmet gasped.

Metal scraps adorned the roof in much the same way as the ground surrounding the shed. But perched on top of it all like a troll guarding buried treasure, and busy admiring his silky, black mask in the back of a large silver serving spoon, sat the largest raccoon any one of them had ever seen. Its folds of skin covered in thick, oily grey fur were splayed out over the edge of the roof where the creature lay languidly, the light from the flashlight not seeming to bother it at all.

Anthony's small face was all smiles. "See, this was what I've been talking about." He was looking at the animal with pride.

Lina was at a loss for words. "Anthony, what am I looking at right now?"

She felt Emmet's large hand on her shoulder. "I think," he cleared his throat, "that our son has found the bandit."

Maya Valenzuela is an avid writer and reader of mystery fiction and loves nothing more than a playfully dark plot and eccentric, unexpected characters. She is a member of Capital Crime Writers and lives in Ottawa with her husband and twin boys. Masked Hysteria is her first published work.

ABOUT THE EDITORS

Mike Martin is the author of the award-winning Sgt. Windflower Mystery series and the main organizer of this project. His main role has been to assist the main editor, Bernadette Cox, in putting this collection together. "This has been one of the most interesting projects of my writing life. I am grateful to have the opportunity to work alongside Bernadette and these amazing authors and to pay homage to the city that we all call home."

Bernadette Cox turned to independent editing, proofreading and writing after a 32-year journalism and public relations career spanning community newspapers and national agriculture organizations. "Thank you Mike and all the authors for placing your trust in me. Editing fiction is both challenging and gratifying because there are few hard and fast rules. Each author's unique style must be respected."